FINAL
EXAM

Also by Carol J. Perry

Bells, Spells, and Murders

It Takes a Coven

Grave Errors

Murder Go Round

Look Both Ways

Tails, You Lose

Caught Dead Handed

FINAL EXAM

CAROL J. PERRY

KENSINGTON PUBLISHING CORP.

www.kensingtonbooks.com

KENSINGTON BOOKS are published by

Kensington Publishing Corp.
119 West 40th Street
New York, NY 10018

All Kensington titles, imprints, and distributed lines are available at special quantity discounts for bulk purchases for sales promotions, premiums, fund-raising, educational, or institutional use. Special book excerpts or customized printings can also be created to fit specific needs. For details, write or phone the office of the Kensington sales manager: Kensington Publishing Corp., 119 West 40th Street, New York, NY 10018, attn: Sales Department; phone 1-800-221-2647.

KENSINGTON BOOKS and the K logo are Reg. U.S. Pat. & TM Off.

ISBN-13: 978-1-4967-1460-2
ISBN-10: 1-4967-1460-1

First printing: March 2019

10 9 8 7 6 5 4 3 2

Printed in the United States of America

Electronic edition: March 2019

ISBN-13: 978-1-4967-1461-9
ISBN-10: 1-4967-1461-X

For Dan Perry, my husband and best friend.

Oh, what a tangled web we weave,
When first we practice to deceive!
—Sir Walter Scott

CHAPTER 1

As a field reporter for WICH-TV in my hometown of Salem, Massachusetts, I rarely report the news from an actual *field*. But on a sunny afternoon in early May, there I was, knee deep in weeds—including some hay fever–inducing goldenrod—chasing down a not-too-reliable lead.

I'm Lee Barrett, née Maralee Kowalski, thirty-three, red-haired, Salem born, orphaned early, married once, and widowed young. My aunt, Isobel Russell—I call her Aunt Ibby—raised me after my parents died, and we share the old family home on Winter Street with our cat, O'Ryan.

I'm WICH-TV's newest and youngest field reporter, and I know I have a lot to prove—to myself and to others—about on-the-spot, breaking news reporting. That's why camerawoman Francine Hunter and I had just climbed partway up a steep hill, through a rusted barbed-wire fence, past several beat-up No Trespassing signs and a couple of No Swimming signs that looked as though they'd been used for target practice. I stumbled over a pile of empty beer cans—shiny, bright colors gleaming through crabgrass and ragweed. Clearly, there'd been recent sign-ignoring trespassers in this bleak landscape besides us. I just hoped our source—Francine's roommate's brother's personal trainer—was right about what might be going on in the abandoned granite quarry just ahead. He said he'd overheard it in a dive shop. Something underwater, he'd said. Something the police were looking for.

"Look," Francine whispered, pointing to a blue Chevy truck, half hidden behind a small grove of maple trees. "Somebody braver than me drove on that godawful, pot-holey, overgrown road and made it all the way up here. Maybe it's divers."

"Bet it is. Anyway, I think leaving the station's only mobile van safely parked down on the street was the right thing to do," I assured her. "I'm sure our beloved station manager wouldn't enjoy sending a tow truck to rescue us if anything went wrong."

"Oh, sure." Francine positioned her shoulder-mounted camera and started toward the Chevy. "Since Doan doesn't even know we're here, barring a van wreck, what could go wrong? We're trespassing on posted land trying to interview some divers who might be cops, who could be looking for something under a couple hundred feet of water—all on a tip from some guy's personal trainer we've never even met who hangs around in a dive shop."

"Come on," I said. "Where's your sense of adventure?"

"I think I left it in the van with the bug spray,"

Francine grumbled, aiming a swat at her ankle. "Let's get this over with."

I gave the handheld mic a quick testing tap, adjusted the lanyard with my plastic-coated press pass on it, and hurried to keep up with her. She was right about the divers. As we drew closer to the blue truck, discreet lettering on the door was visible: S.P.D. DIVE TEAM. So she was right about them being cops too. My police detective boyfriend, Pete Mondello, had told me about these full-time police officers who volunteer to become divers so they can help in water rescue operations and even search underwater for evidence to help with investigations.

"They really *are* looking for something—or *somebody*—in the quarry," I said, "and it looks like we're the only news team here."

We pushed our way through weeds surrounding the maple trees and circled around the Chevy, emerging onto a broad ledge just a few feet above water. We were at the lowest possible access to the abandoned granite pit, facing a semicircle of geometric gray stone megaliths, looming far above us like a vertical moonscape over the lake of blue water below. I took an involuntary step back.

"Weird," I said, with a little fake laugh.

"Beautiful," Francine declared. "Look at that sunlight and shadow contrast." Stepping dangerously close to the edge of the wide outcropping where we stood, she panned her camera in a semicircular motion. "Beautiful," she repeated.

I squinted, still not moving any closer to the edge, my back to the Chevy, trying to see the beauty she saw in this dreary gray environment, which I'd probably soon need to describe for my audience.

The voice came from directly behind me. "Hey. What are you doing here?" The man wore scuba gear, a dark blue wetsuit with two air tanks on his back. A mask dangled from his left hand. He walked toward me, flippers *slap-slapping* on the rough granite ridge. He didn't smile. I did, and lifted my ID badge to his eye level. "Hi," I said, speaking into the mic, "Lee Barrett, WICH-TV News. We had a call about SPD working up here today. How's the search going?"

Francine had moved closer to us and I held the mic in his direction. He gave me a head-tilted, quizzical look and didn't answer for a long moment. Dead air. "Oh yeah." Finally he nodded. "Lee Barrett. I know you. Saw you with Detective Mondello at the PAL Pee Wee Thanksgiving hockey tournament."

"Right," I said. "Nice to see you again Officer . . . ?"

"Andrews," he said. "Bill Andrews." He reached to shake hands and I made a quick switch of the mic to my left and grasped his. "Hey, are we on TV now?" He glanced at Francine, frowning.

"WICH-TV News," I repeated. "Not a live broadcast. Just gathering material right now about the search. How's it going?" I asked again, still fishing for information that might give us a clue about what was happening underwater. "Any luck?"

He looked at a wide yellow band on his wrist. "My buddy is still down. Got about a minute left on this dive."

"How long has he been under?" I moved one step closer to the edge, peering into the blue, blue water.

"Thirty minutes," he said. "Then it's my turn again."

"Very deep, I suppose," I said, still fishing.

"Some say the pit is bottomless." He smiled. "Actually it's probably around two hundred feet at the deepest point. We're looking at around a hundred, hundred and fifty."

"Why there?"

"The tipster who contacted the chief said the car went into the water from up there." Officer Andrews pointed upward, to the mountain of gray stone looming over our heads. "Probably the same tip you got, huh? We figure we know about where it might have landed." He waved the hand holding the mask. "God only knows how many cars have been ditched down there in that murky mess."

"Ditched?" I asked.

"Sure. For the insurance money. Course, not all of them have human remains inside."

CHAPTER 2

I tried not to look surprised. Francine didn't even try, just kept on filming, eyes wide, mouth open. Fortunately, our new diver friend had already flipper-flopped down to the next level of the ledge, about a foot closer to the water, and was no longer paying attention to us. Bubbles appeared on the surface, a few at first, then a veritable flood of them. Like some otherworldly sea creature, a second diver, wearing a mask with huge insect-like lenses and protruding mouthpiece, burst through their foamy center and launched himself onto the granite ridge at his fellow officer's feet.

He yanked the mask off. "Got it!" he shouted. "Hundred twenty. She's stuck sideways under a big chunk of rock. Gonna be a pisser to get out of there. Hard-hat guys and a crane will have to take over." He noticed us then, jerking a gloved thumb in our direction. "Who are they?"

"TV newspeople," Andrews said.

"Oh, boy. The chief's not gonna like that." He looked away, ignoring us, removed his flippers, then lifted a small yellow camera from a pocket. "Got a few pictures. Wicked dark down there though."

"Yeah. Tell me about it. Could you tell what color it is?" Andrews seemed to be ignoring us too. Francine kept filming. I kept recording.

"Couldn't tell much, but I'm pretty sure it's an old Mustang. Still got that little horse on the front grille. Maroon or red maybe" Sea-monster diver looked in our direction. "You girls better run along now. Nothing to see here."

"She's Mondello's girlfriend." Andrews offered. "Did you see . . . you know, anything inside?"

"Not much. Anyway, if there *was* a body there wouldn't be much left of it by now, would there? Listen, Chief's gonna be steamed if this winds up on television." He frowned. "Say, this isn't one of those live-shot things, is it?"

I ducked the mic behind my back. "No sir."

"Good thing it isn't. Say, how'd you get onto us being here anyway?"

"They're gathering material," Andrews said, quoting me. He had removed his flippers and tucked them under his arm. "They got a tip. Same as the chief."

Not exactly the same, but sort of true.

Sea-monster diver scowled. "Does Mondello know you're here?"

I bristled at that. "Of course not."

"Well, you two better scram out of here. We have a permit. I'm guessing you don't?" He didn't wait for an answer and with a quick shake of his head, motioned for Andrews to follow him. The two men stepped easily over the two ledges onto the edge of the field and disappeared into the maple tree grove. Francine and I picked our cautious way across the rough granite ridge, slippery from the divers' dripping wetsuits.

"You sure my kitchen countertops started out like this crap?" Francine grumbled as we made our way over the final outcropping, and onto the field.

"I know," I said. "Not so pretty close up, is it? And imagine someone deliberately driving off that huge cliff."

"Kids used to jump off of it all the time," she said. "That's why they have all the No Swimming signs."

We'd reached the Chevy where the divers, who'd stripped down to T-shirts and shorts, were busy stowing their gear into a long metal locker in the truck bed.

Andrews looked up and gave a little salute. "Nice to see you again, Ms. Barrett," he said. "I'll tell Pete we ran into you."

"Thanks, Officer," I said, forcing a smile. Pete might not be too happy about me messing around with police business. He worries about me. *Too bad. Police business is also news business.*

Francine and I trudged across the weedy terrain, Francine grumbling and me sneezing. *Darn goldenrod.* We were only about halfway to the top of the rut-filled excuse for a road we hadn't dared to drive on when we heard the Chevy start up.

"Think they'll give us a lift down to the van?" I wondered.

"Doubt it," Francine was still scowling. "They'll

probably be in trouble for telling us anything about what they were doing."

"Which wasn't much," I said, "Enough for a teaser maybe. Let's take what we've got back to the station and get Marty McCarthy to edit. She's the best. Have to take out the part about Pete and all the dead air. The most interesting thing is that they're looking for a body—or remains of one. I'll do a voice-over. Explain that it's an ongoing investigation."

"Why don't you just call Pete?" she said. "Maybe he'll tell you what they're looking for. And *who* they're looking for.

"Maybe I will." *And maybe I won't.*

The Chevy passed us with both divers looking straight ahead. "See?" Francine sputtered. "Told you they wouldn't stop. Big jerks. But look. They must have cut the barbed wire over there. Let's follow them. At least we won't have to climb through it."

"They probably didn't have room for us with all that equipment," I reasoned. "Anyway, I don't think police are supposed to transport random people unless there's a problem."

We changed direction and followed the path the Chevy had taken. It was downhill, and without the barbed wire seemed much easier than the way we'd come up. The WICH-TV van was a welcome sight and we hurried toward it.

We stowed the mic and camera, then climbed into the front seats, Francine behind the wheel. I pulled a notebook and pen from a side door pocket and stared at a blank page. "I wish I knew more about diving," I said as we pulled away from the curb.

"Ever try it yourself?"

"Just some snorkeling down in the Keys," I said. "You?"

"Sure. I'm certified."

"No kidding? I should have let you ask the questions."

"Not me. I like my side of the camera better than yours. You did great. I like the way you acted as though we were actually supposed to be there!"

"One of the first things I learned. It fools most people. I couldn't have faked it much longer though. I'm going to have to do a lot of research on this one."

"For instance?"

"'Hard hats and a crane,' the man said. I need to know exactly what a hard hat is and how a crane works."

My phone buzzed and I smiled when caller ID revealed my Aunt Ibby's name. "Hi," I said. "What's up?"

"Hello, Maralee. Where are you right now?"

"Route 128."

"Perfect," she said. "Do you have time to stop in Gloucester for a minute?"

I looked at Francine and mouthed, "Gloucester?"

She nodded okay. "It's a little out of the way, but sure we can," I told my aunt. "What do you need?"

"My class reunion committee is coming over this evening and I haven't had time to bake. Could you stop by Virgilio's and pick up a dozen cannoli and a dozen of those cute Italian cookies?"

On the open page I wrote *Virgilio's—12 cannoli, 12 cookies*. "A dozen of each. That all?"

"Yes, dear. Thank you."

"I have to go back to the station for a while. See you a little after five. Okay?"

"Perfect."

"And Aunt Ibby, if you have a minute, would you check and see if we have any books on diving. Scuba diving? I'm working on a story."

"I'm sure we must," she said. "Seven-nine-seven I should think. I'll check on it." (Not many home libraries are arranged according to the Dewey decimal system, but ours is.) We said our goodbyes and Francine looked over at my notes.

"Virgilio's? Cannoli and cookies? Somebody having a party?"

"Class reunion. My aunt's forty-fifth. There's a committee meeting at our house tonight."

"Oh my God. That's so cute! A bunch of old people drinking tea and eating cookies and looking at their yearbook pictures."

I shook my head. I don't ever think of Aunt Ibby as old. Her hair is still red, her figure still a trim size ten, and her computer skills are amazing. "I haven't met her classmates yet," I said, "but I understand that one of the men was a star hockey player and another was a basketball coach at Boston College. Oh yeah, one of the women still models in TV tea commercials, and one guy is running for Congress. Not too stodgy a group, I guess."

"Wow. Cool. I'll bet there aren't any coaches or congressmen in that bunch of party animals I graduated with." Francine grinned. "Think you'll get to meet them all tonight?"

"I think so. I mean, I won't be sitting in on the meeting, but I guess I'll at least be introduced around the table." We'd arrived in nearby Gloucester and Francine double-parked on the narrow street while I ran into the bakery.

"Get me a loaf of that Italian bread too, please," she called after me. "I can smell it from here."

She was right. I succumbed to the fresh-bread aroma and bought a loaf for myself along with Aunt Ibby's treats. If Pete came over after work we'd have it with the nice olive oil bread dip I'd finally mastered. I ordered a dozen of the cute cookies for us too.

Francine had already sent our material ahead, so when we arrived back at the station Marty and Wally, one of the production guys, were already set up and waiting for us. I was glad to see Marty. We'd worked together many times. Actually, my first—and short-lived—job at WICH-TV had been as the late-night show call-in psychic. The show was *Nightshades*. I'd dressed as a fortune teller and called myself Crystal Moon. It had been pretty much a disaster in every sense of the word, but Marty had proven to be a good and trusted friend—even though she still occasionally called me Moon.

"You kids had a busy day so far, huh?" Marty asked, gray curls bobbing as she tapped and twirled myriad dials facing a triple-screen monitor. "I don't suppose we can get hold of the pictures that diver took, could we?"

"I kind of doubt it. He wasn't too happy to see us. I guess you could tell that." I peered at the first screen where Francine had recorded our ungraceful trek across the field toward the blue Chevy. "Officer Andrews was okay about us being there, but the guy with the camera, not so much."

"A real grouch, that one," Francine said. "One of those by-the-book cops. Can't bend the rules for anybody. Never does anything outside the box. Even asked us if we had a permit to be there!"

I didn't comment on that. Pete is one of those by-the-book cops too. And sometimes I'm so far outside the box it's a wonder he puts up with me.

"The North Shore pits." Wally leaned toward the second screen where the soaring gray granite walls Francine had found so beautiful appeared. They still looked menacing to me. "I used to go there when I was a kid," he said. "Jumped off one of those seventy-footers once on a dare." He pointed. "That one right there, I think."

"No kidding?" Marty gave him a playful punch on the arm. "Seventy feet?"

"Yep. Caught a little edge of granite just when I hit the water. Tore a furrow down the side of my leg. Wanna see the scar?" He reached for his right pant leg.

Three of us spoke at once. "No thanks."

"Lotta blood," he said. "Whole lotta blood."

"So, what's all that about a body, Moon?" Marty asked. "We lost some sound when you stuck the mic behind your back. Did we miss anything there?"

"Not a thing," I said. "From what little they told us, it's been down there a long time though."

Marty nodded. "I think we'll do a little post-production magic with the green screen. For your intro you'll stand in front of that footage of the pit showing the highest side." She pointed to the middle monitor. "Beautiful shot, by the way, Francine. We won't use any of the sound though. Maybe dub in a few birds. None of the conversation with the divers. Action shots only. Like the guy coming up out of the water. Jeez. That was great. You'll do the voice-over, Lee. Just facts. This'll be really short. Just a teaser; a minute, two, tops. We'll try to jam it in at the bottom of the five o'clock news."

"Got it," I said. "Let me make a few notes." I have a fondness for lined index cards for note taking and always have a stack of them handy.

"Right," Marty said. "Not too much about the body. And do something with your hair."

CHAPTER 3

I already had a general idea about the high points of our excursion that I could use in the teaser. Not that there was a lot to work with. We'd had a tip that some police divers were looking for something in the abandoned granite pit. That turned out to be true. We learned that the search was for a car and that they believed they'd found it. It was an old vehicle. A Ford, probably a Mustang, and maybe red or maroon. The most important thing was that they had reason to believe it contained human remains. I made some notes, then scribbled about half of them out. "Not too much about the body," Marty had said. I wished I knew more about hard-hat divers and giant cranes. And I wished I knew exactly what to do about my hair.

It took longer than I'd thought it might, but after fifteen minutes with the edited footage on the monitor, another ten writing a script, five more taming curls-gone-wild, I was in front of the green screen.

"I'm Lee Barrett, at the site of a long-abandoned granite pit. There was some police activity here this morning, and WICH-TV will be on hand to keep you up to date as this story unfolds." At Marty's signal I stepped away from the green screen, watching the monitor where a smiling Officer Andrews gestured toward the water and the 101 Strings played "Summertime" softly. A few birds chirped. I began my voice-over. "Two scuba divers from the Salem Police Department spent part of the morning below the surface of the deep pool of fresh water you see here. Reputed to be two hundred feet deep, this area has been closed to swimmers for many years, largely out of concern for young daredevils who dove from those towering seventy-foot granite cliffs. According to a WICH-TV source, this morning's underwater investigation concerns an automobile, which may have long ago plunged from one of those precipices into the depths below. The car in question may be a vintage red Mustang. And," I paused here for effect, "there may be human remains inside. Stay tuned to WICH-TV for more developments in this ongoing story."

Marty signaled cut, and I looked at the studio clock. "Good job," she said. "One minute right on the button."

"Lucky we got that much," I said. "They didn't give us a lot to work with."

"Just enough to make the audience want more," she said. "Doan will love it." She shrugged. "Of course, now you have to get to work and find out who the car belongs to and who the stiff is."

Francine snickered. "You were just saying how you want to learn more about diving. Here's your big chance."

"You're both right," I agreed. "I'll start doing a little reading tonight and maybe later I'll see what Pete has to say about it." *Fat chance he'll say anything. Just put on his cop face and tell me he can't discuss police business.*

Francine snapped her fingers. "Hey. I'll see if my roomie can get the number of her brother's trainer. Maybe the guy overheard some more dirt at that dive shop."

"Yeah. Do it. Doan's going to expect a follow-up on this.

"He's going to expect it pronto," Marty watched the teaser while I looked over her shoulder. It looked pretty good. Even my hair. "This is perfect for now," she said. "We'll run this on the five o'clock and again at eleven tonight. Doan will want a lot more by tomorrow though. This little bit will tip off the other stations to what's happening over there."

Tomorrow. Oh boy.

"No problem," I lied. "We're on it."

It was a few minutes before five when Francine and I clocked out in the second floor reception area. Rhonda, the way-smarter-than-she-looks receptionist, glanced up from her *People* magazine. "Hi kids. Hear you were over at the pits today. Something exciting happening over there?"

"I'm not sure yet," I admitted. "Right now it's just interesting. Some divers found an old car underwater. But if they find there's somebody dead inside the car—that's when it gets exciting."

Rhonda put her magazine down. "You mean people are still diving off those high cliffs? I think that's against the law."

"Not people," Francine said. "Not *regular* people anyway. It's police department scuba divers, and they were down on the low part."

"Oh. They're looking for a body in there?"

"'Human remains,' they called it," I said. "But one of the divers said there wouldn't be much left of it."

"So they'll have to pull the car out of the pits so they can look inside?" Rhonda's eyes looked even bigger than usual. "So they can get whoever is in it, out?"

"We think so." I headed for the door. "We'll know more tomorrow." *I hope we'll know more tomorrow.* "One of the divers said we might need a permit to go in there. It's posted with no trespassing signs."

"It's posted with no *everything* signs," Francine added.

"Right. It is. Rhonda can you check with City Hall and see if you can get us permission to be at the site? By tomorrow morning?"

"Pretty sure I can," she said. "I know people."

I had no doubt about Rhonda's ability to get things done. "Super. See you in the morning."

"See you then."

Francine and I rode in the ancient elevator down to the lobby, crossed the black and white tiled floor, stepped out onto Derby Street and walked together to the parking lot. She carried her wrapped loaf of Italian bread under one arm. As she opened the door to her truck she looked back at me. "Just what is it we're going to do tomorrow?"

"If you can find out how to get in touch with that dive shop, maybe we'll start there," I said. "I'll see what I can find out about what the police already know, and we'll probably go back to the pit and see if there's any heavy equipment there yet. It probably will take a pretty big crane to lift up an automobile."

"Yep. They won't be able to hide it. Good photo op even if we don't get to see the remains." She closed her truck door and rolled down the window. "What do remains look like, exactly?"

I shrugged. "Bones, maybe?"

"Oh, jeez. What a great shot that would be. A skeleton behind the wheel. Awesome. See you in the morning."

I climbed into my almost-new, Laguna blue Corvette Stingray. I know, the car is a bit much for a fledgling reporter, but the income from my parents' estate totals far more than my salary at WICH-TV will ever be and the Vette was a rare extravagance. I put the paper bags from Virgilio's onto the seat beside me and took a deep breath of the fresh bread aroma filling the car. The late afternoon sun lent a golden glow to the harbor beyond the granite seawall as I backed out of the lot onto Derby Street and headed for home.

I parked in the garage behind our house on Winter Street, picked up the two bags of bakery treats, and started along the brick pathway leading to the back door. Spring flowers bloomed behind the wrought-iron fence surrounding Aunt Ibby's garden—hydrangea, Queen Anne's lace, lilacs, violets, forsythia. As I approached the steps a cat door popped open and our big, yellow-striped male cat O'Ryan rushed out to greet me with loud purrs and happy *mmrrrupps*, wrapping himself around my ankles.

I bent to pat him, pulled keys from my purse, unlocked the door, and stepped into our downstairs back hall. O'Ryan immediately ducked through another cat entrance, this one leading into my Aunt Ibby's kitchen. I deposited my bags of bread and cookies on the nearby stairs leading up to my third-floor apartment, put the one containing the cannoli and cookies under my arm, and knocked on her door. "It's me, Aunt Ibby. I've got your goodies."

"Come right in, Maralee. It's open," she called. My aunt's kitchen is a wonderfully warm, welcoming place. Visitors usually wind up there, in comfortable captain's chairs at her round oak table, sipping coffee, tea, or wine. I put the bags on the long butcher-block counter and gave her a hug.

"You look pretty," I told her. "All ready for your classmates?"

"Thank you, dear. Yes, I think so." She patted her hair, smoothed the skirt of her pale green silk dress, and opening the door of a glass-fronted china cabinet, removed two platters. "I'm thinking of using the Spode Blue Indigo porcelain for the cookies, and the Blue Willow for the cannoli. What do you think?"

"They're perfect of course. And let me guess— Grandmother Forbes's Flow Blue china plates and cups?"

"Exactly. And the cobalt wineglasses." She gestured toward the oak table. "There'll be just six of us, so I think we'll do the plotting and planning at the big table in the dining room, and then come out here for refreshments."

"Do you need any help? What time do you expect them?" I asked.

"Six o'clock," she said, glancing at her watch. "And it's past five already. You could help me arrange these lovely pastries on the platters so I can just pull them out of the refrigerator when it's time to eat."

"Glad to," I said, reaching for the Blue Willow. "I'll do the cannoli. Want to turn on the news? Francine and I did a little teaser story that should be on pretty soon."

"A teaser? How fascinating. I never get over what a delight it is to see you on TV." She picked up the remote and the small wall-mounted TV clicked on. Phil Archer, the evening news anchor, does the half-hour show on weeknights. He'd just begun a piece on shelter pets, highlighted with video of adorable puppies and kittens. O'Ryan looked up from his red bowl of kibble, watching intently. He likes kittens.

Aunt Ibby had finished arranging her cookie platter and had already begun covering it with plastic wrap while I still debated about which way to angle the sugar-dusted tubes with their creamy fillings on mine. "I'll just put these in the fridge," she said. "Oh look. There you are." She paused on her way to the Frigidaire, watching the screen. Francine had filmed me from the back as I trudged across the weed-filled field. "Where in the world were you?"

"At the old North Shore Granite Works. Watch. It gets better," I promised as I finished my cannoli arrangement. "Look. Scuba divers."

We watched together and I heard my own voice. "According to a WICH-TV source, this morning's underwater investigation concerns an automobile, which may have long ago plunged from one of those precipices into the depths below. The car in question may be a vintage red Mustang, and there may be human remains inside."

I heard the crash as the Spode platter shattered. Colorful cookies rolled among blue and white porcelain shards on the tile floor. My aunt stood over the wreckage, green eyes wide, complexion ashen.

CHAPTER 4

I reached for her arm and led her to a chair. "What's wrong? Are you okay?" She made a helpless gesture toward the mess on the floor. "Don't worry about that," I said, taking her hand. "I'll sweep it up. Your hands are freezing. What is it?"

She was silent for a long moment. I rubbed her hands, felt her forehead, watched as the color came back into her face. "Aunt Ibby?" I whispered. "Do you feel better now?"

She suddenly sat erect, pulling her hands away, folding them in her lap. "Oh, dear, Maralee. I've broken that lovely platter. It's part of a set, you know. How clumsy of me. Here. I'll clean it up. I expect all the pretty cookies are ruined too." She attempted to stand, but I held her shoulders.

"Please. Sit for a minute." I peered into her eyes. "I'll sweep up. There's a china replacement store in Boston. We can get another platter."

She shook her head and gave an apologetic smile.

"I'm such a klutz. And carrying on like that over a dish and some cookies! I'm embarrassed. Not like me at all, is it? Must be what they call a 'senior moment.'" It wasn't one bit like her and I didn't like to think about her having a "senior moment." *Does this portend anything serious going on in her mind?* I shook the dreadful thought away.

Within minutes the sparkle was back in the green eyes, her smile was sincere and genuine, and when I released my grip on her shoulders she stood as gracefully as ever. "You just sit back down and take it easy for a minute," I said, pulling the broom and dustpan from the utility closet. "Have a nice cup of tea and relax."

I swept up the debris and dumped it into a wastebasket, while my aunt quietly—and surprisingly—did exactly as I'd suggested. She microwaved a cup of water, dunked a tea bag into it, and calmly took a seat at the round oak table. O'Ryan climbed onto her lap and she stroked his fuzzy head with one hand, stirring the tea with the other.

"I bought an extra dozen cookies," I said, still watching her closely. "And I have a pretty Wedgwood hibiscus platter upstairs. Not old, but it'll go with your blue theme. If you'll be all right for a minute, I'll run up and get it."

"That's so thoughtful of you, dear," she said. "Yes, thank you. And you bought extra cookies? How fortuitous!"

"Couldn't resist them," I said. "Now you just take it easy. I'll be right back." I glanced at the clock on the wall. Five thirty. The TV was still on, but the newscast was over. A *Golden Girls* rerun was playing—one of my aunt's favorite shows. With the tea, Bea Arthur, and the cat on her lap, she'd probably stay put for the couple of minutes it'd take me to run upstairs and grab the platter.

I snatched the bakery bag from the bottom of the staircase and raced up two twisty flights of stairs to my apartment. Unlocking my door, I passed through the living room, hurried down the narrow hall to the kitchen, and threw open the door to my china cabinet. The platter was at the bottom of a pile of serving pieces that had to be removed carefully, one by one. Leaving graduated bowls, soup tureen, cream pitcher, and sugar bowl in an untidy cluster on top of my Lucite kitchen table, I picked up the box of cookies and balanced it on top of the platter. The kitchen door offered a faster route back down to the first floor, so, heart pounding, carrying platter and cookies, I raced down the wide and quite handsome oak staircase curving gently from the third floor landing down to a spacious foyer opening into Aunt Ibby's living room. I slowed down and approached her kitchen at a more decorous pace. My aunt had stayed pretty much exactly as I'd left her except that the teacup was empty and O'Ryan had moved to a chair beside her.

"Feeling better?" I asked, placing the platter carefully on the table. She reached across and touched it.

"What? Oh yes. I'm fine. Just feel a bit silly. Lucky you bought extra cookies, and the Wedgwood is perfect. Oh my, look at the time. They'll be here soon." She stood, smoothed her dress, and carried her teacup to the sink. "Want to arrange the cookies while I freshen up a bit?" She headed for the little powder room off the kitchen.

"Sure," I said, still watching her carefully. *What am I so worried about? She dropped a darned plate of cookies. Big deal.*

I rinsed and dried the platter. It had, after all, been in my china cabinet—unused—for a couple of years It was wedding china, and I just hadn't felt like using it since my husband Johnny died. I arranged the cookies, covered the platter with plastic wrap, and put it into the refrigerator beside the cannoli.

The front doorbell chimed "The Impossible Dream," and I looked around for my aunt. Her voice issued from the powder room. "Would you get that, Maralee? I'll be there in a minute."

I passed the dining room on my way to the living room and the foyer, turning on lights along the way. Peeking into the room, I smiled at the way Aunt Ibby had arranged materials on the long mahogany table— pens, markers, paper, glue sticks, tape. It reminded me of my middle school project days.

O'Ryan had reached the front hall before I did, his pink nose pressed against the narrow window next to the door. A quick look through the same window revealed a tall man with a good tan and a neatly trimmed gray beard. I recognized him from newspaper pictures. He was Steve Overton, one of my aunt's most successful classmates, class president forty-five years ago, and now a candidate for the U.S. Congress. I pulled open the door. "Hello! Please come in. My aunt will be here in a moment." I stuck out my hand. "I'm her niece, Lee Barrett."

"Steve Overton," he said, shaking my hand vigorously. "So very pleased to meet you. Ibby speaks so highly of you."

"Did I hear my name? Hello, Steve!" My aunt appeared in the living room's arched entrance.

"Ibby," he said, holding out both arms and moving toward her. "As lovely as ever." They did one of those over-the-shoulder air-kiss things people their age do. He was right. She looked absolutely lovely, without the slightest hint of her recent "senior moment" or whatever the heck that thing was.

"I see you've met my niece," she said. "Perhaps you recognize her from television?"

"I do indeed," he said, turning to face me once again. "I expect I'll be seeing you fairly often, young lady. I've been working on an advertising schedule with Bruce Doan. Running for a congressional seat, you know."

I nodded, smiling, and turned back to the door as the bell chimed again. "That'll be Betsy," my aunt said, reaching for the doorknob. "I saw her Mercedes pull up a minute ago."

Betsy Leavitt was the tea commercial model. Aunt Ibby had pointed her out to me several times—always on the big national channels, not the locals like WICH-TV.

Betsy whirled into the foyer in a cloud of Chanel Gabrielle and Oscar de la Renta black silk. "Ibby! Oh, Ibby, what a joy to see you." The two women hugged and Betsy turned to me. "You're Maralee. You look like your mother," she said with a dazzling smile that showed why the tea company liked her. "So pretty."

"Thank you. You knew my mother?"

"Of course. Ibby's little sister Carrie." She flashed that professional model smile again and extended a perfectly manicured hand to the aspiring congressman. "Hi, Steve." He took her hand.

"Hi, Betts," he said.

"I have the dining room set up for our projects." My aunt beckoned to her friends to join her. "It's almost six now so the others should be along any minute. I'd like to start on time. We have so much to accomplish. Maralee, will you mind the door for us and direct the others to the dining room?"

"Sure, glad to." O'Ryan had hopped onto the seat of our antique hall tree, which is quite a spectacular piece of furniture. It's about eight feet tall, made of walnut with age-darkened metal hooks at various heights along both sides of a big, bevel-edged mirror. The seat is convenient for pulling on or taking off boots, and it lifts up for storage. The mirror is handy for a last-minute check of your appearance before admitting guests. All in all, a well-designed and useful item. I took a quick glance in the mirror, wishing I'd had a chance to change from jeans and a pale blue cotton sweater to something more appropriate. *Oh, well.* I gave my hair a token fluffing, nudged the cat gently, sat beside him, and waited for three more members of Salem High School's class of 1974 to arrive.

My phone buzzed. "Hi, Pete. What's up?"

"Chief's on a tear. How come you—"

The doorbell chimed. "Hold on a sec," I said, standing. "Gotta answer the door."

Reaching for the doorknob, I glanced again at the mirror. Big mistake. In an instant, I saw the flashing lights and swirling colors.

I'm what's known in paranormal circles as a "scryer." My friend River North calls me a "gazer." River happens to be a witch, and she knows all about such things. Anyway, I'd found out fairly recently that I have the weird ability to see things in shiny objects—things that have happened or are happening and even things that could happen in the future. River calls it a "gift." I don't think of it that way. It had come in handy a few times, but mostly all it had shown me was death and dying—and the visions always start with those damned flashing lights and swirling colors.

CHAPTER 5

Fast priority assessment. First, answer the door. Next, see what Pete wants. Finally, hope that whatever's in the mirror goes away.

Two more of Aunt Ibby's classmates had arrived. A very tall man who had to be the basketball coach, and a tiny-by-comparison blond woman. I welcomed the pair, introduced myself, and learned that the coach was Warren Whipple ("You can call me Coach, sweetheart"), and the woman was Penelope Driscoll, who, she informed me, had been friends with my aunt since first grade and had brought along her yearbook so that they could copy the high school pictures for name tags. "Some of us have changed a little since seventy-four," she said with a shy smile. "It might help to have a photo to jog the old memory."

"Good idea," I said and escorted the pair to the dining room. I'd be interested to see that old yearbook myself. I wondered if Aunt Ibby had kept hers. I was pretty sure I'd never seen one around the house.

The arrival at the table of Coach and Penelope produced another round of hugs, greetings, and air-kisses. That made five. One more classmate to go. I excused myself, returned to the bench, and, carefully avoiding the mirror, pulled my phone from my pocket.

"You still there, Pete?"

"Yes. What's going on?"

"Tonight's Aunt Ibby's class reunion committee meeting. Bunch of people coming over."

"Oh yeah, I'd forgotten about that. Listen. What I was trying to tell you, Chief Whaley says you were over at the pits interfering in police business. Then Andrews tells me he saw you there and you were taking pictures and recording him and his partner? That right?" Pete was using what I call his "cop voice." That means serious stuff.

"Francine and I were following a tip about SPD looking for something underwater over there. That's all. Why?" I knew that sounded a little defensive and I tried to soften my tone. "We didn't learn much of anything."

"Well, when the chief got hold of it, he got on the horn with your boss and told him not to air any of whatever you got."

Un-oh. Too late. "And he found out we'd already aired it on the five o'clock."

"Right. He's not happy."

Chief Tom Whaley is rarely happy with me. I seem to get on his wrong side more often than not. It's been that way since practically the minute we met, right after I discovered Ariel Constellation's body floating in Salem harbor. (Ariel was a witch and

O'Ryan used to be her cat—some say he was her "familiar"—and in Salem a witch's familiar is always respected and sometimes feared.)

"Did Mr. Doan agree to spike the story?" *I can't believe he did.*

"Just for tonight's eleven o'clock news." Pete admitted. "How much do you have about—um—about what they're looking for anyway?"

"Red Mustang with possible human remains," I said. "Wedged sideways down about a hundred and twenty feet. They're going to need hard-hat divers and a crane to get at it."

"No kidding." I could hear the smile in his voice. "You're getting pretty good at this, babe."

"Really? That's not very much to go on, is it?"

"It's a pretty darn good start if you ask me." Short pause. "But you're not going to ask me, right?"

"Come on over after work," I said in my best Marilyn Monroe imitation. "I'll ply you with fresh Italian bread and the dipping sauce you like. Maybe even some wine."

"Ice cream, too?"

"Absolutely. Want to pick up an antipasto at Bertini's on your way?"

"Sure. I'll get out of here around eight," he said. "But seriously, you know I can't discuss police business with you."

"It's also news reporter business, Pete. You know I'll be poking around, looking for information."

"I know. See you in a couple of hours. Love you. Bye."

"Love you too. Bye." I checked the phone for messages—River North wanted me to call her ASAP.

River is not only my best friend but a fellow employee at WICH-TV. After my unfortunate experience as a phony phone-in psychic on *Nightshades,* River—a tearing beauty and an expert tarot reader—took over that late-night time slot. *Tarot Time with River North* became one of the station's top-rated shows.

Still deliberately avoiding looking at the mirror, I remained at my post by the front door. I'd call River just as soon as the tardy classmate showed up. At twenty past six, Aunt Ibby appeared at the dining room doorway. "Looks like Bobby couldn't make it, dear," she called. "You go along upstairs. If he shows up, I'll let him in. Thanks for your help."

"No problem." I stood, facing the stairway. O'Ryan left the bench and padded across the living room to follow her. "Will you need me in the kitchen later?"

"Nope. We'll be fine. You've had a busy day. See you in the morning."

"Have a good meeting," I said. "Good night."

She and O'Ryan disappeared into the dining room. I started up the stairs, then thought I heard a car pull up. *Has the missing Bobby arrived?* I turned back toward the door.

Toward the mirror.

The swirling colors and flashing lights had stopped, but the vision was stark and clear. Moonlight shone on dark water etching shadowy designs on the face of gray cliffs. Then, as if in slow motion, a car lurched from the highest point, slowly revolving as it fell. The picture faded away before the vehicle hit the water. Too dark to see color or details, but I had no doubt that the damned thing was red and that there was a little horse on the front grille.

The doorbell chimed. Reaching for the doorknob, I shoved the vision out of my mind. I was getting pretty good at doing that. The man standing outside was slim with salt-and-pepper hair, big brown eyes, a warm smile, and a strong smell of alcohol. "Hi there," he said, stepping inside and offering his hand. "I'm Bobby Ross. Have they started the party without me?"

I shook his hand, dodging the fumes. "Just getting started," I said. "I'm Lee Barrett, Ibby Russell's niece. Come on. I'll show you where they are."

"Hello, Lee Barrett," he said, falling into step beside me. "You look like her. Like Ibby's sister."

"Thank you," I said. "Here you go."

The group gathered around the table called out happy greetings. Steve pulled out a chair and motioned for Bobby to sit next to him. "Glad you could make it, Bobby. You're looking good." There was a chorus of "Good to see you," and "How was San Francisco?" and "You haven't changed much." I gave my aunt a little wave and started for the stairs again with O'Ryan tagging along behind me. I dared a glance at the mirror. Nothing there but my own reflection.

I hurried up the two flights. Even though the apartment was in the house where I was raised, the space my aunt had designed for me was uniquely my own. It felt like home. From the 1970s Lucite table and chairs set to the vintage Fiestaware in the kitchen, the glass-fronted barrister's bookcase in the living room to the chest of drawers with secret compartments in my bedroom, I was surrounded by things that made me happy. A glance at the Kit-Cat Klock on the wall told me I had an hour or so to return River's call, get a shower, and change clothes if I was going to be presentable—with warmed Italian bread and fresh dipping sauce on hand—when Pete arrived.

A little multitasking was in order. Once in the bathroom, I put the phone on speaker and hit River's number. "Hi, River. You called?" I began to strip off my clothes and put them into the laundry chute.

"I did. Saw you on the news in that creepy place."

"You think it's creepy, too? Francine thinks it's beautiful."

"Yeah, well, different strokes. Listen," she said, using her on-the-air card-reader voice. "It creeped me out enough that I did a reading for you. I need to talk to you about it." I turned on the shower and stuck my hand into the stall, testing the temperature. "Hey! You're not in the shower are you?"

"Not yet. Pete's coming over. Can the reading wait until tomorrow?"

"It can." She dropped her voice. "But Lee, I think this one might be really important. Tomorrow for sure?"

"Now you're creeping me out. But yes, for sure," I promised.

Later, showered, dressed, hair brushed, and even blushed and glossed, I had a few spare minutes to check the 797 shelf in the study for books on scuba diving. O'Ryan followed me into the book-lined room, but spent his time looking at the occupants of Aunt Ibby's saltwater aquarium swimming languidly in and out of a turreted castle and over treasure chests. I found two books that looked helpful, called the cat, and closed the study door and returned to my apartment.

O'Ryan ran to the living room door as soon as he

heard Pete's key turn in the lock, and I was right behind him. I'd changed into a new cotton minidress in a cheerful sunny yellow with some cute white Birkenstock sandals. The look of approval in his dark eyes told me I'd made a good choice. He put the Bertini's bag on the coffee table, and we exchanged a long, satisfying kiss. "You smell good," he said, still holding me close.

"That might be the rosemary I put in the sauce," I said. "But thanks." After a little more kissing we eventually made it to the kitchen. I arranged the antipasto in an orange bowl, slipped the bread into a brown paper bag, and popped it into the already warm oven while Pete started the coffee.

"Chief Whaley isn't mad at you, is he?" I asked. "Because of me, I mean."

"No. You know the chief. Bark's worse than his bite. He just doesn't much like surprises, and this dumped car thing came right out of left field."

"Really?" I pulled the loaf of bread out of the oven and began slicing. "How so?"

"Anonymous tip. He hates 'em. Half the time they don't lead anywhere, and this one will be expensive to follow up on."

I thought about what little I knew about divers and cranes. He was right. Getting that car out of the water-filled granite pit would surely make a dent in the department's operating budget. "He must think the tipster has some credibility, I suppose, if he's gone this far with it." *Unapologetic fishing expedition.* I set out plates, silverware, and wineglasses and arranged thick bread slices beside the bowl of warm dipping oil.

"Think it's the same person as your—um—unnamed source?" he asked.

"I doubt it. The chief has more credible sources than I do." I said, confident that Francine's roommate's brother's gym rat personal trainer didn't have Chief Whaley on his radar at all.

Pete changed the subject. He's good at that.

"Some pretty fancy rides out front," he said, ticking them off on his fingers. "A Mercedes, a BMW, a Lexus, and a Jag. Your aunt's classmates must be a bunch of most-likely-to-succeeds."

"Could be," I said. "So far I've met a college basketball coach, a model, and a candidate for Congress."

"Overton?"

"Right. You know him?"

"Not really. I've seen him around the station a few times. Chief knows him."

"Friends?"

"I don't think so. But he's asked Chief Whaley for his endorsement, and the chief said yes. Overton's a big law-and-order guy."

"That's good, I guess. He told me he'll be doing some advertising on WICH-TV."

Pete poured pinot noir into our glasses. "I suppose he'll be all over TV by next fall."

Back to fishing. "You know, if they pull that car up, and there *are*—um—human remains inside, that'll be all over TV too. Including WICH-TV. Including me."

"I know." He divided the antipasto neatly onto

our plates, making sure I got extra artichoke hearts. "That's why I have to be extra careful about talking about it with you." He broke a slice of Italian bread into pieces and dipped a big chunk of it into the sauce. "Oh, babe. This is the best ever."

"Virgilio's," I said.

"I meant the sauce."

"I know. I'm trying to soften you up."

"I know. Good try." He reached over and put another piece of artichoke heart on top of my salad. "I'm planning to soften you up too."

"For information?"

"Nope." He did his Groucho Marx eyebrow thing. "For later tonight." We both laughed and—for the moment at least—I gave up prying for police department data and focused my attention on food.

"Tell me some more about this class reunion of your aunt's," Pete said. "I've only been to one of mine. Ever go to yours?"

"Never have. I was in college when the first one came along, then I went to work in Florida. I wouldn't mind going though. Looks like it could be fun."

"Well, if you need a date, I'm available," he offered. "I can't promise you a ride in a Lexus or a Mercedes though.

"Thanks. I'll definitely take you up on that," I promised. "Hey, wait a minute. You mentioned four cars out front. Five people showed up. Maybe two of them came together. Must have been Coach and Penelope. The others came in one at a time.

"Did you meet all of them?

"Just barely. But yes. I was official door answerer. Met 'em all."

"And?"

"And what?"

"And what do you think of them? You're an investigative reporter. You must have formed some sort of impression of each one." He put down his fork. "Five quick character sketches. Go!"

I put my fork down too. A challenge! Could I do it? At Pete's suggestion I've been taking an online course in criminology. There'd been a recent exercise on making quick analyses of people, and Pete knew it. He's a couple of semesters ahead of me in the same course and likes to toss these little pop quizzes at me once in a while.

"Okay. First one here was Steve Overton. He was president of Aunt Ibby's class and now he's running for Congress."

"You already knew all that beforehand. Come on. You can do better."

"A lot of self-confidence," I said. "Pleased with himself. Very good clothes. *GQ* stuff. He'll probably be a good candidate."

Pete nodded. I continued "Betsy Leavitt is an oversixty professional model. Beautiful smile. Gorgeous silver hair. Great designer clothes." I thought about Betsy's arrival. "She knew my mother."

"More," Pete prodded. "You can do better."

I closed my eyes. "The relationship between Betsy and Steve seemed strained. No hug. No air-kisses. They just said hello to each other."

"Good observation," Pete said. "Who's next?"

"Coach Whipple," I said. "Typical jock. Called me 'sweetheart.' Thinks he's more important than he probably is."

"Interesting," Pete said. "You don't like Coach Whipple?"

Excellent question. "I don't actually dislike him," I admitted. "He just didn't make a good first impression."

"Okay. Go on. You say Penelope arrived with him?"

"I'm just guessing at that," I told him. "They were on the front steps together when I opened the door. They made an odd-looking couple though. He's pretty tall and she's a tiny little thing. She and my aunt have been friends since first grade."

"More," Pete said.

"She seems shy. She's probably efficient at whatever she does. She remembered to bring her old yearbook so they could copy pictures from it to make name tags."

"Good detail. That's four. Who's the last one?"

"Bobby Ross. He arrived late. He'd been drinking. Friendly. He was probably good-looking when he was young. Nice smile. Maybe he was nervous about the meeting and had a few drinks to work up his courage."

"Nice going. I'll make a cop out of you yet," he said. "Ready for ice cream?'

"Yes, to the ice cream. No thanks to the cop job," I said. "I like being a reporter."

CHAPTER 6

I'd set my alarm for 6:00 a.m. to be sure Francine and I could get an early start on the granite pit story. Would they already have a crane in place? Hard-hat divers? Would the other news outlets be there ahead of us? Had Rhonda been able to score the permits we'd need?

Pete was already up, dressed, and ready for work. *He must have a busy day planned too.* I put on slippers and followed the fresh morning coffee aroma wafting in from the kitchen. "Good morning," I said, reaching for my *New Hampshire Speedway* mug. "You have an early day, too?"

"Yeah. Chief called a six-thirty meeting. Detectives, dive-team rep, CSI, and forensics."

"Is this about . . . you know?"

"He wasn't specific. I guess after your spilling the beans on the five o'clock, he wants to get out ahead of it. Before the questions start coming."

"Just doing my job," I said, sitting in the chair closest

to the window and pouring half-and-half into my coffee.

"I know that." He planted a kiss on top of my head. "Chief knows it too. Even if you hadn't spotted the divers yesterday, somebody's surely going to notice the giant yellow crane that's going to show up over there today."

"The crane? Do you know approximately what time that's going to happen?"

He paused for a moment before answering. "If I was to guess, I'd say around eight."

I decided to push my luck a little. "Educated guess or random guess?" I was sure Francine and I could easily be there, cameras and sound equipment in place, by eight. On the other hand, if there wouldn't be any action until say, noon, I didn't want to stand around sneezing for a couple of hours knee-deep in goldenrod.

Another pause. "Around eight should be good," he said, "if I was to guess."

I nodded. "I suppose it would be a pretty big crane, wouldn't it?" *Still fishing.*

He laughed. "Pretty big." He rinsed his coffee mug, put it in the dishwasher, and started down the short hall to the living room. "I'll call you later. Love you."

"Love you too." I showered and dressed quickly in jeans, long-sleeved WICH-TV white T-shirt, and cordovan booties, texted Francine that I was on my way, poured a to-go cup of coffee, and grabbed a granola bar from the Red Riding Hood cookie jar.

I checked my watch on the way down the back

stairs. There'd be time to stop by Aunt Ibby's kitchen to see how her meeting had gone. I knew she'd be awake. She was probably already halfway through the *Boston Globe* crossword. I knocked gently. O'Ryan exited the kitchen through the cat door and wound himself around my boot top.

"Come in, Maralee," my aunt called. "It's open."

"Hi. I just wanted to pop in for a sec to see how the reunion meeting went." O'Ryan and I entered together.

"Very well, I should say." She put the paper aside and laid her pen on the table. (Yes, she does the *Globe* crossword in ink.) "Everyone was quite enthusiastic. They all seemed to enjoy the treats. Of course Betsy is on a perpetual diet, and Penelope is so tiny she barely eats, but the men made short work of them." She pointed to the butcher-block counter. "Your platter is right here. Want to take it now?"

"No. I'll pick it up later if that's all right. Kind of in a hurry this morning. I enjoyed meeting your friends. Quite a distinguished group." I smiled. "Pete noticed the four expensive cars parked out front. Not to be nosy, but are Coach and Penelope an 'item'?"

"Warren and Penelope?" Her eyes widened. "Good heavens, no. Whatever gave you that idea?"

"They arrived at the front door at the same time." I shrugged. "Five guests, four cars. I just assumed they were together."

"Oh, Bobby didn't bring his car. He came by Uber. Steve drove him home, though."

I refrained from saying that it was just as well Bobby

hadn't been driving. "How did the name tags work out? Using the yearbook photos is a good idea."

"Yes," she said. "We have to make them and slip them into those plastic pin-back things. The girls are going to get together some afternoon soon to do it. The boys are going to get the invitations designed, finalize the guest list, take care of the postage. Then we'll all get together again to figure out the theme and the decorations and the menu."

"Sounds like you have your work cut out for you. Let me know if I can help." I headed for the door. "Oh, do you have a copy of your yearbook? I'd love to see it sometime."

"Hmm. It's probably around here somewhere." She looked down at the table, her smile fading. "It's not very interesting."

What an odd thing to say.

I backed the Vette out of the garage onto Oliver Street, thoughts of my aunt's reunion duties driven away by my current plans for discovering the fate of a waterlogged red Mustang and the identity of its deceased occupant. I wished I'd had time to study the books I'd left on my bureau.

Francine was already at the station. Her truck was parked in her usual spot, and the mobile van was ready and waiting in front of the building. I parked, hurried inside, and rode the clanking elevator up to the second floor. Through the glass door I saw Rhonda at her desk, Francine in one of the turquoise chairs, and Mr. Doan standing in the doorway of the office marked MANAGER.

Mr. Doan was the first to spot me. "There's our reporter now," he said. "Listen, Barrett, you seem to have pissed off our police chief with your teaser yesterday, but I have no intention of backing off this story. Freedom of the press, First Amendment rights and all that. I want you to really concentrate on this one. Palmer will help with your regular schedule if you can't handle both. Use a clip mic today. You can't stick it behind your back and mess up the sound like last time. You and Francine can use the mobile unit." He pointed in Rhonda's direction. "Rhonda's pulled all the permits you'll need to avoid getting pinched for trespassing. Just try not to do any of the other stuff they've posted over there. Got it? Okay." He backed into his office and pulled the door shut.

"Well, there's your marching orders." Rhonda flashed a dimpled smile. "Scotty's not going to be too happy about working around your schedule, I'm guessing. Anyway, here're your permits. You both have permission to use all the roads leading to the pits, the access areas, and any unposted outbuildings. Wear your press passes. Naturally, you can't go into the water, and you have to respect any orders from the divers, police officers, and heavy equipment operators. Good luck!" I accepted the sheaf of papers, each one bearing the official seal of the city of Salem, tucked them into my purse, and clipped my press pass to the neckline of my T-shirt

"Let's roll," Francine said. "The van's out front."

"Saw it. Let's take the stairs. Faster than old clunky."

We clattered down the metal staircase, tumbled

out into the lobby, and raced across the black-and-white tile to the front door. Within minutes we were on our way to Route 128 and the North Shore Granite Works.

"Did your detective tell you anything about what's going on?"

"Not much. Did you notice that they didn't use the teaser on the late news?"

"No. I was sound asleep by then. Rhonda told me about it this morning though." She tapped the horn in a friendly toot as a Volkswagen work van bearing the WICH-TV logo passed on the opposite side of the street, heading toward Derby Street. "That'll be Scott Palmer's ride for the day with Old Eddie driving. We're going to have both Chief Whaley *and* the senior field reporter mad at us."

"Neither one will be anything new to me," I said. "I'm not popular with either of them, though I don't usually offend them both on the same day."

"Don't worry. They'll get over it."

"I know. Want to turn on the radio? WESX does local news every half hour in the morning. Maybe they have something."

"Hope not," Francine tapped the radio button. "I want us to be first."

"We have permits, and I'll bet not many others thought of that." We rode quietly for a while, listening to the radio, commenting occasionally on bits of local news here and there. The thirty-minute segment was nearly over when I picked up the words "granite pit." "Listen!" I reached for the volume control, but Francine got there first.

". . . seeking to salvage a vehicle believed to be submerged in one of the area's deepest pits. Sources say that a vintage automobile, possibly a Ford Mustang, may contain human remains."

"Big deal," I huffed. "Their source is us! But anyway, there's no mention yet of a giant yellow crane on the old granite pits road."

"How do you know it's yellow?" Francine asked.

"Pete mentioned it last night."

"So," she said, smirking just a bit, "you got him to shake loose with a little bit of information after all."

"*Very* little. He's always been careful about that—more so since I got the field reporter job."

"Even so," she said, "It's good that he drops a few hints sometimes. Anyway, I hope we get to see it when they pull it up out of the water. That'll be a great shot." She waved one hand. "It'll be all dripping, with slimy mossy stuff on it—maybe the skeleton will be in the driver's seat—what a great picture!"

I remembered the vision I'd seen in the hall tree mirror. I don't know what it will look like when they pull it out. But I know how it looked when it went over that cliff. It was red and shiny and had a little horse on the grille. It tumbled toward the water below. No skeleton though.

"I think I'll try using that old road this time," Francine continued. "Those cops made it in their truck, and with the barbed wire down we should be fine."

"Whatever you think," I agreed. "You're the driver."

We'd reached the entrance to the site. There was a 2011 Crown Vic parked in the space our mobile unit had occupied the previous day. *Unmarked police car? A newer model than Pete's*. Francine was a skillful driver and I admired the ease with which she maneuvered the van on the uneven road, dodging tree roots and potholes. We'd come to the first No TRESPASSING sign when I noticed some fresh cuts on the trees as we climbed upward. "Looks like some limbs have been trimmed since yesterday," I pointed out.

"You're right. Maybe that's to make room for a big yellow crane," she said, pointing. "Uh-oh. Cop ahead."

She was right. A uniformed officer with white-gloved hand upraised in the traditional "stop" position stood just ahead of us with legs braced, feet firmly planted in the middle of the road. We pulled to a halt. Francine set the hand brake and rolled her window down while I pulled the permits from my purse.

"No trespassing, ladies," he said, indicating the faded sign. "You can turn around right here."

"We have permits, officer." I reached across Francine and handed him the paperwork. "I'm Lee Barrett, WICH-TV."

He nodded and proceeded to study each page. Carefully. At length. Time passed. I imagined that I could hear crickets.

"Any other press here?" Francine asked. "Boston stations?"

He shook his head. "Nope. You're the first."

"Is the crane in place yet?" I asked.

That brought a questioning look and another long pause. "Yep. Brought her in last night. Big one." He shuffled the papers, tapping them on the side of the van so that the edges were all even.

I reached for them. "So we're good to go?"

"Maybe." He pulled a phone from his belt and, still holding our permits, turned his back and stepped to the side of the road.

CHAPTER 7

Francine turned the radio off. I opened my window, straining to hear the officer's words. Francine didn't even try to be discreet—just stuck her head out the window as far as she could. I couldn't make out even a single syllable, and from my partner's puzzled expression I guessed she hadn't fared much better.

The officer faced our direction once again. Still holding our signed and sealed official permits, he returned to the driver's side window. "Can I see your IDs please?"

We handed them over. "Is there a problem, officer? I asked, maintaining a friendly tone. He didn't reply, but passed each license in front of his phone. *He's sending pictures of our IDs somewhere? Why?*

He spoke into his phone once more, then handed the licenses and permits back to us. "Okay, ladies," he said. "You're good to go." With a casual salute, he stepped out of the way.

Francine released the brake, put the van in gear, and we resumed our slow, upward trek.

"What do you suppose all that was about?" I whispered, although we were far out of earshot of the law.

"Beats me," she said, also whispering. "But it looks as though there's more going on up there than we thought."

"It looks that way to me, too," I said resuming a normal tone. "Maybe the human remains aren't just from any old human. Maybe they're looking for some famous missing person."

Francine laughed. "Like D. B. Cooper? Amelia Earhart? Jimmy Hoffa? In the North Shore pits? I don't think so."

"I guess you're right. Whatever it is though, at least we're the first media here." We'd reached a small clearing and over the treetops I spotted part of what had to be the yellow crane. "Look! There's the crane," I said.

We drove directly onto the field we'd crossed on foot the day before. The barbed wire was gone, but all of the "No" signs were still there. No diving, no swimming, no trespassing. The empty beer cans were still there too. So was the goldenrod. There were two identical blue Chevys where there'd been one before. Next to them was a good-sized RV, and dominating the scene was the humongous yellow crane, way larger than I'd even imagined it would be. A group of people were gathered near the thing, dwarfed by the long row of enormous tires.

Francine was already out of the van, camera in hand,

running toward the crane by the time I'd opened my door. I clipped the new mic to my shirt next to the press pass, grabbed a handheld mic, too, and climbed out into the weeds. I began talking as I moved toward the granite pit. "Lee Barrett here for WICH-TV. We're on-site at the old granite pits where yesterday divers from the Salem Police Department's dive team, working on an anonymous tip, discovered a sunken vehicle over one hundred feet underwater. Heavy equipment has been deployed to this area to facilitate bringing the automobile—reportedly a Ford Mustang—to the surface." I'd caught up with Francine, and her camera included me in a long shot of the crane.

As I moved closer to the giant yellow machine, I recognized a few of the people gathered there—city councillor Lois Mercer, who I'd interviewed several times on city business; Officer Andrews and his sea-monster dive buddy from the day before, today dressed in plain clothes; and Doc Egan, the medical examiner. The others—some in business attire, some casually dressed—didn't look familiar. "A source close to WICH-TV tells us that there may be human remains inside the sunken vehicle," I continued, fudging a little about the closeness of the source. "These granite pits were once popular with swimmers and young daredevil divers. But because of the danger of diving from the reportedly seventy-foot-tall granite cliffs, this entire area has for many years been closed to the public." I moved past the twin Chevys to where we'd stood before, on the low ledge overlooking the water.

I remembered what sea-monster diver had said about the cliff they thought the car had fallen from. (That matched the picture I'd seen in the hall tree mirror, so there was a darned good chance it was correct.) Still, I didn't want him to get into trouble for talking to me about what the tipster had told the police. So I'd decided to use the "confidential informant" source the network reporters always use. *Why not?*

Francine once again stood close to the edge of the ledge, aiming her camera upward. "WICH-TV has learned that the vehicle in question may have long ago plummeted from one of the seventy-foot granite crests here," I said. I saw Francine move the camera slowly downward, undoubtedly trying to give the viewers a feeling of plummeting from that gray, forbidding rock facade. I motioned to her to follow me back to where the crane was poised, pretty sure that city councillor Lois Mercer would allow an interview even if the others were too busy or too important to share information with my viewers.

I moved close to the crane and called softly to the councillor. "Ms. Mercer? Lee Barrett. WICH-TV. Could I ask you a few questions?"

"Hello, Lee," she said. "I was sure I'd see you here."

"You were?"

"Of course." Big smile. "I saw your spot on the news yesterday evening, then we all got the text this morning from Chief Whaley.

"A text from the chief?" I hoped I didn't sound as clueless as I felt.

"Yes. He's quite anxious to get the news out about this sunken car, isn't he?"

That's news to me. He sure wanted it spiked yesterday. "Yes, well, that's why WICH-TV is here," I said. "We like to keep our viewers informed."

"You and your photographer are the first media people here," she said. "WBZ called me before I got here this morning. Anyway, I didn't really have anything to share with them yet. Said they had to pull some permits to get their equipment onto the property. That can take a while."

Bless you, Rhonda!

I motioned for Francine to join me. "Could you answer a few questions on camera, Ms. Mercer?" I checked the time. "I believe we can still make the morning news."

"Glad to," she said. "This is quite exciting, isn't it?"

"Seems so. Shall we stand in front of the crane?" I rehearsed questions in my mind while Francine arranged us to her liking. I handed the councillor the hand mic and began. "I'm speaking with city councillor Lois Mercer. As you know, Ms. Mercer, members of the Salem Police Department dive team, on a tip from an anonymous person, discovered a vintage automobile at close to one hundred twenty feet underwater here at the abandoned granite pits. Can you tell us about the city of Salem's interest in this matter?"

"Yes, Lee. According to what we've learned so far, there may a body—that is, there may be remains—of a Salem citizen inside that car. A citizen who may have met with foul play."

"Foul play?" *Really?* "Like murder?"

"That term has not been used." She frowned.

I decided to pursue another angle. If there was murder involved, Pete would have to tell me about it. No sense annoying my best city hall contact at this point.

"The informant must be a credible one," I said, feeling a tickle in my throat, and stifling a sneeze. "Pulling up a vehicle from that far underwater must be expensive." I tapped the side of the crane.

"Indeed it is. That's why I'm here, representing the city."

"Do you know who the 'deceased Salem citizen' is?"

"I do not." Lois Mercer's smile was gone. I pressed further.

"Do the police know who it is?"

"If they do, they haven't shared that information with me." Her expression told me that our conversation was over. It was becoming clear that if Chief Whaley wanted people to know about this underwater car, he apparently wanted a sanitized version of it. I wondered if I could get a look at that text.

"Thank you, Ms. Mercer. WICH-TV will keep our viewers informed as this story unfolds." I turned to Francine and checked my watch again. "Morning news will be over in ten minutes. Let's send what we've got so far back to the station. We'll stick around here and see what else we can dig up for the noon edition." I patted the crane again. "If they get this baby fired up maybe we can go live."

"Maybe we'll be jockeying for position. Look at the

parade of mobile units coming up the hill." She was right. There'd been some serious permit-pulling going on. One by one, they parked in a row next to ours—two Boston units, one all the way from Worcester, the WESX radio van, and a sweet Jaguar with a red, white, and blue OVERTON FOR CONGRESS bumper sticker bringing up the rear.

I wonder if they all got the same third degree we did before we were allowed up here.

CHAPTER 8

It didn't take long for our competition to get their
equipment and personnel into broadcast mode. But
Francine and I still held our front-row positions, close
to the crane and the people gathered around it. Doc
Egan had noticed me there and made eye contact. I
moved in closer with every intention of taking advantage of long acquaintance. "Hello, Ms. Barrett," he
said. "Somehow I'm not surprised to see you here."

"Good morning, Doctor Egan," I extended the
hand mic. I wasn't surprised that *he* wasn't surprised.
Doc and I had met before, usually in the presence of
the recently deceased. This was a little different.
"Could you share a few words with our audience?
Councillor Mercer has suggested that the remains of
a Salem citizen may be in the underwater vehicle,
and that the person may have been the victim of foul
play. Is that what brings you here this morning?"

"Always glad to cooperate when I can, Ms. Barrett,"
he said, "but in this case, if there is a case, I have not
viewed any remains, if there are any remains, and

cannot comment on foul play, if there was foul play."
He nodded toward the camera. "Sorry."

*Bummer. Glad we didn't go live with that bunch of
nothing.* I glanced behind us at the rapidly advancing
representatives of rival media and took one more
shot at our original source, sea-monster diver, whose
name I still did not know.

"Good morning, Officer," I said. "I understand that
you are a member of SPD's elite dive team." (I threw
in the "elite," not sure if it fit, but it sounded good.)
"Have you actually seen the underwater subject of
this investigation?"

He frowned, as if trying to place me, with recognition
dawning on his face seconds later. "Yes, Ms. Barrett,"
he said. "I dove on the wreck yesterday. Hard-hat divers
take over now."

"Can you give us your name, and tell our WICH-
TV audience a little about what the hard-hat divers do
differently from what you did yesterday?" *And at the
same time educate me on the subject?*

"I'm Paul Linsky. Hi," he stuck out his hand and we
shook as though we'd just met. "Want to meet a couple
of hard hats?" he said. "They came up from New Bed-
ford just for this." He turned toward the group now
congregating at the payload end of the crane where
a hook dangled from a cable high above our heads.
"Hey, Ben, Terry. Come on over and meet the TV girl
I told you about."

What a break for me! "Thank you, Paul," I said, and
signaled to Francine to get a shot of the two men approaching. "So these are the divers who'll help to get
the vehicle attached to the crane?"

"Yep. Ben and Terry are the working divers for this

job. They're part of a team—a *real* elite team. There're also the standby divers, the chamber operator, the life support tech, the systems tech—they're all here too. It takes a bunch of people to pull off a stunt like this, you know." He greeted the two men with a salute. "They'll tell you. Guys, this is Lee Barrett."

So began my education into the underwater world of professional divers. It turns out that hard-hat divers take special advanced training courses to learn a whole new set of skills. Ben and Terry knew how to cut and weld metal under water, even to use pneumatic drills. Ben had flown by helicopter to work on offshore oil rigs, and Terry was also a medical tech and could deal with emergencies like decompression sickness. The two gave the WICH-TV audience (and me) a clear and concise picture of how the task at hand—the raising of the Mustang—would be accomplished. Hopefully today. *Doan is going to love this segment!*

Francine transmitted it all back to the station, with a promise of more to come, for the noon news. We got permission to broadcast the actual raising of the car live, no matter what time of day it happened.

After our interview with the hard-hat divers, some of the reporters from other stations approached them. Ben smilingly waved them off. "Time for us to suit up," he said. "Sorry." I watched as he and Terry headed for the RV in the maple grove. We'd scored an exclusive! I thanked Paul Linsky—maybe a little too profusely—and turned my attention back to the rest of the group assembled beside, in front of, and behind the giant yellow crane. The supporting members of the dive team Paul had told me about had followed the divers to the RV. Lois Mercer was being photographed for the *Salem News*. A sizable cluster of reporters were gathered around a somewhat familiar figure. It took a few seconds before I recognized Steve Overton. Of course. The Jaguar with the bumper sticker.

"Come on. Let's go interview Overton," I told Francine.

"Who?" She fell into step beside me.

"Steve Overton. He's running for Congress. He was at my house last night."

"Auntie's classmate?"

"Sure is." My nose began to itch and I felt a sneeze coming on. "I don't know what he's doing here, but I'm sure he's good for an interview."

"Politicians show up wherever there's a camera. Doesn't matter a damn what it's about," Francine stated flatly. "You'll see. He probably doesn't even know what's going on here."

Francine and I wiggled and elbowed our way into the front row of the people surrounding Steve. He answered shouted questions from the crowd carefully and thoughtfully. Francine moved in for a close-up. Most of the questions were about what he planned to do when and if he got to Washington, so maybe the answers were scripted. I was impressed anyway. I'm not very good yet at shouting questions, but I'm good at making eye contact. I learned that from O'Ryan. Stare at someone long enough and they have to look at you. It's true. Ask any cat. Within a minute I got the expected meeting of the eyes and the follow-up warm smile. "Ms. Barrett," he said. "How nice to see you again. Couldn't miss that red hair." *Okay. Maybe it's the hair and not the eyes. Whatever works.*

"Mr. Overton," I said, going for local human interest instead of rehearsed campaign promises. "When you were a boy, did you ever dive from that seventy-foot monster?"

My question drew a short laugh. "Just once," he said, his expression suddenly boyish despite the gray-at-the-temples hair. "If somebody double-dog-dared you, you had to dive. It was kind of a rite of passage. Fortunately, once was enough to prove—whatever it was we were trying to prove."

I had a follow-up question ready. "Were you scared?"

"Absolutely terrified!" There was a smattering of good-natured laughter from the group. It was the right answer. I searched my mind for another question, but the sound of the crane's big engine turning over made all of us focus on the task ahead.

Things began to move very quickly, and once again I was glad that Francine and I were at the forefront of the action. I felt a little more confident in narrating what was going on, too, since I'd picked up information about the upcoming dive along with enough of the divers' jargon to sound somewhat knowledgeable about it all.

Two hard-hat divers had emerged from their RV. They, looking like space creatures, along with half a dozen assistants, made their way to the same ledge where we'd first met our scuba diver friends. By the time the crane was in place, its giant hook suspended by thick cable above the water, I was sure WICH-TV viewers would have a ringside seat for whatever was going to happen. Hard-hat divers use surface-supplied breathing equipment instead of the tanks we'd seen on Bill and Paul, and as the first diver disappeared below the water's surface, I told the viewers about the special mixture of gases used for a dive of such depth and how the divers would attempt to attach the wedged vehicle to the crane's cable so that it could be retrieved safely.

The recovery took only a couple of hours. Bill Andrews told me later that we'd witnessed a textbook-perfect dive operation. As Mr. Doan had promised, we went live on the air when the dive supervisor finally signaled the crane operator to lift the long-submerged burden. When the old Mustang broke the surface, I remembered how Francine had imagined it. "It'll be all drippy and slimy with mossy stuff on it," she'd said, and she'd been right about that. Of course, she'd also thought there'd be a skeleton sitting behind the wheel.

CHAPTER 9

It had been an exhilarating day. I'd seen something I'd never seen before and I was confident that the WICH-TV audience had too. Marty assured us that she had plenty of material and was already editing for a feature piece on the nightly news. Francine continued filming, and I continued talking for quite a while after the live segment was over. We were sure we'd have enough material for at least a ten-minute chunk of the nightly news, and with luck, maybe some of it would get picked up by one of the big networks.

While we'd all been focused on the action down by the water, a flatbed truck had moved into position beside the crane. All the media, including me, had ducked involuntarily when the dripping, mossy, slimy car swung slowly over our heads toward solid ground. Francine, with her keen photographer's eyes, had raced toward the truck in time to capture the shot as the Mustang was lowered onto the flatbed, the cables detached by a waiting crew. The years with my NASCAR driver husband Johnny had made me a bit of a car buff. *Ford Mustang Fastback,* I thought. *Nineteen seventies.* I followed close behind her, squinting as I tried to decipher the numbers on the license plate. No luck. Rust and time and slime had obscured whatever was there. In what seemed like seconds the whole thing moved away from us, down the hill to the street, the car by then completely covered with canvas, preceded by the same Crown Vic we'd seen earlier, this time with lights flashing

"Stay here or follow it?" Francine asked.

"Follow," I said and together we raced across the field toward our mobile unit, me sneezing all the way. We'd lost sight of the truck by the time we got to the bottom of the hill, but the sound of the police car's siren led us in the right direction. We caught up with it on 128 and followed at a discreet distance—if riding in a long van with a TV station's call letters emblazoned on both sides can be considered discreet—to a row of warehouses just over the Beverly line. We were stopped at the entrance to the place and no amount of pleading, permits, or press cards could get us past the uniformed officer this time.

That was a letdown after the earlier excitement, and we were both quiet as Francine headed the van back toward Salem. I broke the silence. "You called it right about how the car would look when they brought it up. River would probably say that you're psychic."

That brought a smile. "No skeleton in the front seat, though. Maybe I'll call her show tonight and ask her where the heck my skeleton went."

"I'm supposed to call her later today," I recalled. "She worries about me."

"Really? You believe in that stuff?"

"I'm not exactly sure," I admitted. "But sometimes she's so spot-on it's scary."

"My roommate watches *Tarot Time* most every night. Believes every word of it. Her brother thinks she's nuts. Kids her about it all the time."

"That the brother with the trainer who hangs around with the divers?"

"That's him."

"Maybe he can find out about what's inside the Mustang. Maybe he can even find your missing skeleton." I was just kidding about the skeleton. But I was curious to know exactly what was hidden under all that canvas.

"The hard-hat divers might know what's in there," she said. "They had a pretty good close-up look in the windows today."

"Why don't we skip the middleman and just start hanging around that dive shop ourselves?" I asked, in a sudden burst of inspiration. "It'd be research for the story, wouldn't it?"

She snapped her fingers. "Bingo! You should probably do that anyway," she said with a sly smile. "Though you've been faking it pretty well so far. Today you sounded like an expert on diving procedures."

"Faking it is right," I agreed. "Today I used up every shred of information I have on the subject. I need to hit the books and learn about how they attached the car to the crane. And about the gas mixtures the hard hats use. If we're going to try to talk to divers, I can't sound like a total ditz."

"Doan is going to want a lot more on this."

"I know. And if there *is* anybody—or remains of anybody—in that car, he's going to want to know how they got there," I said. "And maybe the first thing we need to find out is who the car belonged to."

We rounded the corner onto Derby Street and pulled into the WICH-TV parking lot. "Since Scott Palmer picked up our regular schedule, looks like we're through for the day. You've got a lot of studying to do. I'll run in and clock out for both of us, and fix up tomorrow's schedule with Rhonda—including a visit to the dive shop first thing," Francine said as she let me out beside my car. "See you in the morning."

"Uh-huh. See you. Don't forget to watch the news tonight." My mind raced as I started the Vette. *I'll bet Pete already knows who that Mustang was registered to. I wonder what River saw in that reading that creeped her out. Did the divers see "human remains"?* I headed down Derby Street, turned onto Hawthorne Boulevard, past the Salem Common and onto Oliver Street. (Our house faces Winter Street, but our property goes all the way through to Oliver Street, and that's where the garage is.)

First things first, I thought as I pulled into the garage and parked beside my aunt's Buick. *I'll call River and get the reading out of the way.* O'Ryan sat on the back steps waiting for me and accepted my head pats and chin chucks with happy purrs, then followed me into the hall. I was about to knock on Aunt Ibby's kitchen door, thinking I might pick up my platter and even mooch a bite of late lunch, when I heard women's voices inside. Raised voices. I recognized my aunt's unmistakable New England accent.

"Listen, Betsy." Her tone was serious. "It's none of your business. It wasn't your business then and it isn't now. I'm telling you, stay out of this."

Betsy. Must be Betsy Leavitt. She must have parked that fancy Mercedes on the Winter Street side of the house.

The answering voice was lower, more modulated, but with a decidedly angry edge. "I know more than you think I do, Ibby. And maybe I just intend to make it my business. I'll see you later." There was a click of high heels on the tile floor, then silence.

I looked down at O'Ryan. He looked up at me. Together we started up the staircase leading to my apartment. Whatever was going on between my aunt and her old school chum Betsy was certainly none of *our* business.

It was four-thirty, still a little too early to call River—I'd worked that late-show time slot and I knew she wouldn't be awake yet. It was also pretty late for lunch and I was hungry. My refrigerator didn't yield much of interest—nothing new there—so I made a peanut butter sandwich, poured a glass of milk, and opened *The Scuba Diving Handbook*. I'd just started the chapter on "lifting heavy objects" when my phone buzzed. Caller ID showed River North.

"Hi, River."

"I thought you were going to call me."

"I didn't think you'd be awake yet," I said, surprised by the urgency in her voice.

"Never mind. I woke up thinking about your cards," she said. "I left them on the table last night and I'm looking at them right now. I don't like what I see."

"I guess you'd better tell me about them then," I told her, working to keep my own voice even.

"I started with your card, the Queen of Wands, same as always." She'd chosen that card for me the first time she read my cards. The red-haired queen sits on a throne holding a staff and a sunflower, facing a cat. We agreed it was an appropriate choice on several levels. She continued. "Okay. Ask a silent question or make a silent wish."

I'd already done that. "Question," I said. "Go on."

"The Ten of Swords covers your queen. The meaning here is ruin and pain, affliction and tears, and possible heartbreak. I'm sorry, Lee."

"That's all right. Not your fault. Go on."

"Next comes the Ace of Cups. A new beginning." I knew that. Aces always mean beginnings.

"In this case it's about the beginning of new love," River said. "Is everything okay with you and Pete?"

"Yes. As far as I know," I said. "You sure this is about me?"

"It can involve somebody close to you. Maybe that's it. Anyway, next comes the King of Cups, reversed. A powerful man. Watch for deception. He's crafty. Clever."

A powerful man. Like a congressman?

"Next is the Queen of Swords. She's quite beautiful. Maybe a widow. Here she's reversed though. She's artificial, gossipy. Do you know who she is?"

"Nope," I said. "So far this doesn't sound too good, does it?"

"It doesn't have to be bad, you know," she said. "It just gives you some ideas of what to look out for. Who to avoid. Anyway, next one is the Star. Insight, inspiration, and hope. If you listen carefully, the truth will come out."

"Listen to who?"

"I don't know. Keep your ears open. Do you have the deck of tarot cards I gave you?"

"Of course I do." The beautiful cards were in one of the secret compartments in my bureau.

"Put the Star card where you can see it every day. Look at it once in a while. It might help," she said. I promised that I'd do as she asked, and she moved on to the next card. "The Six of Cups. This can bring someone from the past with new knowledge. Maybe a new opportunity,"

"That sounds good. Is it?"

"I think so. Keep your ears open on that one too. Now here's the one that worries me. The Eight of Swords. Do you happen to remember what it looks like?"

"I'm not sure. I wish I'd brought my deck of cards out here to the kitchen with me. Is it the blindfolded lady standing in water?"

"Right. You're getting good at this, Lee. Anyway, it can mean restricted surroundings. Like some kind of imprisonment. The classic translation is fear to move out of a situation." River paused. "I just don't like this one at all. I wouldn't even mention it to a caller on my show. But I care about you, and you need to be careful."

"I'm always careful, River. What about the rest of the cards?"

"Pretty ordinary, actually. I'll take a picture of the layout and I'll read it to you later, It was just the first few that concerned me, so now you know. Oh, the last card was the Nine of Wands, so the answer to your question will be delayed.

That figures. And now I know what? Watch for new

love for somebody? Pay attention to a gossipy widow and a powerful guy who's crafty? Concentrate on a pretty tarot card and don't get blindfolded while standing in water?

"Thanks, River." I said. "I'll be careful about everything you said. By the way, was Pete's card there this time?" The card River uses to represent Pete is the Knight of Swords. He shows up in my readings quite often.

"Not this time," she said. "But that doesn't mean he won't be there to protect you. That's not what you're thinking, is it?"

"Of course not. I didn't think that at all," I lied. "Thanks again. Talk to you soon."

I fished into my purse and pulled out my package of index cards. I selected one and quickly listed the cards River had just told me about before I had a chance to forget them. The Queen of Wands, the Ten of Swords, the Ace of cups, the King of Cups, the Queen of Swords, the Eight of Swords, the Nine of Wands, and, of course, the Star. Did they mean anything? Maybe. I labeled the card "Tarot reading" and added the date.

I went back to my book on SCUBA diving and tried to focus on atmospheric diving suits. Would a suit like that comprise "restricted surroundings?" I put the book down, my train of thought by then totally derailed, and looked toward my kitchen window where O'Ryan lay sprawled out full length along the windowsill.

"I wonder what Aunt Ibby and Betsy were talking about." I said aloud. O'Ryan opened his eyes, acknowledging my comment. "You think they were arguing about something?" He made a sound in his throat that sounded remarkably like "duh."

"Yeah. That's what I thought too. You think maybe Betsy is what you'd call 'gossipy'?"

No cat response. I tried another idea. "I wonder if she's a widow." That brought a tail swish and a low growl. "How about the new beginning? The new opportunity?" O'Ryan stretched, opened his mouth in a big yawn, and closed his eyes. End of conversation.

I went back to my book. Read the sentence three times about the helmet including a microphone so that hard-hat divers can talk to the crew on the surface. I was sure I wasn't retaining any of it. I put the book down again and looked over the cat and out the window.

"Make a wish or ask a question." River had given the usual pre-reading command. My question had probably been the same one everybody in Salem was asking.

Are there really human remains in that old car? Whose? And why?

CHAPTER 10

Pete and I hadn't made any specific plans for the evening, but we keep in touch daily by phone or text. I was doing a bit of overdue dusting in my living room when my cell buzzed. "Hi Pete" I said. "You still at work?"

"Just left. You up for pizza at Greene's Tavern? And maybe a movie after?"

"Absolutely. What time?"

"Pick you up in about an hour? Around six?"

"Perfect. See you then."

Greene's Tavern is a cozy, casual, everybody-knows-your-name kind of place and one of our favorite date destinations. I gave a final flick of the fluffy duster and headed back down the hall to the kitchen. Kit-Cat Klock showed a few minutes after five. I'd barely have time for a quick shower, and a change into fresh jeans and top. I gathered up the books, index cards, and Post-it Notes, and returned them to the bedroom. Remembering River's advice about putting the Star card where I'd see it every day, I removed the deck from its special compartment in my antique bureau and studied the card. A beautiful nude woman kneels with one knee on the land and one foot in the water. In the sky are seven small stars and one large one. *I'll figure out where to put this later.* Leaving the card on top of the books, I padded down the hall to the bathroom.

Showered, shampooed, with too-curly hair towel-dried, I pulled on white jeans and a navy turtleneck. Mascara and pink lip gloss would do for makeup, and white sandals with kitten heels were cute and comfortable. O'Ryan abandoned his windowsill post and ran for the living room door at exactly six, letting me know that Pete had arrived.

With the purring cat doing figure eights around our ankles, we shared a long, delightful kiss—the kind that can interrupt pizza plans indefinitely if we let it. But the fact that all I'd had for lunch was a peanut butter sandwich and the additional knowledge that Pete planned to spend the night again prompted me to whisper an unromantic, but sincere, "I'm starving."

"Let's go get that pizza," he said, taking my hand. "You've had a busy day, babe. I saw the live shot of the Mustang coming out of the pit. I didn't know you knew so much about underwater recovery."

"I'm learning as I go along," I admitted as we headed out into the hall with O'Ryan leading the way. "Let's stop at Aunt Ibby's for a minute so I can tell her where we're going. See if she wants us to bring her a pizza."

O'Ryan ducked into his cat door and I knocked. "It's me, Aunt Ibby. Pete and I are going to Greene's. Just want to see if we can bring you anything."

"Come in, dear. It's open."

Pete frowned. "I wish she'd keep her doors locked," he said softly. "She's much too trusting." I pushed the door open and greeted my aunt with a hug.

"Smells good in here," I said. "What's cooking?"

"Oh, just a small spinach quiche." She wiped her hands on her red-and-white striped "Kiss the Cook" apron. "Penelope's coming over later to use my copying machine. It's faster than hers, and we have to start on those yearbook pictures for the name tags."

"Was it a big graduating class?" Pete asked.

"Not too big," she said. "Around two hundred of us. Small enough so that we knew just about everybody."

"Do you have any idea how many will show up for the reunion?" I wondered

"Not yet. We'll know when the RSVPs start to come in."

"You said earlier that the men would be ordering invitations and that the women would be making the name tags." I watched her face. "Is the other woman, Betsy, coming over to help with the copying?"

Her expression didn't change. "No. We invited her, but she had other plans. She stays busy. Said she'd help when we do the pin backs for the pictures."

"Well, you girls have fun," I said, "and I guess if you have quiche cooking you don't want pizza."

"Thanks anyway," she said. "Have a good evening."

Pete pulled the door open. "Ms. Russell," he said. "Do me a favor and keep this door locked, will you."

She smiled. "I'll try to remember that, Pete. I go in and out of it so often it seems like too much trouble to keep locking and unlocking it every time."

"I understand." Serious cop voice. "But there's so much crime in the news lately you can't be too careful."

"Speaking of the news, Aunt Ibby," I said as Pete and I stepped out into the hall, "did you catch my feature story about the car they pulled out of the granite pit?"

She turned to face the stove and picked up a pot holder. "Sorry, dear. No. Too busy, haven't watched TV or even turned on the radio today. Oh, look. Here's your platter" She handed it to me. "See you tomorrow."

Pete closed the door and put his finger to his lips. I put the Wedgwood platter on the bottom step of the flight leading to my apartment. Then we waited there quietly until we heard the click of the lock sliding into place.

Greene's Tavern is located in a circa 1800s house on a side street in one of Salem's oldest neighborhoods. The parking lot and the entrance to the bar are in the back of the place. Proprietor Joe Greene's daughter Kelly greeted us warmly at the door. Kelly had been a student in my very first television production class at the Tabitha Trumbull Academy of the Arts and was currently an intern at a major Boston TV station. She sometimes worked evenings, helping her dad at the tavern. I was proud of her and often told her so.

Kelly led us to our favorite booth in the corner closest to the giant fieldstone fireplace. We ordered two light beers and our usual pepperoni with extra cheese. When our food arrived and we were alone, Pete leaned across the table. "What's going on with Ms. Russell?" he asked.

"I'm not sure," I said. "You noticed it, too?"

"Nothing specific," he said. "But—something isn't right."

"I know." I told him about the conversation I'd overheard between my aunt and Betsy. "'It wasn't your business then and it isn't your business now.' That's what she said."

"And Ms. Leavitt said she intended to make it her business?"

"Words to that effect," I said.

"You were pushing her buttons a little with that question about Betsy helping with the name tags."

"I guess so. Was it obvious?"

"To me. You're starting to sound like a cop."

"A reporter."

He nodded. "Kind of the same thing, I guess. Aren't you getting ready to ask me some questions about today?"

I nodded back. "What's in the car?"

"We don't know yet."

"Do you know whose car it was?"

Little smile. "Yes."

"Can you tell me?"

"Not yet. There may be people to notify."

That set off one of those imaginary light bulbs over my head. *Notification of family usually means there's a body.* "So, they've found—um—remains?"

He leaned back in the red leather upholstered booth. "Whew, babe. You're getting pretty good at this. No comment on remains. Right now we're trying to identify the owner of the car."

CHAPTER 11

I tried to dig a few more scraps of information from Pete, but we've been together long enough for him to know exactly how to dodge my questions. I gave up before our pizza was even half gone. Proving that he has a lot more experience in the interrogation department than I do, I found myself telling him about what I'd seen in the mirror.

Early in our relationship I'd kept quiet about being a scryer, afraid he'd think I was some kind of nutcase. When I finally began sharing some of the things I saw, I knew he was uncomfortable about this strange ability of mine. I fully understand that. I'm still not very comfortable with it myself.

"So you think you saw the Mustang at the actual moment when it fell into the pit?"

"I do. River says the visions can be from the past, the present, or the future."

He leaned toward me. "Can you describe exactly what you saw?"

That was a surprise. He doesn't usually ask for details about what I've seen.

"Well, just what I told you. It was like a slow-motion clip from a movie. The car fell all the way from the top of one of the tallest granite cliffs."

"Did it fall straight down?"

I closed my eyes trying to bring the picture back. "It was kind of a twisting motion," I said. "Straight down but turning at the same time."

"Okay. Day or night?"

"Oh, night. Definitely night." I was sure about that. Eyes still closed. "And there was a moon. Moonlight."

"Good. Now think carefully. At the top of the cliff, did you see any people at all?"

I shook my head and opened my eyes. "You know? I don't actually see the very top. The car is already in motion, tumbling down beside the granite cliff wall when the vision starts."

"Okay. It's not important. I'm just curious about how those—things—how they work."

"Me too. If you ever figure it out let me know," I said. "Is Chief Whaley feeling any better about—um, everything?" I meant was he feeling any better about me releasing the news about the sunken car before he was ready. Pete knew what I meant. He knows me pretty well.

"He hasn't mentioned anything about you and that five o'clock news teaser. At least to me anyway. You know how he is." He reached over and took my hand. "He'll get over it. Always has."

"I know." It was true, but it's an uncomfortable feeling having the police chief ticked off at you, and this was far from being the first time I'd been in that position. "He'll get over it," I echoed Pete, and tried for another subject change. "I guess Aunt Ibby didn't watch the piece Francine and I did from the pits today. Did you happen to catch it?"

"I didn't. Sorry. There wasn't anything in it to piss off the chief again, was there?" A tiny worry frown creased his forehead.

"Don't think so." I reached for the second-to-last slice of pizza. "They'll probably use some of it on the eleven o'clock. The shot of the car coming out of the water was the best part. Otherwise it was pretty much just me interviewing the people who were there. The hard-hat divers. The crane driver. City hall people. Steve Overton was there. Francine says those political types show up wherever there's a camera."

"She's probably right about that." He checked his watch. "If we catch the eight o'clock movie at Cinema Salem we'll get back to your place in time to see the news. I'll be interested to see that shot of the car coming out of the pit. Quite a sight, huh?"

"It was. And then the crane swung it right over our heads and onto a flatbed where they covered it with canvas so fast it was all covered by the time Francine and I got back up there."

"Probably took it right to a secure location so the forensic people and the doc can get a look at it."

"Yep. We followed them. It's at a warehouse in Beverly."

"So much for security," he said. "I don't suppose they let you in, did they?"

"Of course not! But it was worth a try."

He picked up the last slice of pizza and smiled.

"You sound more like a cop every day. Want to leave now and catch the new Avengers movie?"

"Certainly. The perfect date, You, pizza, and Robert Downey Jr. Life is good." We sipped the last of our light beer, Pete paid the tab, we wished the Greenes a good night, and we stepped outside into the mild spring evening.

Cinema Salem is a popular destination for all ages and tastes with such a good variety of films to choose from that Pete and I usually flip a coin to see who picks the movie. We both like the Avengers so we were flip free. We agreed on the popcorn too. The kind dripping with real butter.

By ten thirty, with pizza, beer, movie, and popcorn finished, we were back at the house on Winter Street. O'Ryan greeted us on the back steps. The lights were out in Aunt Ibby's part of the house, so I picked up my platter from the bottom step and Pete and I tip-toed up the staircase trying hard to be quiet—which naturally always makes both of us laugh.

Smothering giggles, I unlocked the door to my living room. "We made it in plenty of time for the late news," I said. "I hope they'll at least show the part where the car comes up out of the water—all drippy and slimy and creepy."

"Want me to make a pot of decaf?" Pete asked. "I hope they'll show the whole part you and Francine did. Wish I could have been there, but it's really not exactly my case yet."

"Yes to the coffee," I said. "And I wish it was your case so I could interview you. Are you working on anything interesting? I mean anything interesting that you can talk with me about?" *Not his case* yet? *What does that mean?*

We walked down the hall to the kitchen, where O'Ryan was already sitting on the windowsill. Pete filled the Mr. Coffee with water and measured coffee into the basket. "Chief's got me working a couple of cold cases. I like that kind of investigation. Working on something nobody else has been able to figure out so far."

"I think it's every bit as interesting as the wet Mustang, although that's an old mystery, too, isn't it? Like why was it underwater at all? Did somebody ditch it for the insurance money? Officer Andrews said that happens sometimes."

"He's right." Pete put our coffee mugs on the table. "And it's possible that's the case with this one. That's the part I'm checking, and why I want to find the owner of record. Did he—or she—collect insurance money on it?"

I hadn't given the insurance question much thought. "The car has been missing for a real long time. Whoever owned it could be dead. What'll you do then?"

"One thing at a time, babe. I'll follow procedure."

"You're not going to tell me what the procedure is, are you?"

"Nope."

"What about the tip the department got? It wasn't about insurance was it? It was about 'human remains.' That's what everybody's saying anyway."

Pete opened the refrigerator. "Got any cream?"

"I'm out. There's some of the fake stuff in the pantry," I said. "Hey. What if that tip is fake stuff?

What if it's just a case of insurance fraud after all? No body. No remains."

He shrugged and put the jar of creamer on the table. "Then we spent a whole lot of money on divers and cranes and detectives' overtime for nothing. You got any cookies or anything?"

"There's still a package of Girl Scout cookies in the cookie jar." I reached for the Red Riding Hood cookie jar and emptied a sleeve of Samoas onto the Wedgwood platter. "Chief must have a lot of confidence in the tipster then, to risk so much money on an anonymous tip."

"Uh-huh," he said.

"It was anonymous wasn't it?"

"Far as I know. Now cut it out. No more shoptalk. It's almost time for the news."

We carried our coffee and cookies back to the living room. The big flat-screen model in there is bigger than the kitchen or bedroom sets. We settled ourselves on the couch and turned on WICH-TV. The night anchor, Buck Covington, read the first commercial— flawlessly, as usual. Covington's main claim to TV fame, other than being incredibly handsome, was his ability to read absolutely anything—cold off the teleprompter, with no rehearsal—perfectly. He was however, according to Mr. Doan, otherwise "dumb as a brick." So he was never required to comment on the news or to voice any opinion that hadn't been prepared for him and posted on the teleprompter. He was so gorgeous that virtually all the women—and likely some men—in the WICH-TV audience were in love with him, but he had eyes only for River North— who fortunately, found him fascinating, and not dumb at all. He read a brief tease for my story, showing the clip from the previous day when Francine had slowly panned down the entire rock face of the gray granite precipice. "Whoa!" Pete said. "Watching that could make a person seasick, couldn't it?"

"I know. I can't imagine all those kids who jumped off it."

"They all kept their eyes shut on the way down, I promise." He crossed his heart, grinning.

"You jumped, too?"

"Sure. More than once. Hey, look. Let's watch the weather."

Buck introduced Wanda the Weather Girl. If Buck Covington was eye candy for the ladies in the audience, Wanda was all that and more for the gentlemen. (The night's attire consisted of purple short-shorts and a pink crocheted peek-a-boo crop top.) Wanda posed prettily and as provocatively as legally possible in front of her weather map and promised another beautiful spring day with only a slight chance of rain. (Wanda has a degree in meteorology and another in climatology but undoubtedly would have been hired without them.)

My feature about the submerged Mustang was next, and it ran in its entirety. We'd done a damn good job on the segment and I was proud of it. "You know something, Pete," I said when it was over and Buck had moved on to a report on a big flounder a nine-year-old had caught at the Ultimate Kids Fishing Camp in Marblehead. "I don't want to wish anybody dead, but I can't help hoping you *do* find remains so I can keep this story going."

"Don't blame you, babe." He pulled me close. "I'm

so proud of you. And," he whispered, "you're right about the chief having confidence in the anonymous tipster. The guy may have been a witness to exactly what happened to that old Mustang."

I looked up at him. "Is that why you wanted to know about the vision I saw in the mirror? If I saw anybody on top of the cliff when the car went over?"

"Yep." He pointed at the TV screen. "Hey, speaking of spooky old cars, want to watch River's show? Look at what movie she's running tonight."

Of course, it was *Christine*.

CHAPTER 12

We carried the coffee mugs and cookie platter (empty) back to the kitchen and moved the late-movie watching to the bedroom. O'Ryan joined us on the big bed. He loves River and seems to enjoy watching her on TV almost as much as he does being with her in person. She began the show as usual with a tarot reading for a call-in follower.

"River did a reading for me this afternoon," I told Pete, as we watched River arrange cards on her table. I quickly added that I hadn't requested one. "It was her idea. She called me because she—well—she said she didn't like what she saw."

He turned down the volume on the TV and faced me. "Which was what? What did she see?" The question surprised me. Pete doesn't often show a lot of interest in River's "hocus-pocus."

"Pete, the things River sees in her cards make just about as much sense as the things I see in my visions. It's all up to the interpretation. She warned me about a gossipy woman and a deceptive powerful man.

She mentioned pain and tears and a scary bit about imprisonment." I watched his eyes. "She asked if things were all right between you and me. They are, aren't they?"

"More than all right," he said, his voice husky "and getting better all the time." He pulled me close. "Do you really want to watch *Christine*?"

He didn't need to wait for my answer. He clicked off the TV, and in the darkness I heard O'Ryan jump off the bed and head out of the room, back to his windowsill.

In my heart I knew that, just as Pete had said, things were more than all right between us and getting better all the time. I was still a tiny bit concerned though that Pete's card, the Knight of Swords, hadn't shown up in that reading to protect me from gossipy women, powerful men, and that poor blindfolded soul with her feet in the water.

I'd set my alarm for six thirty, allowing plenty of time for both of us to get ready for the workday ahead—and guaranteeing that, considering the depleted state of groceries in both refrigerator and cupboard, we could eat breakfast elsewhere.

As Wanda had predicted, it promised to be a pleasant day, weather-wise. I wore faded jeans, a white silk blouse, and a red cardigan with cordovan booties. Pete dressed casually too. "Plainclothes detail today?" I asked, admiring the way his tight jeans and long-sleeved Boston Celtics T-shirt accented his flat abs and cute butt.

"Right. Have to do a little blending into the background. Listening, mostly. These cold cases mean dredging up things people might have forgotten about—sometimes on purpose.

Dredging up? Does Pete's cold case involve something underwater?

We'd decided on our favorite early morning breakfast spot, an out-of-the-way two-story clapboard house on a side street, identified only by a neon OPEN sign in one window. Any weekday morning there'd be a variety of vocations represented at the assorted tables, booths, and counter in the long, warm, good-smelling room. Pete and I frequent the place so often that we've become "regulars," and have a passing acquaintance with many of the other repeat patrons—fishermen, nurses leaving the late shift, kids' hockey teams who had early ice-time practice, cops, cab drivers—a cross section of Salem's "morning people."

We headed for our favorite table in the back of the room. Two white ironstone mugs of steaming coffee appeared as though by magic along with a plastic-covered menu. "Be right back for your order, kids," our waitress Helen said. "Today's special is ginger pancakes with orange sauce. Wicked good."

We took the suggestion and each ordered the special. Our very first bites proved Helen right. Wicked good. As she topped off our coffees, I glanced around the rapidly filling room, and tapped Pete's arm. "One of Aunt Ibby's classmates just came in," I whispered. "He's the one in a blue windbreaker, sort of slumped over at the end of the counter. He doesn't look too good." I wasn't exaggerating. The man's complexion looked almost gray.

"Sure doesn't look good," Pete agreed. "Which classmate is he?"

"That's Bobby Ross," I said. "The man I told you about who smelled of booze when he arrived for the meeting."

Pete's brow creased in a small frown. "Bobby Ross? Name's familiar. A drinker, huh? Probably just has a hangover. A little coffee, a little food, and he'll feel a lot better."

While enjoying the breakfast and the company of my favorite man in the world, I stole an occasional peek at the man at the end of the counter. I decided that Pete's assessment was probably correct. By the time I'd poured the last of the orange sauce onto the last triangular wedge of my pancakes, Bobby's color had returned and he seemed to be enjoying the food on his plate. Pete had noticed too.

"I see that your aunt's friend seems to be recovering."

"Yes. He's even chatting with the guy next to him. You were right."

Pete smiled. "Food is a great healer," he said. "You about ready?" He tapped the face of his watch. "After I drop you off I have to pick up a rental car for the day. The Crown Vic is a little obvious for undercover work."

"I should think so. Hey, if I ever want to cover a story incognito I might have to switch cars too. My Corvette is a little on the obvious side, don't you think?"

He laughed and we got up to leave. "It's quite a bit more obvious than mine. Between the bright blue convertible and that red hair you'll probably never be in demand as a spy."

"That's okay. If I need to I can pull a hat down over the hair and borrow my aunt's nice nondescript Buick." We approached the counter and while Pete paid the bill I looked over toward the stool closest to the door where Bobby sat. I wondered if he'd recognize me. I even tried the cat-stare trick, but the man didn't look in my direction.

"Aren't you going to say hello to your aunt's classmate?" Pete said, taking my elbow and gently steering me toward the door. "I'd like to meet him."

That was puzzling. "You would? Okay." When I reached the end of the counter I attempted an oh-my-gosh-I-just-noticed-you expression. "Mr. Ross? Hello. I'm Lee Barrett, Ibby Russell's niece."

His smile was immediate and genuine. "Ms. Barrett. Good morning. How nice to see you again." He looked up at Pete and stuck out his hand. "Hello there. Bobby Ross. I'm one of Ms. Russell's high school classmates."

Pete grasped the extended hand. "Pete Mondello. Good to meet you. I've heard your name before. Played some hockey, didn't you?"

"I did, a long time ago." He glanced behind me. "But, hey, we're holding up the line here. Good to see you both." He turned back to his coffee and Pete and I proceeded to the exit.

"What was all that about?" I asked as soon as we were outside. "He's a hockey player? Should I have heard of him before?"

"No reason you would have," Pete said, holding the passenger door for me. "I knew the name was familiar. I remembered my dad talking about him. Ross played for UMass back in the seventies when my dad was there. Back then most teams had what they called an 'enforcer.' Tough guy. A fighter. Ross was that guy. Master of the Gordie Howe hat trick."

"A goal, an assist, and a fight, all in one game," I supplied. "Did he ever play professionally?"

"Nope. Wrecked a knee playing in college. Too bad." He shook his head. "My dad said Ross never graduated. Quit in his junior year and moved out west somewhere."

"San Francisco," I said, recalling the comments of the classmates when I'd brought Bobby to the dining room. "His high school friends all seemed glad to see him."

We turned the corner onto Winter Street. Pete looked at the clock on the dashboard. "Gonna have to drop you off in front of the house, babe. Chief's not going to be happy to see me if I'm late. Call you later." He leaned across the center console for a quick kiss and I climbed out onto the brick sidewalk and saw O'Ryan peeking from the tall window beside the front door. Hurrying up the steps, I unlocked the door and was greeted with the usual ankle rubs and happy cat noises.

Finished with his welcome home ceremony, O'Ryan trotted into my aunt's living room, pausing to look expectantly back toward me—a clear invitation to follow him. So of course, I did. "Aunt Ibby," I called. "It's me. O'Ryan invited me in."

"Good morning, dear. You're up and about early," she answered. "Coffee's on." She looked up from her *Boston Globe* as I entered the kitchen. "Been out for breakfast?"

"Yes. Ginger pancakes. Yum." I selected a Blue Willow mug, poured my coffee, and sat opposite her. "Know how to make them?"

"Of course. I haven't thought of ginger pancakes for years. Your mother used to love them."

"Did she? I wish I remembered more about her. Your friend Betsy thinks I look like her."

"You do. More and more every year." She put the newspaper down and stood to refill her coffee cup. I pulled the paper toward me. "Oh look." I pointed. "The *Globe* got some good shots of that car they pulled out of the granite pit yesterday."

"Really?" she said. "I hadn't noticed."

CHAPTER 13

We chatted for a few more minutes about my parents and pancakes and Betsy Leavitt's clothes and Steve Overton's run for office. I told her that we'd seen Bobby Ross at the restaurant. "Pete says Bobby was a good hockey player when he was young."

"Oh my, yes," she said, smiling. "He was quite the athlete. Won a scholarship to the University of Massachusetts. He and Betsy were high school sweethearts, you know."

"No kidding. I'll bet they were a cute couple. Did Penelope leave her yearbook here? I'd love to see some old pictures of you all."

"Sorry, no. She took it along with her."

"Oh well, let me know if she brings it back." I was disappointed. "I guess you haven't located yours?"

"Haven't really looked for it, but if it turns up I'll let you know." She opened another cabinet and pulled down a box of O'Ryan's favorite kibble. "Come on, kitty. Breakfast time."

I put my mug into the sink. "I'd better be on my

way. Francine and I are going to visit a dive shop this morning and see if we can learn anything new about the mystery Mustang."

She didn't comment. I kissed her cheek. "See you later today, then. Have a good day."

"You too," she said. "I'll be working at the library all afternoon, and Rupert and I have plans for the evening. North Shore Music Theater. They're doing *Mame.*"

"That sounds lovely. Have fun then. See you tomorrow." Rupert Pennington had been my boss when I taught TV production at the Tabitha Trumbull Academy of the Arts, and he and my aunt had hit it off beautifully. They're both old movie buffs and enjoy stumping one another with lines from the golden age of film.

I ran upstairs once again to pick up the grocery list I'd started, yanked a comb through my hair, and reapplied lip gloss. The Star card from the tarot deck was still on top of my bureau. I picked it up and looked at it carefully. In the sky above the woman were seven small eight-pointed stars and one large one. I'd thought about tucking the card into the frame of my oval mirror but decided if I was going to look at it often—as River had suggested—I'd rather it not be near a reflective surface. I decided to use that old standby—the refrigerator magnet. I attached the card to the front of the tall (and darn near empty) Frigidaire with a Cape Ann Whale Watch magnet, then hurried down the back stairs and out into the yard.

It was such a pretty day I put the convertible's top down. Since Francine and I were more or less "undercover" for the morning, we wouldn't be using the station's mobile unit and I was sure she'd enjoy the ride too. There was plenty of room in the big trunk for any equipment we might need if we lucked out at the dive shop with a good interview subject. When I reached the WICH-TV building, I parked next to the studio side door. Francine's truck was already in the lot so I called her. "What do you say we visit the dive shop in my car? With the top down. I'm at the side door. Grab the small camera and a mic and come on down!"

I didn't have to ask twice. With an excited "I'm on my way," Francine accepted and appeared in the doorway in less than a minute, camera, mic, and a couple of the navy blue nylon hooded WICH-TV jackets the station occasionally uses for promotions. "Wanda says there's a little cold front coming, maybe with showers," she explained. I popped the trunk open and she stashed the equipment.

"You'll have to give me directions," I said. "Diver's World, right? In Danvers?"

"Yep. Real nice people. You'll see." She gave me directions punctuated with comments about what we'd learned so far about the mysterious red car. "I'll bet they found those remains in it." She nodded vigorously. "Yep. I'm sure they did. They were sure in a big hurry to cover that car up and truck it away."

I agreed with her. "Looks like they've got some pretty tight security around it at that warehouse too."

"Right. Did your boyfriend tell you anything new about what's going on over there?"

"Not really. It's not his case, you know. But he kind of let it slip that the chief thinks there may have been a witness who saw how the car wound up in the drink in the first place."

"Wow! That's a game changer." She pointed to the right. "Over there. Near the pet store. Did he have any idea who the witness is?"

"I'm pretty sure he doesn't, but he wouldn't be able to tell me even if he did." I pulled the Vette as close to the show windows of the place as I could. I like to keep an eye on it, especially when the top is down. I locked the trunk and we went inside. The store was bigger than it looked from the outside, and it was packed with merchandise—some things I recognized, like flippers and face masks and snorkels, but some things looked alien—in every sense of the word.

Francine was greeted by name by several of the guys and girls inside. She introduced me, and our idea of being undercover disappeared almost immediately when several of them recognized me from the news shows and at least one remembered me as Crystal Moon. One of the men, who Francine identified as Fred, the manager of Diver's World, asked if we were there to do a feature about the store.

Francine and I looked at each other. *Why hadn't we thought of that in the first place?* I almost laughed out loud. Here we'd been trying to make a simple local interest topic into some kind of secret investigative-reporting event when all we actually wanted was some pro diver information about a recent underwater dive. *Duh.*

I hurriedly agreed with Fred that we had indeed hoped to get his permission to do such a story. Francine ran out to the car to get the camera and mic while I called the station to get Doan's okay. Rhonda relayed the message and we got a fast yes from the boss. As our friend Marty often says, "Piece of cake."

We decided to begin the segment with a tour of the store with Fred doing most of the talking. He turned out to be a natural narrator as we walked from display to display. All I had to do was pop in with a question here and there. We moved from boots to buoyancy compensators, watches to wetsuits. He explained uses of clips and reels, the importance of weights, lights, and hoses. It could have been eye-glazingly boring, but Fred made the topics interesting even to a diving know-nothing like me.

We reached a big and beautiful built-into-the-wall aquarium and Fred paused in his narration. "This is wonderful, Fred," I said, peering at a variety of colorful fishes, darting among miniature sunken pirate ships, treasure chests, and a pair of tiny hard-hat divers. "We have a small saltwater aquarium in our study, but nothing like this." I pointed to the little figures. "I happened to be on scene recently when some divers discovered a sunken automobile in a local granite pit, and I learned a bit about the skill and expertise and special equipment it takes to work in the deep water. Would you tell our audience something about it?"

His eyes narrowed just a tad, then without missing a beat, Fred delivered a short, succinct, and understandable, even to me, explanation of the special breathing apparatus, the required mixture of gases, and the particular challenges of deepwater diving. He did it, however, without making any reference to the recovered Mustang. Between the narrowed eyes and the slight change in tone of voice, I decided it would be wise not to press the issue.

We approached a glass display case filled with knives. Fred unlocked the case so that Francine could get a clear shot of the assortment. There were knives of varying sizes in the case, most with both cutting and serrated edges, some with saber-like points, all very shiny, very sharp. A pair of nearby mannequins dressed in scuba gear each had a sheathed knife—the girl had one strapped to her leg, the man wore his on his wrist.

"Are the knives really necessary?" I asked, "Or are they kind of a diving outfit fashion statement?"

"A good dive knife is important," he said, lifting a particularly lethal-looking one from the case. "You'd rarely use it, but when you do it's usually a life-or-death situation."

"Really? Life or death?" I repeated, picturing an enraged giant purple octopus bearing down on the girl mannequin.

Fred smiled. "Chances are you won't need it to fend off enemy divers or swamp creatures. No. But it'll cut you free from fishing lines and rope and other stuff that can trap you underwater."

We moved on to less threatening merchandise in the Dive Apparel Alcove. Here, T-shirts and jackets, hats and bags, bracelets and beach towels bearing logos familiar to divers—EVO, Aqua Lung, Dive Rite—made an attractive and undoubtedly profitable display. I thanked Fred and gave the address and website for Diver's World while Francine panned around the large showroom, where customers and clerks smiled and waved at the camera.

With camera and mic once again stashed in the trunk, Francine and I returned to the store as customers. Francine bought an underwater selfie stick. I picked out two T-shirts with sea creatures on them for Pete's nephews, all the while listening to conversation going on around us. It seemed as though everyone there was talking about the Mustang, and apparently had been all morning. This clearly wasn't going to be the glamorous covert secret agent chicks' operation we'd pictured for ourselves. *Sounds like everybody in Salem knows more about it than we do, and we were on scene with camera and sound.*

I spotted Officer Andrews standing beside the aquarium and hurried across the room to speak to him. He wasn't in uniform, so I figured he was off duty, a customer, just like me.

"Hello Officer. Lee Barrett. Remember me? We met the other day at the granite pit."

"Of course I remember you." Big smile. "It isn't every day I get interviewed by a beautiful redhead and get my face on the news. My mom was so excited!"

"Everybody here seems to be talking about what went on over there," I began my fishing expedition. "Human remains and all that. Is that why they were in such a hurry to cover the car and take it away? Did they see—um—something in it?"

He dropped his voice. "I didn't see it myself, but Paul did. Creeped him out big-time."

So there was a body in the car—or at least whatever remained of one. I took a quick look around the room, hoping to locate Paul Linsky. No luck. Not that he'd probably tell me anything anyway. I decided to press my luck with Officer Andrews. "Did he tell you exactly what he saw?"

A different look crossed Bill Andrews's face, replacing the smile. I recognized the look. *Cop face.* Maybe I'd pressed too hard. I waited. "Guess you'd have to ask him that," he said. "Nice seeing you again, Ms. Barrett." With a half salute in my direction, he headed for the front door. Oh well. I tried. If Bill Andrews and his dive buddy had known all along that there *was* a body—or something creepy—in the Mustang, Pete had known it all along too. Maybe by now Pete even knew who—or what—it was.

Francine appeared at my side. "Wasn't that one of the diver cops? Find out anything new?"

"Yep." I feigned deep interest in the aquarium occupants and Francine did the same. "He said that Paul, the other diver, saw something in the car that creeped him out," I whispered. "I'm thinking that could have been your skeleton."

"Bet you're right," she said, "and they must have cleaned that license plate by now so I guess they know who my skeleton is—was."

I thought about that. "Maybe. If the skeleton was driving his—or her—own car."

"True. Could have been a car thief—or the owner's girlfriend—or his mother—or . . ."

"So they might not know yet. Pete might not even know yet."

"Right. They're probably checking dental records. Checking for DNA. All that stuff they do on *CSI.*"

"I suppose we'll just have to wait along with everybody else until they announce it," I said. "You don't suppose your roommate's brother's contact has come up with anything, do you?"

"I don't know. We could stop by the gym on our way back to the station and see if he's there," she said.

"Guess we'd better head back that way now. We can turn in the footage we got on the dive shop. I think I'll give my aunt a call too. She's going to be at the library most of the day. She's a whiz at digging up old newspaper records. Somebody in Salem must have reported a red Ford Mustang Fastback missing. By the style of the car I'd guess it has to have been sometime in the early seventies."

We thanked Fred for his time and excellent presentation, reminded him to watch WICH-TV news at both five and eleven, and headed toward Salem. We did, as Francine had suggested, stop at the gym where her roommate's brother worked out. He was there, taking a spin class. Unwilling to stop cycling—he was in the middle of an uphill sprint—he told us that he'd heard from a warehouse security guard that the cops had put a one-bay rental garage under twenty-four-hour armed guard because they have a car in there with a bunch of bones in it. "Human bones," he practically shouted over the noise of speeding wheels.

That pretty much confirmed what we'd already figured out, even if the account we heard came from what might surely be considered an unreliable source. Naturally I couldn't admit that on the air. I mentally debated between using "a confidential informant" and "an unnamed source" for my report about human bones being found in the mystery car. I had every intention of covering that story, and I intended to tie the information to our dive shop segment. After all, it had been divers who'd set the whole story in motion. I was pretty sure I could work all of this into a darn good piece for my occasional late-news investigative-reporter spot.

I could hardly wait to meet with Marty to begin weaving the earlier footage of Andrews and Linsky, followed by the lifting of the Mustang from the depths of the North Shore granite pit, along with the Diver's World segment about deepwater diving, tied together with the announcement that there was indeed—according to a "confidential WICH-TV informant"—a dead human in the waterlogged wreck being kept under wraps in a local warehouse. Doan would love it. Chief Tom Whaley wouldn't.

CHAPTER 14

I had put the top up, remembering Wanda's warning about possible showers. Francine once again pulled her camera and mic from the trunk. I punched my password into the pad beside the downstairs studio door and together we entered the long room. Coming in from the sunshine, it always takes a moment or two for my eyes to adjust to the dim lighting in the studio with its black walls.

"Hey, Moon, Francine. Come on down to the cooking show stage." Marty's voice rang out in the semi-darkness, and we made our way carefully along the center aisle past sports, finance, fashion, and *Tarot Time* sets to the gleaming kitchen with its white appliances and oak cabinets. "Get anything good from the divers?" she asked, moving a green jadeite bowl full of plastic pears to the center of a butcher-block counter.

"I think so," I answered. "At least we know more than we did yesterday."

"Did they ID the body yet? That's what Doan is waiting for."

"Jeez, Marty," Francine added. "It's a freakin' skeleton. They're working on it."

"The cops must know by now." She added a plastic apple and a banana to the fruit bowl. "I suppose they have to do the next-of-kin thing." I wondered how fast my aunt could do the newspaper search. I'd love to have the name of the Mustang owner before the official release came. Francine had sent the morning's filming earlier, and Marty was ready to begin editing. "Why don't you two check in with Rhonda? I'll meet you in half an hour upstairs in the newsroom and show you what we've got."

I told her about my idea for the investigative-reporter piece. "I think Doan will like it. Maybe for tonight's late news with Covington?"

"Good thinking, Moon. We'll do your dive shop interview on Scotty's North Shore News segment, and patch the good part about the bones into your late news story. I'll get to work on it pronto."

We took Marty's suggestion and checked in with Rhonda. It was nearly noon and we were scheduled for a few afternoon assignments beginning at one o'clock. That would give me an hour to grab some lunch and call my aunt about finding out who'd reported the Mustang missing in the early seventies. I'd seen her work magic on similar requests with the library's sophisticated newspaper search software. I told Francine what I was doing and she volunteered to pick up burgers, fries, and milkshakes for both of us while I adjourned to the WICH-TV break room.

I pulled a folding chair up to the scarred and cigarette-burned Formica-topped table and called my smart, hip, and super-techie librarian aunt.

She didn't answer her cell, so I tried the library's main desk number. A few minutes passed before she answered. "Isobel Russell. Research desk. How can I help you today?" came the usual cheery voice.

"It's me, Aunt Ibby," I said. "Do you have time to do some newspaper research for a story I'm working on?"

"I don't know, Maralee," she said. "We're pretty busy here today. What do you need?"

"Early nineteen seventies North Shore area stolen vehicle reports."

"That's a big order, dear. There'd be thousands of them. I don't have time for a search like that. Sorry."

"I can be specific about make, model, and year," I began. "It's a red—"

Dial tone.

"Hello. Are you still there?" She wasn't. I didn't try to call back. My aunt had hung up on me and I knew it. She wanted nothing to do with the recovery of the Mustang from the pit. I'd already ignored too many indications of that simple fact. Too many not-too-subtle signals. Perhaps I didn't want to believe that my adored aunt was somehow connected to this complicated mystery, long hidden deep underwater. But inexplicably, she was.

Had Pete figured that out already? Was he keeping it from me? As long as I was in my investigative-reporter mode, I figured I might as well find out. I called him. He answered on the first ring. "Hello, babe? Are you inviting me to lunch?"

"Nope. Too busy. Francine's bringing back take-out. Listen. I need to know something. Does my aunt have anything to do with the sunken car?"

Long pause. Little sigh. "We're looking into that possibility. It has to do with one of my cold cases. A missing person."

"A missing person? And Aunt Ibby has something to do with that?"

"I'm sorry, Lee. Yes. The missing man was one of her classmates. Why do you ask? Has she told you anything about this?"

Is that what Betsy was talking about? The thing that was none of her business then and still isn't?

"No. She seems to be avoiding the subject," I said. "Pete, is the missing man—the um—is he the one in the Mustang?"

"Looks that way. But we don't have a positive ID yet."

"Was the car his?"

Another pause. "Maybe. It's complicated. Chief will schedule a presser as soon as we have something to share with the public."

"Got anything you can share with me?"

"Nothing you won't learn pretty soon anyway." Another little sigh. "Okay. Here it is. It's quite likely that I'll be talking to your aunt about her association with the missing man," he said. "It might be helpful to everyone concerned if you could kind of prepare her for that happening."

"You said this wasn't your case. That you were working on cold cases," I said.

"It's mine now. One of my cold cases was the missing guy. The same guy who might have been driving the Mustang," he admitted. "Looks like your aunt and all the people on her class reunion committee knew him, and it's a good bet that all of them recognized that car the minute it came out of the pit."

And maybe Steve wasn't just looking for publicity when he showed up at the site.

"Is that why you wanted to meet Bobby this morning?" I wondered. "And why you wanted my character sketches of the rest of the committee?"

"Just curious," he said. "It's highly unlikely that any of them, or any of the other members of the Salem High School class of 1974, have anything to do with this—including your aunt. But one or more of them may know something that can help us figure it all out."

"This is weird," I said. "You and I are investigating the same case. Can't we just this once call a truce on the sharing information thing? I'll promise not to release any police information about this without permission, no matter how much I want to, and I'll tell you everything I overhear at class reunion committee meetings."

"That sounds so reasonable," he said. "I hate it when I can't talk with you about police business, but I know you understand."

"I do," I said, "but just this once? Because my aunt is involved?"

"Just this once," he said, "and within reason. I'll call you later."

Francine appeared with our hearty, though not remotely healthy, lunches and joined me in the break room. "Learn anything new?" She pulled up a chair. "Did your aunt figure it all out for us?"

I stuck a paper straw into my chocolate shake. "Afraid not. If we thought this was confusing before, it's now *really* complicated." I gave her a quick rundown on what I'd learned from Pete about the possible involvement of the class of 1974.

"Wow. Who'd ever have thought of that?" She looked as surprised as I felt. "So you think your aunt might have recognized that car when it came out of the water?"

I thought about that. "You know something?" I pictured a shattered Spode platter and spilled cookies on the kitchen floor. "She recognized it *before* it came out of the water."

CHAPTER 15

Marty did her usual amazing job of cutting, splicing, and editing words and pictures, making our work the best it could be. The Diver's World piece, shortened to five minutes, would air on the five o'clock news and Buck Covington would introduce me with my investigative report at eleven fifteen that night. Rhonda had been busy, too, scheduling the afternoon's field report sites for Francine and me. We had two destinations. An exhibit of new works at the Punto Urban Art Museum, Salem's amazing open-air museum featuring giant murals by artists from all over the world—and a visit to Flower Fantasy, a high-end floral design business. Both stops would provide the kind of spot that could be used anytime. Doan liked to have a few of these on hand for slow news days. This time we left the Vette in the lot and took the mobile unit.

The two were within about ten minutes of each other, and we decided to visit the exhibit on Lafayette Street first. "Do you still have your high school yearbook?" I asked Francine.

"It's at my mother's place," she said. "In my old bedroom. Why?"

"I know where mine is too. But my librarian aunt, who's numbered and cataloged all the thousands of books in our house, claims that she doesn't know where hers is. Almost as though she doesn't want me to see it."

"Why don't you try Classmates.com? They might have it online. I know mine is."

"Really?" I did as she suggested and there it was. I flipped through the virtual pages for the alphabetically posted photos—boys wearing suit jackets and ties, girls with sweaters and pearls. L-M-N-O-P-Q-R. Russell. Isobel Russell. Easily recognizable, a pretty young version of my aunt smiled from the screen. Under the photo it said "Pretty Ibby has a mind to contrive, a tongue to persuade, and a hand to execute any mischief." The photos were laid out seven to a page, with a candid photo at the lower right corner of the page. The girl in the candid shot wore a striped mini and posed leaning on the front fender of the car. The smiling boy leaning from the window was blond and handsome. The car of course was a 1971 Mustang. The caption read: Cutest couple. Ibby and Ted.

We looked at each other. Neither of us spoke the words. *Is Ted the skeleton?*

It wouldn't be difficult now to study the photos of all the handsome blond boys in the book to find Ted. While Francine drove, I scanned page after page. It didn't take long. I found him in the Ts. Theodore Thorne. The saying under his picture was, "Not afraid of work but not in sympathy with it."

I phoned Pete. "Is the body Theodore Thorne?" I asked.

"You'd make a good cop, babe." he said. "How did you do it?"

"Yearbook picture. How did you?"

"DMV, dental records, and his wallet. Easy ID."

"Can I use it on the eleven o'clock news?" I crossed my fingers. "Have you notified his family?"

"Chief told his mother this afternoon. She doesn't believe it. Insists we have the wrong boy."

"Why?"

"She says Ted ran away in 1974 and has been sending her postcards, greeting cards, ever since."

"How is that possible?"

"It isn't.

"A cruel joke?"

"Looks that way."

"She's his mother. She must have known his handwriting. How did he sign them?"

"There was never a written message'" he said. "The address was on a printed label. Signature was just a capital *T*. Could have been anybody. But, she's his mother. She wants to believe."

"So sad. Talk to you later. Bye."

We'd reached the Point Neighborhood with its fifty large-scale paintings and it was time to put thoughts of the muddy Mustang, the cutest couple, and cards from a dead son aside. Time to concentrate on my job. Time to tell the WICH-TV viewers about this walkable arts district. From there we went directly to Flower Fantasy. If the second appointment went as smoothly as the first, I'd have time to prepare for my appearance on Buck Covington's late news show. I had to pick out an outfit to wear, do makeup, and—hopefully—do something about my hair.

On the way to Flower Fantasy I studied some more yearbook pictures. A much thinner Coach had been the star center on the school's basketball team, leading Salem to a 19–4 season. Bobby had a similar winning record as a defenseman on the ice hockey team. There were no girls with last names Leavitt and Driscoll, so I assumed those were married names. Betsy wasn't hard to identify by studying photos. A cheerleader forty-five years ago, at sixty-five she could easily pass for twenty years younger. Penelope had been chubbier back in 1974 and had always been an organizer. She was a member of the student council and the guidance assistants. I'd known that my aunt had been class secretary, captain of the library corps, and valedictorian. I hadn't known that she was also a member of the school orchestra and played both piano and flute.

Steve had been the class president. My aunt had told me that. He was also a member of the geographical society, the student council, and the chess club. A corner-of-the-page photo showed the whole group, Steve, Coach, Bobby, Penelope, Betsy, Ted, and my aunt in the school cafeteria. Seven smiling, happy, successful high school stars sitting together at what was undoubtedly what kids today call "the popular table."

Seven stars? Like the ones on the tarot card on my refrigerator?

Mr. Belechek, manager of Flower Fantasy, was a few minutes late, but clearly delighted to see us. "I'd been looking forward to this ever since Bruce Doan called me. We're lodge brothers, you know. Sorry I'm late, but I had to call on a client who'd had some dreadful news. You know of course about the body in that car they pulled out of the granite pit." I nodded. "Of course you do. What am I thinking? You're a news-person. Anyway, the mother of the boy is a longtime client—and a friend. Several customers have sent flowers of condolence to the house. I felt that I should make the deliveries personally.

"Did you know him? Ted Thorne?

"Yes. I remember him well. Used to play with my kids when they were all little. A good boy. So devoted to his mother. An only child too." He shook his head, eyes downcast. "She refuses to believe he's gone." He looked up. "She says he's been in touch with her all these years. She says he ran away just before gradua-tion after a terrible row with his father."

Francine interrupted. "I've got the lights set up here, Lee. Mr. Belechek. Let's do a fast mic test and then we can shoot the spot."

"Of course." He stood and hurried to where Fran-cine waited with a lapel mic. I followed, arranging my own mic as I walked across the sweet-smelling, color-ful, blossom-filled space and thought of poor young Ted Thorne's many years in that cold, dark, muddy resting place.

If that actually *was* Ted Thorne's body in the Mus-tang. His mother didn't think so. And now that the always active Salem grapevine had leaked the news well enough that people were actually sending flowers, I wondered if my aunt knew. Pete had said they might want to talk to her. I couldn't let that be the way she learned that her old friend had been identified.

I held up my hand. "Hold it a sec, Francine." I moved to the corner of the room, behind an artificial hibiscus, and tried her cell once again. This time she answered. "Oh, Aunt Ibby, I'm so sorry about your friend." I blurted it out. "Pete says they've identified him."

Her voice was surprisingly calm. "His mother called me," she said. "She's sure it isn't Ted."

"I understand. It must be very hard for her to accept."

"I told you. She doesn't accept it. He ran away because of his father. I know Laura Thorne very well. She's been a trusted friend since I was in high school. She serves on my bookmobile board of directors for heaven's sake. All of us on the reunion committee know her."

Francine's impatient face appeared through the branches of the fake hibiscus. "Let's go, Lee. Rhonda says they might need this one for tomorrow because of Mother's Day coming up. Because of the flowers, you know."

Mother's Day. That poor woman!

"We'll talk tonight when you get home from the theater," I told Aunt Ibby, and followed Francine to where Mr. Belechek stood surrounded by roses. I invited him to tell our audience about his business. He talked about flowers for special occasions. "If there's an occasion where you'd send a card," he said, "why not make it extra special and send flowers?" We wrapped it up with an outdoor shot of the storefront and headed back to the studio with our assignment sheet completed.

On the way I thought about what he'd said about card-sending occasions, and Ted's mother's insistence that the cards he'd sent proved he wasn't dead. My aunt, too, sounded as though she doubted that the human remains were Ted's.

The very idea defied logic. Dental records don't lie. *Do they?*

CHAPTER 16

I knew that if Aunt Ibby and Mr. Pennington were going to see *Mame* at the music theater, she'd have to come home from the library to change clothes. I hoped we'd have a little time together so that we could talk about Ted Thorne. I had some questions about the reunion committee too. I understood that the six friends had varied chairmanship over the years. If they'd held a reunion every five years, excluding Bobby who'd lived too far away to participate, that meant the last time Aunt Ibby had hosted the group had been twenty-five years ago, when I'd been seven. Did they all believe Ted had run away from home? And since the group of friends had obviously once included Ted, had they always expected that someday he'd return?

The thoughts were disturbing.

Our assignments completed, we returned to the station. I stopped to see how Marty was doing with my expected eleven o'clock appearance. I told her I planned to give Ted Thorne's name as the deceased passenger in the long-sunken Mustang. "After all, it's possible that Chief Whaley might call a press conference later this afternoon and release the information anyway," I said. "I'm sure Scott Palmer will cover it if it happens. Either way the news will be out tonight."

We checked in with Rhonda. "Looks like you two are done for the day" was her good news. "Scott covered a swim meet at the rec center this afternoon so he'll be back soon. He's directing for Covington tonight, so he'll be on hand if anything important breaks." With the clear conscience that comes from a day's work well done, I headed for the parking lot.

I made a quick stop at Shaw's Market, determined to save time by keeping my purchases down to ten items so I could use the fast lane. Bread, milk, cat food, bagged salad, frozen pizza, ice cream, hamburger, hamburger buns, Pop-Tarts, and a twelve-pack of Pepsi. Made it in and out in twelve minutes covering all the basic food groups.

I still had plenty of time to dress for the eleven o'clock news, and if I could arrange it, I'd come in early enough to get River's makeup guy, Carmine, to do my face and hair. Heading my car for Winter Street, I let my thoughts go back to the 1974 Salem High yearbook. I meant to bring it up on my laptop screen—a lot bigger than the tablet—and study every page. I was pretty sure that the seven seniors I'd seen at the cafeteria popular table—six of whom I'd seen at my aunt's dining room table—would have been prominently mentioned and photographed throughout.

I pulled the Vette into the garage, noting that my aunt's Buick wasn't there yet. O'Ryan met me at the back steps with his usual happy-to-see-me greetings. He purred and meowed and rubbed against my ankles. I put the two bags of groceries down on the top step, bent to pat him, and fished in my purse for my keys. Once we were both inside, the cat sniffed at the cat door leading to Aunt Ibby's kitchen, then trotted ahead of me up the twisty staircase to the third floor. I followed, balancing bags and purse. He scooted through his cat door into my living room while I entered using the traditional unlocking and knob-turning human way.

Hurriedly stashing my food purchases, I carried my laptop to the kitchen table and once again brought up the Classmates.com site and the 1974 yearbook. This time I read the captions under each of the photographs more carefully and learned a few more facts about each one. Steve, not too surprisingly, had been voted most likely to succeed. Coach Whipple had lettered in two sports, basketball and track. Bobby was voted most handsome boy and captain of the Salem Witches hockey team. Betsy was head cheerleader. Penelope was class treasurer. Ted Thorne and my aunt were nominated for prom king and queen. All three of the girls and Steve had made National Honor Society.

That gave me some things to think about. It appeared that my aunt and poor dead Ted were a couple, and it was likely that Betsy and Bobby were too. It was time to start making notes about what I'd begun to think of as "the seven stars." Opening a fresh package of lined index cards, I put the name of each one of the seven on a separate card. I spread those cards out on the tabletop, thinking as I did so about the way River laid out the beautiful tarot cards for a reading. But at least each of the tarot cards had meaning.

Obviously, the one I knew most about was my aunt, so I put her card aside for the moment. I knew a little about Steve so I began my note taking with his card.

> *Steve Overton:*
> *Running for Congress.*
> *Was present when the car got pulled out of the pit.*
> *Was first arrival at reunion meeting.*
> *Was class president; most likely to succeed.*
> *National Honor Society.*
> *Gave Bobby a ride after the meeting.*

Since I'd just mentioned Bobby, I chose his card next.

> *Bobby Ross:*
> *Hockey player in high school. (Most handsome boy.)*
> *Scholarship to UMass; dropped out after junior year.*
>   *(Because of knee injury?)*
> *Lives in San Francisco? How long?*
> *Dated Betsy in high school.*
> *Drinking problem?*
>
> *Betsy Leavitt:*
> *Model for tea company.*
> *Was head cheerleader in high school.*
> *Dated Bobby in high school.*
> *Had argument with Aunt Ibby.*
> *("None of your business then and none of your*
>   *business now.")*
> *Seems unfriendly with Steve.*
> *National Honor Society.*

Coach Warren Whipple:
Two-letter man in high school (basketball and track).
Arrived with Penelope. (Aunt Ibby says not an item.)
Kind of full of himself. (Personal observation.)
Was basketball coach at Boston College.

Theodore (Ted) Thorne:
May be the body in the sunken Mustang. (Pete has
    DMV records, dental records, wallet.)
Ted and Ibby dated in high school. Cutest couple.
The florist delivered flowers personally to his mother.
Chief Whaley delivered news of death to his mother.
Mother refused to believe he is dead, says he "ran
    away because of his father."
Mother claims he's sent her greeting cards and
    postcards for years.

Penelope Driscoll:
Efficient, well organized. Was class treasurer.
National Honor Society.
Brought her yearbook to make copies for badges.
Came to our house a second time to make photo
    badges.
Arrived at meeting same time as the coach.

Not much to go on there.

I moved Aunt Ibby's card to the foreground. Then
just stared at it. O'Ryan choose that minute to race to
the living room door. I heard the cat door flap and
knew that Aunt Ibby had arrived home. I stacked the
cards into a pile, put a rubber band around them,
and followed the cat, hoping to get a few minutes
with my aunt before she had to leave for the theater.

I paused in the back hall and hesitated, thinking
maybe she'd prefer to be alone considering the bad

news she'd received. O'Ryan had obviously barged right in, though; his cat door was still swinging back and forth. So I knocked. "It's me, Aunt Ibby," I called.

"Come right on in, Maralee," she answered. "It's unlocked."

I shook my head, remembering Pete's very recent admonition, and turned the knob. I'd scold her about locking doors some other time. I knew she had some disturbing things on her mind just then. "Hi," I said. "Just popping in for a minute. You okay?"

"Why yes, thank you, dear. I'm holding up just fine, I think." She turned on a faucet and proceeded to fill a Revere teakettle. "Just about to have a nice cup of tea. Please join me. We were right out straight at the library today. Hustling every minute right up until closing."

"Yes. I could tell you were busy when I called earlier."

"Sorry if I sounded short with you, Maralee. We had people lined up three deep at the checkout desk." She put two chintz-patterned teacups on the table, dropping a tea bag into each one. "I never did get around to looking up those old stolen car references for you. Sorry."

"No problem," I said. "I found the information I was looking for."

"That's good." The tiniest frown crossed her face. "How was your day?"

"All right so far," I said. "We did a piece on the urban artists in the Point Neighborhood and one on Flower Fantasy, but my day's not over yet. Doing a short piece on the eleven o'clock news tonight."

The frown was real now. "Are you still reporting about the granite pit thing?" Her hand shook slightly as she poured hot water onto the tea bags in our cups.

"Yes. It's the headline story in Salem right now. I understand that the victim was a classmate of yours, and the whole topic must be painful for you." I took the teakettle from her and returned it to the stovetop. "When I called you about the stolen cars I had no idea about any of that."

Her voice was so soft I had to lean forward to hear. "How did you find out? Did Pete tell you?"

"Nope. I found a yearbook online. I saw the picture of you and Ted Thorne and the Mustang. 'Ibby and Ted. Cutest couple.' You must have known right away it was his car." I thought of the broken platter. "That's why you dropped the cookies."

"Yes." She nodded sadly. "We all thought he'd run away in that car. I even imagined that maybe someday he'd drive back here in it." Her eyes were misty. "When I heard you say that the diver had seen a Mustang, right away I knew in my heart that it was Ted's car."

"And you suspected that Ted was—well—not coming back?" I prompted.

"No." Her headshake was vehement. "No. I wasn't ready for that. Maybe I'm still not ready for that. Cream?" She passed the silver cream pitcher.

"You all expected that he'd be back someday?"

"Oh yes," she said. "After his father died we all thought for sure he'd show up that year."

"Because Ted didn't get along with his father? Someone said they'd had a 'terrible row.'"

"Oh, dear. More than one." She tsk-tsked. "It was a constant thing. Ted just never could seem to do anything right, according to Mr. Thorne. He was never good enough. Oh, he tried so hard to please that dreadful man." She sighed. "He tried so hard." Again, she seemed to be fighting tears.

Good time for a subject change.

"So, you and Mr. Pennington are going to see *Mame*?"

"Yes. We've both been looking forward to it." She looked up at the kitchen clock. "Oh, look at the time. Come on up to my room and help me decide what to wear, won't you? Maybe you can look through my closet while I jump into the shower. I'm usually better organized than this, you know. It's just that the past few days have been so hectic. I haven't even had a chance to get my hair done."

"It looks lovely," I told her truthfully. Hers is red, too, but of a paler shade and not all curly and wild like mine. "I'll be happy to help you decide what to wear. Remember how I used to love watching you get ready for special evenings when I was a little girl?"

"I do. Let's get started, shall we?" She picked up our cups and saucers and put them into the dishwasher. I clicked the lock on the kitchen door and we walked together through the living room and into the front hall. O'Ryan followed, pausing in front of the hall tree, jumping up onto the seat. As my aunt and I started up the broad, polished staircase, I turned, looking back at him. "Come along, cat," I said. But he'd turned his back on us and sat upright looking into the mirror. "What's so interesting, huh?" I looked around the furry haunches.

Big mistake.

The twinkling lights and swirling colors were already there. A scene began to take shape.

CHAPTER 17

I looked away quickly, but not quickly enough to erase the image from my consciousness.

Aunt Ibby's room is on the second floor, a few doors down from my own childhood room. We climbed the broad polished staircase together. The cat remained on the hall tree seat, golden eyes still focused on the mirror. I've been seeing these visions long enough so that I've learned to mask my reaction to them. I was kind of proud of that, sure that Aunt Ibby had no clue that I'd just taken a peek into her past. And so, I presumed, had O'Ryan.

We reached my aunt's doorway and entered her pretty room. It was larger than mine, done in soothing shades of green, and had always seemed sunnier, even though we each had the same number of windows. She waved a hand toward the closet. "It's going to be cool tonight, according to Wanda, and she says the rain she'd expected has passed us by. I'm thinking maybe one of my dressy pantsuits? Something with a little glitter? Pick one please." She disappeared into her bathroom and almost instantly I heard the shower running.

I deliberately concentrated hard on the task at hand, shaking away the memory of the vision I'd so recently seen in the hall tree mirror. Like most of the scenes this unwelcome "gift" showed to me, it made no particular sense. I'd deal with it later.

I selected a two-piece suit in soft gray lightweight wool. The jacket was longish, almost Edwardian, the pants slim and straight. The desired glitter was provided by threads of gold woven into the fabric of a silky sleeveless V-necked top. I hung the outfit on her closet door and added cute and comfortable-looking gray suede shoes with open toes and kitten heels. I sat in a cream-colored wing chair, pleased with my selection. I'd leave the rest of the accessorizing up to her.

She emerged from the bathroom in a pink terry robe and bunny slippers. "Perfect, Maralee," she said as soon as she spotted the gray outfit. "Good thing we have similar tastes. Now for a handbag and jewelry, and I'll be all set."

My aunt doesn't wear a lot of jewelry. Never has, in my memory. But there are a few choice things, mostly family treasures, that she wears for special occasions. She doesn't have a proper jewelry box, although I've offered to buy her one. As far back as I can remember, she's kept her jewelry in a miniature wooden cedar chest on top of her dresser. I watched as she reached into the box and produced Grandmother Forbes's gold wristwatch. I remembered it from my childhood. I'd always known it was old because it's the kind you have to wind. No batteries. It's a dainty thing with real diamonds marking the six and the twelve.

"You know, Maralee, my jewelry will be yours when I'm gone," she said. "There are some of your mother's favorite pieces here too. I've always meant to give you her emerald ring, but I'm just not quite ready to part with it yet."

"I understand," I smiled because she'd told me the exact same thing every time I happened to be around when she opened the chest. "I'm in no hurry," I told her, which was exactly what *I* said every time. She selected a small black cross-body bag from her closet and put a comb, some cash, a package of tissues, and a roll of Life Savers into it.

"There," she said. "I guess I'm ready. Thanks for your help, dear. I'll just jump into these clothes and be ready when Rupert comes to pick me up. Showtime is eight o'clock and he likes to be early."

"Have a wonderful evening," I said. "I'd better go upstairs and figure out what I'm going to wear for the late news show." I'd already just about decided on a turquoise French terry pullover with beaded neckline and Mexican silver earrings. I'd be seated behind the news desk with Buck, so it didn't matter what was on my bottom half. I wanted some alone time to think about that vision in the mirror. I needed to make out an index card for it, too, while it was still fresh in my mind.

O'Ryan had left the hall tree seat while I was assembling my aunt's theater wardrobe and was already inside my apartment, sitting on the table all nonchalant and innocent looking. *I'll tell Pete later all about the vision.*

Like most of the other pictures I've seen in various

reflective surfaces, this one didn't make much sense to me, didn't relate to anything I'd noted on the index cards so far. Unlike the usual images, this one was black-and-white, like some of the yearbook photos. Two girls sat close together on a rustic bentwood bench. I recognized them immediately. They each looked remarkably like late-twentieth-century teen-aged versions of me. My mother and my aunt. No question about it. Orphaned at five, I had few memories of my parents, but I'd seen albums full of photos of them both.

Selecting a fresh card from the stack, I picked up my pen.

Vision in hall tree mirror #2
B&W scene shows my mother and Aunt Ibby—
*   probably in the 1970s.*
Girls are wearing shorts, sneakers, collared blouses.
*   (Summer camp?)*
They appear to be on a porch or some kind of outdoor
*   shelter.*
Rustic bentwood furniture: Bench and square table.

I stared at the card for a moment, hoping to re-member something more. Nothing. O'Ryan, was still on the table, (Yeah, I know most people don't let cats walk on the kitchen table, but they do it when you're not home anyway.) He moved close to the stack and put his nose on the card I'd just added, then looked up at me with a quizzical, head-tilted pose and said, "Mmrup?" I don't speak much cat, so I couldn't inter-pret the remark.

"I'll leave for the station at ten, if I'm going to get Carmine to do my hair," I told O'Ryan. "I guess I'll take a shower, grab a snack, and watch TV for a while, We'll talk about this later. Okay?"

He moved over to the windowsill and proceeded to lick his paws. I put the turquoise pullover into a garment bag, makeup, hair straightener, and brush into a canvas tote in case the Carmine appointment didn't work out and tossed a few blank index cards and a pen into my purse for incidental random thoughts. I took my shower, put on a robe, heated a bowl of Dinty Moores beef stew, and turned on the TV.

At exactly seven o'clock O'Ryan made a dash for the kitchen cat door, announcing Mr. Pennington's arrival. Still too early to head to the station and there wasn't much of anything of interest happening on TV. I turned off the sound, still thinking about the two girls on the bench. Pulling the card headed *Vision #2* from the growing stack, I laid it on the table and frowned at it.

"Concentrate," I told myself aloud. "Think of details." Squeezing my eyes shut, I tried to bring the picture back. Sometimes that works for me. Sometimes it doesn't. This time it worked. Slowly at first, then with more detail. The girls smiled at the camera. Behind the bench I could see part of a window. Lacy curtains. There was something hanging there behind the glass—something that gave off a little sparkle. A decoration of some kind? I imagined myself moving closer to the scene. It was a star. Crystal maybe? But definitely a star. Something else too. The picture had those little black paper corners on it—the kind people used to use to stick photos in albums.

I turned in my chair and faced the refrigerator and the tarot card, the Star, sure that this meant something. But what? I reached for my phone.

"Pete? You busy?"

"Nothing that won't keep. I'm in the records room, looking up some old stuff. What's going on?"

"I saw another picture in that hall tree mirror tonight," I said. "Can't figure it out. Maybe you can help."

"I can try, babe. Is it a bad one?"

"No. It's kind of nice," I said, looking at the index card as I spoke. "It's like an old black-and-white snapshot of my mother and my aunt when they were girls." I described the picture the best I could, trying not to leave anything out. I told him about the Star in River's tarot reading, too, and how she'd told me to keep it where I could see it every day.

"You noted what you'd seen in the mirror as soon as you could after you'd seen it, right?"

"Yes. I helped my aunt pick out some clothes and then I filled out the card," I agreed.

"Uh-huh. Then after a while you tried to remember what you'd seen and discovered details you'd missed before."

"That's exactly what happened," I said. "The first time I missed the star in the window and the photo corners."

"Of course I don't even pretend to understand the things you see when these things pop up," he said. "I told you I'm in the records room looking at some testimony in one of those cold cases I told you about."

"Yes, you told me that." *And what does that have to do with my vision in the mirror?*

"Sometimes, actually fairly often," he said in what

I call his patient-cop voice, "when we question a witness more than once during an investigation, his recollection of the event changes with each interview."

"I've heard you say that before. But in this case, I'm the only witness to something that may or may not have ever happened," I explained. "I mean except for O'Ryan. He watched it too."

Pete laughed. "I'll ask him about it. But seriously, I'm suggesting that maybe as you thought about what you'd seen in the mirror some other things kind of crept into the memory. For instance, that star in the window. Couldn't that have been because of the tarot reading? And maybe the photo corners you remembered were a result of your thinking that the black-and-white image looked like an old photo."

It happens fairly often. Pete's good, straightforward cop-thinking makes sense out of my sometimes highly imaginative way of looking at things. (On the other hand, there've been plenty of times when visions and tarot cards and a witch's cat have helped Pete out, too!) But this time I guessed he could be right. *I've been thinking a lot about those stars, and just tonight I thought about the pictures of my parents in Aunt Ibby's albums.*

"You're probably right," I said. "I'll concentrate on the two girls. Never mind the background."

"Good," he said. "But you still don't know what the girls are trying to tell you, do you?"

"Nope. Back to square one on that puzzle" I turned my back to the Star card on the refrigerator. "Right now I have to concentrate on tonight's late-news segment on the car they pulled out of the pit. I'm doing a roundup of what we've learned so far about it. Any clues you want to share with a struggling girl reporter?"

I could tell he was muffling another laugh. He thinks it's hilarious when I say "clues," or "case." I don't deny that I was a huge Nancy Drew fan, and some of Nancy's vocabulary slips into my conversation occasionally. "Very funny," I said.

"Sorry, Nancy," he teased. "Do you have a book name yet for this one?"

Actually, I did. "Thought you'd never ask. I'm calling it *The Mystery of the Muddy Mustang*."

"Perfect," he said. "You're right about the mud. The inside of that car is full of it. Messy, gritty, black sludge. The guys at the warehouse are going through it with a fine-tooth comb. Literally."

Reporter alert! "Looking for anything specific?" I asked, trying hard for a casual tone.

"Not exactly," he said, his tone just as casual as mine. "Personal belongings. More bones of course. We're looking for anything that might help the guy's poor mother accept the fact that it's definitely her son's remains in the car."

"Aunt Ibby's a little bit on the fence about that, too," I said. "Isn't that part of the 'denial' stage in this sort of tragedy?" As I spoke, I scribbled "sifting through mud for clues" on a fresh card.

"Guess so. But we'll be ready to release the remains shortly I think. She's going to have to make funeral plans I suppose, and she's all alone. Husband's dead and there were no siblings. But she thinks he's been sending her cards all these years."

"Have you seen the cards? His classmates have

believed all these years that he ran away because of his father."

"She won't show them to us. Says they're all she has of him now. I sure wouldn't want to be the one who has to subpoena birthday cards from a grieving mother."

"Don't blame you. I wouldn't, either. Thanks Pete, for making sense of the mirror thing. I'm going to head for the studio soon. Carmine's going to try to do something with my hair and face."

"They're both perfect the way they are," he said. "Love you. I'll be watching the news."

"Good night. Love you too."

I picked up my garment bag and laid it on the living room couch so it'd be handy when I left for the studio. A pair of tan flats would be comfortable and no one would see them anyway since most of my commentary would be off camera. Rhonda had printed out a transcript for me of all of my on-air comments so far from the day we first met the divers right up until I talked about hard-hat diving. I planned to add the information about the mud in the car too. By nine o'clock I was ready to leave the house. O'Ryan escorted me down the stairs and out into the yard. He watched from the back steps as I opened the garage door. When I pulled my car out onto Oliver Street I looked over the fence. He was still there. I waved to him and headed for WICH-TV for the second time that day.

Carmine was waiting for me in the revamped dressing room in the downstairs studio. The pink and white room with professional chairs, wonderful lighting, and a wall full of professional beauty products was a far cry from the dim, dusty dungeon with its one dressing table and chipped mirror my Crystal Moon persona had used.

"Ah, Ms. Barrett," Carmine clapped his hands together. "It is such a delight to bring order to your wonderful hair." I put my purse and sweater into the cubby with my name on it and sat in the white leather salon chair.

"I'm delighted, too," I said. "It can surely use some order."

For the next half hour I relaxed under Carmine's capable care of hair and face, and at the same time, mentally rehearsed my presentation for the late-news audience. I felt that my chronological approach to the unraveling of the question of how and why the Mustang had been hidden underwater for so many years would interest the viewers—and please Doan. It interested me enormously and I knew that there was a lot more to learn about this story.

"Ted Thorne," I said, then realized from Carmine's questioning look that I'd spoken out loud. "A story I'm working on," I said. "Ted Thorne was the person they found in that old car in the granite pit."

"I know," he said. "I've been following that story myself. My dad says he went to middle school with the guy."

I sat up straight, disturbing my cooling, pale green refresh-mint facial mask. "Really? Does your dad have any ideas about what happened to him."

"Dad says he wouldn't try to guess how the kid wound up the way he did. But he's damned sure it wasn't a suicide."

"He's sure? How come?"

Carmine waved his curling iron. "The kid had it all. Good looks, good marks, pretty girlfriend, all the money in the world, the coolest car in the whole school. Kid'd have to be nuts to want to die. Wouldn't he?"

"Well," I said, "when you put it that way . . ."

"I can't see it any other way. You want some highlights?"

"No. It's okay for now," I said. *Funny. I never even thought about suicide.* "I figured an accident. Like, maybe he'd been drinking, you know? It was right around graduation. Party season."

"Maybe," His tone was doubtful. "But now that you mention it, I heard they found a bunch of beer cans in that old car."

Beer cans! How come taxi drivers and hairstylists and gym rats know more about what's going on than a member of the press with a detective boyfriend does?

I tried to keep my voice level, though I wanted to yell. "Where'd you hear that, Carmine?"

"Guy at the gym. Everybody there knows about it." He flexed a bicep and smiled at himself in the mirror. "I try to keep in shape."

"Lookin' good, Carmine," I told him, closing my eyes as he applied eyeliner, and thinking about joining his gym.

By ten thirty, hair tamed and makeup as perfect as only a professional artist can make it, I changed into the turquoise top and headed upstairs to the newsroom.

Scott Palmer was in the director's chair reading *Sports Illustrated,* and Buck Covington occupied the anchor seat, literally watching the studio clock. Wanda sat in lotus position on the floor in front of the green screen, studying what I recognized as an NOAA weather map printout. Her costume du jour consisted of tiny green velvet short-shorts and a gold halter top with her trademark deep-V neckline. Gold thigh-high boots with four-inch heels completed the look. All three looked up, acknowledging my presence with a nod, or wave. I slid into the chair next to Scott, where I'd await my signal to join Buck at the news desk. "Hi, Scott," I whispered.

"Hi yourself, Moon," he said. "Good job on the dive shop story."

"Thanks," I said. "I'm learning about diving, little by little."

"Figured out how the kid got underwater yet?" he asked.

"Not even close," I admitted. "You heard anything new?"

"They say his mother doesn't think it's even him. Says she's sure he's alive."

"It's him." I sighed. "No doubt about it."

The music for the *Nighttime News* began, and Buck Covington turned on his thousand-watt smile and faced the camera. Wanda stood in one graceful motion, and I stuck the notes Rhonda had given me under my chair. Buck moved flawlessly from one local story to another as usual. I watched him on the large monitor. Wanda did her first brief weather segment, promised to be back after the next break, and smiled prettily, bowing deeply. All progressed as usual until a tiny frown crossed Buck's handsome face and he touched his ear—which usually means he's receiving a message from the off-camera control room.

"Ooops," Scott muttered, touching his own headphones. "Breaking news."

I watched the monitor. The late-breaking news banner flashed across the bottom of the screen.

"Stay tuned for Lee Barrett with the latest on that long-submerged Mustang, folks," Buck instructed, and broke for a dog food commercial.

"Jeez," Scott said.

"What? What's going on?"

"They found a spent bullet in the Mustang," he said. "Looks like maybe the kid was shot."

CHAPTER 18

There was a mad dash to get the new information onto the teleprompter. (It was well known that Covington was helpless without it.) Scott managed a printout of the same information for me. A promo for shelter pets followed the dog food commercial, and by the time we'd returned to live camera, the audience would never have guessed that moments earlier there'd been abject panic on display in the WICH-TV newsroom. Buck was once again his usual unruffled self, and I was seated beside him at the anchor desk, my stack of paper cheat sheets in my lap out of camera range. On top of the stack was the new bulletin headed GRANITE PIT VICTIM MAY HAVE BEEN SHOT.

Buck lost no time in turning the broadcast over to me. To unprepared, unrehearsed—but looking pretty darned good—me.

"Here's our investigative reporter, Lee Barrett, with the latest on what's going on at the old North Shore Granite Works. Lee, you've been on top of this case from the very beginning. Catch us up on what's happening, won't you?"

"Thanks Buck," I said, glad my hands were under the table because I knew they were shaking—hoping at the same time that the mic wouldn't pick up the paper rustling. "The community has been riveted for the past few days on the recovery of a vintage Mustang from the depths of an abandoned North Shore granite pit," I began as the giant screen showed sea-monster diver as he emerged from the water, followed by the shot—slowed down for greater dramatic effect—of the vehicle being raised high above the water. I spoke about how North Shore kids for years had jumped from the heights of the granite cliffs, while Francine's dizzying shot of the place rolled. This segued neatly into Fred's description of the importance of the hard-hat divers' part in all of this. I watched the clock. Eleven thirty. Time for a hard break. I looked at Buck, who, with faultless timing and perfect diction, announced that I'd be back in a few minutes with some late-breaking news on this exciting story.

This gave me a little time to consult the new bulletin. It seemed that the forensic team had been sifting through the mud and silt that had accumulated in the car searching for bones when they'd found the spent bullet.

When the break was over, Buck didn't lose any time kicking it back to me. I narrated the part where the Mustang swings over our heads and onto the flatbed. We had no picture of the warehouse where the grisly business was being conducted, and there's no gentle way to say the forensic team was picking through several feet of muck looking for bones, so I simply stated it.

"According to divers on scene, the car had been tightly wedged at an angle on a deep underwater ledge—probably for many years. During that period granite dust, silt, and grime accumulated inside the vehicle, creating a thick layer of black mud. Forensic scientists have been meticulously sifting through this sludge in an attempt to recover skeletal remains. WICH-TV has just learned that during this painstaking process a spent bullet has been recovered, causing authorities to suspect foul play in the death of the victim, who has been tentatively identified as Theodore Thorne, a nineteen-year-old man who was reported missing by his parents in 1974. Police ballistics experts are studying the bullet, and it is expected that Police Chief Tom Whaley will announce their findings soon. As always, keep your television tuned to WICH-TV for the latest developments."

Buck thanked me for my report. I thanked him for inviting me, and it was time for Wanda to predict the next day's weather.

I knew that River would be preparing for *Tarot Time* by then, so I went back down to the ground-floor studio. In the long, windowless, black-walled room River's set was brightly illuminated. I could see Marty moving around there, so I hurried down the center aisle. "Hi, Marty. Where's River?"

"Hello there, Moon." She maneuvered her wheeled camera toward an arrangement of candles and crystals surrounding a greeting card illustration of angels and a rainbow. "Be right with you." She pressed her face to the viewfinder, then popped right out again. "River's in the dressing room. I'm just setting up her first bumper shot. Cute, huh?"

"I like it," I said. "And I liked the editing job you did on the granite pit story. It was perfect. What would we all do without you?"

"Hate to even think of it," she said. "You liking your new job?"

"Very much. But I know I still have a lot to learn."

"Hey, kid. With the way technology moves these days, so do I—and I've been here forty-odd years."

River approached, gorgeous in a strapless pale yellow sheath, with daisies woven into her long black braid. "Lee, Carmine and I watched you on the news. You look beautiful, and your report was so interesting. And now everybody knows who the poor guy in the car was."

"Thanks, River. It's pretty certain that Ted Thorne was the man in the car. It got extra interesting there at the end for all of us," I said. "That bulletin about the bullet they found in the car came in while we were already on the air. I'm sure Buck will tell you all about it."

"No kidding?" Her big eyes grew wider. "You all handled it so smoothly no one would ever guess it was a surprise."

"Now we have to wonder if finding the bullet means the poor kid was shot." We walked together toward the *Tarot Time* set. "And Pete says Ted's mom still hasn't accepted the fact that her son was the boy in the car."

"That's just sad. It *is* him, isn't it? The cops are sure?"

"Oh, yes" I assured her. "No doubt, really. Dental

records, auto registration. They even have what's left of his wallet."

"It must have been awful for her, after all these years." River sat in her high-backed wicker chair and spread a tarot deck, facedown, on the table before her, into a fan-shaped pattern. "Not knowing where her child was. Just awful. What about the father? Does he believe it?"

"Father's dead. Apparently everyone blamed the man for Ted's disappearance. It looked as though he'd climbed into that fast car and run away from a bad home situation."

"Uh-huh," she said, then looked up smiling. "Here comes my man! Hello, Buck!"

The newsman entered the set, sat on the couch (left over from my old *Nightshades* decor), and gazed at River adoringly. I knew that he often joined her at the start of the show, usually shuffling the cards, which he did with Las Vegas flair and style and some-times selecting a random card for her to comment on. The audience seemed to love it.

"Hello, darlin'," he said. "Hi again, Ms. Barrett. Hi, Marty."

"Five minutes to intro," came Marty's muffled voice from behind the camera. "Phone lines are good to go. You've already got a few callers on hold. First commercial is for Wicked Good Books bookstore, then we go right to you. Got it?"

"Got it," River said, arranging her braid over one shoulder. "See you later, Lee. Bucky, stay with me. I need you to pick a card."

I took the hint and hurried back to the dressing room to pick up my purse and sweater. Carmine had left, and the room was in perfect pink and white order. I paused on the way to take one more peek at the magic a professional makeup artist can create. I leaned close to the mirror, fluffed my hair, touched my still-glossed lips, and wondered if I could ever master that smoky eye shadow trick.

I should know better than to linger in front of a mirror, however tempting it is to look. This time the vision developed slowly. My face faded away as the young man's face developed—something like an old Polaroid picture. It was his yearbook picture face, but instead of suit coat and tie he wore a Boston Red Sox T-shirt and faded jeans. As the background came into focus I recognized the rustic bentwood bench.

Then, boom! He was gone. I was staring at my own surprised reflection. The bench was the same one my mother and aunt had occupied in the hall tree mirror vision.

CHAPTER 19

I left the studio quietly, exiting through the green metal door to the ground floor lobby, where, as usual, sound from the current WICH-TV programming issued though a speaker. The last strains of River's theme music, "Danse Macabre," faded away as she recited the Wiccan supplication she often uses before her evening's readings.

"May only the highest spiritual forces be present with us and may I be guided to give true and sensible readings." Short pause. "You all know Buck Covington, our nighttime news anchorman. Before I take your calls, I'm going to ask Buck to pick one card. This is for a special mother, who doesn't know for sure where her child is tonight."

I started for the door, then stopped. Waited. River was talking about Ted's mother. I'd never known her to do this particular kind of reading before.

"Go ahead, hon—I mean Buck. Pick a card and hand it to me." *Oops. River's relationship with the handsome newsman slipped out a little.* I wished there was still a TV in the lobby instead of just sound, but we'd already had one set stolen and Doan doesn't like to waste money. There was a slight rustling sound, then River's voice again. "Buck has chosen the Two of Pentacles for the mother I told you about. Look." (I could visualize her holding up the card.) "See the happy young man dancing. He holds two pentacles held together by a cord shaped like a sideways figure eight. This is the cosmic symbol of eternal life—a comforting sign for this mother. This card also signifies news, messages in writing. I hope the mother receives this blessing and achieves harmony in the midst of change." The music swelled again and River announced the late movie—*The Fog,* the 1980 thriller starring Adrienne Barbeau. I'd always liked that one. Maybe I'd get home in time to catch the beginning. I stepped out into the darkness. It felt like rain.

I pulled into the garage, locked the car and garage doors, and hurried up the path, past the garden. Sometimes at night the plants and bushes, especially the tall ones like sunflowers and hollyhocks, take on strange shapes. There was no moon, or if there was one it was hidden by clouds and pre-rain mist. *Fog?* I moved a little faster toward the back steps, where O'Ryan waited for me. We went into the house together, he through his door, I through mine. He didn't pause outside Aunt Ibby's kitchen, so I guessed that she and Mr. Pennington were still out. The cat and I hurried up the two flights to my apartment.

I turned on the living room lights as soon as we were inside. When Pete works late he usually drives by my place on his way home. If he sees my lighted bay window he knows I'm awake, and he'll call to say good night—or sometimes call to see if I want company.

I put on a pot of decaf, just in case Pete might come over, or in case Aunt Ibby wanted to talk about her evening. I was pretty sure she hadn't seen the news, hadn't heard about the spent bullet in the Mustang. I knew I should take off my makeup, but I was vain enough to leave it on a little longer in case Pete dropped in.

Turned out they both felt like visiting. Aunt Ibby arrived first, all bubbly, excited over her evening out—a favorite musical and late dinner with Mr. Pennington I hesitated about telling Aunt Ibby that a spent bullet had been found in her friend's car—she seemed so happy and I didn't want to be a downer. When Pete arrived, I hurried to meet him with a whispered warning that she didn't know.

We sat in my kitchen enjoying good coffee, chatting about the current theater offerings on the North Shore, Pete's Pee Wee Hockey team's upcoming tournament, and finally my report on the late news.

"You look absolutely wonderful, dear. The eye makeup is perfect," she said. "I'm sure you did a grand job reporting everything you've learned about the poor soul in that car."

I threw Pete a helpless look.

"She did an excellent job," Pete said. "including a late-breaking news story that came in while she was on air."

"Good heavens, Maralee! What happened?"

"Forensics found a spent bullet in the mud inside

the car," Pete explained, as gently as he could. "It's being examined. We hope it can give us some new information."

"You think its possible someone might have *shot* that boy?" Aunt Ibby frowned.

Pete shook his head. "We don't know yet where the bullet came from. Ballistics has it. We'll know in a day or so, the caliber, possibly the type of gun it was fired from. Then we'll take the investigation from there. See where it leads us."

"I understand." My aunt stood, yawned. "I think I'll bid you two good night. I've had a busy day." She smiled. "Coming O'Ryan?"

The cat jumped down from the windowsill and followed my aunt to the door. "I'll let myself out," she said. "See you in the morning."

"Want to watch *The Fog*?" I offered after she'd left. "Adrienne Barbeau and Jamie Lee Curtis. And by the way, I had another vision tonight right after the show."

"No to the movie, thanks. Want to tell me about the vision?"

"Yes," I said. I described how high-school-photo-Ted had materialized in my mirror. "He wasn't wearing his yearbook clothes though," I explained. "He wore a Red Sox T-shirt."

"Oh, boy." Pete sighed.

"Oh boy what?" I asked. "Everybody in Salem has one."

"He was wearing one. The kid in the car. We found what was left of it."

"Jeans too?" I asked.

"Yep."

I wasn't exactly surprised. "In the vision he was

sitting on a bench. It was the same one my mother and Aunt Ibby were sitting on in the first vision."

"But you don't recognize the bench? Or the place?"

"Sorry. I thought about trying to see it again—in my mind, you know? But I'd probably add things, like last time."

"I guess you're right. But be sure to keep me up-to-date on the visions as they come along. Okay?"

"I will. I'm glad I'm finally able to share the darned things with you. For such a long time I was afraid to." I touched his hand. "Afraid you'd think I was crazy."

"We've come a long way together, haven't we?" He turned his hand over and squeezed mine. "I admit, I still can't begin to understand this strange gift of yours, but I know it's real—and important. And I'm sorry that sometimes it scares you—makes you sad. I wish I could fix that part of it."

"It helps a lot to be able to talk with you about it. Like now. It helps to know the vision was right about the T-shirt." *Helps keep me convinced I'm not crazy!*

"It's nothing I can use in a report, but it sure does help validate his identity. Did you notice that your aunt keeps saying 'the boy,' or 'that poor soul' when she's talking about Ted Thorne? According to the yearbook they were a couple, but she refuses to use his name. Same as Mrs. Thorne. Won't say 'Ted.' Or 'my son.'"

"Neither of them wants to accept it." I said. "Eventually they'll have to. Finding that bullet makes it even worse, doesn't it?"

"Maybe. Maybe not. If he was shot, chances are the skeletal remains will tell us so. If not, there's another explanation."

"I hope there is. River did a special reading for Ted's mother tonight. She used only one card, but it was one that represented eternal life."

"That's nice."

"It also represents messages in writing. Maybe that's about the greeting cards his mother told you about."

Pete leaned back in his chair and grinned. "Babe, I'm still learning to figure you out. Understanding River's hocus-pocus is way beyond my pay grade."

O'Ryan chose that moment to reenter the kitchen via his cat door. Barely pausing to acknowledge us, he went straight to the bedroom. We watched through the open door as he hopped up onto the bed, turned around three times, then lay down and closed his eyes.

"I guess that means it's your bedtime, too." Pete gestured toward the refrigerator door where I'd posted the Star card. "Anything in there for breakfast?"

"Is that a hint that you'd like to still be here in the morning?"

"See? I'm easy to read." He did his Groucho Marx eyebrow thing.

"Pop-Tarts," I said.

"What kind?

"Strawberry."

"You talked me into it. I'll stay."

CHAPTER 20

Pete had already left for work (with two strawberry Pop-Tarts and a to-go cup of coffee) when I'd finished loading up my biggest Jacki Easlick hobo bag with all the things I figured I'd need for the day. I'd included the growing stack of index cards in case I got a minute to myself to organize them into some sort of logical sequence. O'Ryan had followed Pete downstairs and had, I presumed, joined Aunt Ibby for breakfast.

The promised rain had finally arrived, so I tossed on a clear plastic rain poncho with the WICH-TV logo on the back and made my way down the twisty staircase to the back hall. I tapped on my aunt's kitchen door. "Good morning. It's me."

"Come in, dear. It's open."

I shook my head and I walked right in. She was in her usual spot at the round oak table. O'Ryan lay curled up on a round braided seat pad in a captain's chair beside her.

"You two look comfy. Hope you don't have to go out anywhere. Wanda says it'll rain on and off all day."

"I don't have to go to the library today, and I have plenty of groceries on hand," she said. "I think I may catch up on some reading. Penelope might come over this afternoon for an envelope-addressing session if the rain doesn't keep her away." She sighed a tiny little sigh. "Betsy's too busy to help us, and anyway her handwriting is practically illegible."

"I don't know what Rhonda has lined up for Francine and me. Hopefully, it'll be indoors somewhere," I said. "If you think of anything you need, though, just give me a call."

"I will, dear. Have you had breakfast? I can fix you something quick."

"Thanks. Already had coffee and a Pop-Tart."

I got the expected tsk-tsk, promised that I'd eat a nice healthy lunch, kissed her goodbye, and locked the kitchen door on my way out.

Salem in the rain isn't a particularly pretty sight, with mouse-gray sky overhead, and bits of litter floating along in rivulets next to the curbstones. But the pleasant *swish-swish* of the windshield wipers, traffic lights reflecting in puddles, along with classics from the good-music station playing on the radio make for a soothing commute to work. I've always liked it.

I got there before Francine for a change, wished for the thousandth time I'd picked a parking space closer to the downstairs studio door, and dashed across the parking lot splashing water onto my jeans and my second-best Chelsea Gloss rain booties. I stamped my feet on the jute mat inside the door, waiting for my eyes to adjust to the dark room, and headed for the metal stairway leading to the second-floor offices, shaking raindrops from my plastic poncho all the way.

Rhonda, with her usual efficiency, was prepared with a list of possible field report ideas, but as she let me know, "not set in stone" locations. Francine arrived just as I was reading through the choices, mentally eliminating new playground equipment at the Collins Elementary School, and the spring flower display at the Ropes Memorial Gardens, both better suited to a sunny day.

"Hey, anything fun and dry for us to do?" Francine closed a wet red umbrella and leaned it against the curved reception desk. "It's a freakin' monsoon out there."

"Sorry," Rhonda said. "I made out the list before I watched the weather last night. But there are a couple of indoor ideas, and I'll keep checking around for more."

"These aren't so bad." I showed the list to Francine. "How does this strike you?" I pointed to the third item.

"A ten o'clock scrapbooking class at the community center." she read aloud. "Why do people need a class to stick stuff in a scrapbook? Scissors, paste, pictures and there you go."

"These days it's quite an art form. Special paper, little 3-D stickers," Rhonda offered. "They say it can run into money if you get into it seriously. The instructor gets there early, so she can brief you on what's going on before you start. It won't be live. We'll run it with the five o'clock."

"Got it," I said. "Hey, isn't Chief Whaley supposed to be doing a presser today on the ballistics report on that bullet they found in the granite pit car? Do we have a time on that yet?"

"Around noon, probably. But that's not firm so it's not on the list." Rhonda said. "I'll text you the minute I hear for sure."

"He usually does those in front of the police station," I said. "I hope we don't have to stand in the rain to cover it."

"I'll bet we do." Francine made a fake pout-face. "There's a covered sidewalk. He gets to stand under the roof. We don't. Better tell Doan we'll need a couple of guys to hold umbrellas over us. Mine to protect the camera, yours to keep your hair from frizzing up."

"How about Scott Palmer and Buck Covington for umbrella holders?" Rhonda suggested.

We all laughed about that. "Let's get over to the community center and get a crash course in scrapbooking," I said, and the two of us headed back out into the rain.

The community center building houses all sorts of pleasant activities for the citizens of Salem. (I still feel a little shiver of uneasiness whenever I walk into the place, though, because of a totally *un*pleasant experience I had there once.) Francine parked the mobile unit close to the front entrance. We grabbed the camera and mics and dashed inside—"running between the raindrops" Aunt Ibby calls it.

We found the scrapbooking instructor right away. The sign on the glass door read GLORY'S SCRAPBOOK HAVEN. She welcomed us to a room furnished with groupings of tables, some round, some square. It looked a bit like a bridge tournament setup, except for the stacks of books of fancy papers, rolls of ribbon and colored tape, cans of spray glue, bottles of rubber cement, and file boxes full of photos.

"I need to run down to the supply closet for a few things," she said. "I'll be just a few minutes. Why don't you just look around? I'm sure these girls don't mind you peeking over their shoulders."

There were already a few women there, each of them clearly engrossed in the open book on the table before her. They each looked up and nodded politely as the woman known as Ms. Glory introduced us. All but one quickly went back to her project. The remaining woman tilted her head and stared at me. "You're Ibby Russell's niece, aren't you? Remember me? Penelope Driscoll? We met at your house."

"Of course. How are you?" I introduced her to Francine. "May we see what you're working on, Ms. Driscoll?" I asked. "This is our first experience with scrapbooking."

"Really? Sure you may! I've made dozens of them. For my kids, grandkids, my church group. It's actually quite addictive and so much fun—gathering the pictures, the mementos, the clippings. Come and see!"

Francine lifted her camera to her shoulder. "Mind if I film this?"

"Will it be on TV? Oh my. Do I look all right?" She patted carefully waved hair.

"You look lovely," I said. And she did.

"This is Ms. Penelope Driscoll," I said into the mic. "She's going to tell us a little about her scrapbooking project. I understand this isn't your first one, Ms. Driscoll." I extended the mic toward her.

"Oh, goodness no. I've made them for family,

friends, organizations." She spread her hands wide apart, indicating a scattering of photos, newspaper clippings, menus, all sorts of paper memorabilia on the tabletop. "I guess you can tell I'm one of those people who never threw anything away." A tinselly giggle. "This book is for my forty-fifth high school class reunion."

"Wow!" The unprofessional exclamation escaped me. "I mean, what a treasure trove of memories this will be for your classmates."

"I hope so." She gestured to the table." I come here early most days because I need to get it finished in time for the reunion in August. There's so much to do, you know, what with invitations, reservations, decorations, food service, photographers. Oh, so much to do!"

"You seem to be off to a good start." I pointed to the open book. "Looks as though you have half of the pages full already."

"I do." Bright smile. "I'll just keep snipping and trimming and pasting and decorating and it will be ready on time."

"I'm sure it will be wonderful." I looked up to see Ms. Glory in the doorway, both arms loaded with boxes, spray cans, and wallpaper sample books. Francine gave the "cut" signal and I put down the mic, hurrying to help the burdened instructor.

Once the supplies were distributed to the various tables and more students had begun to arrive, I realized that I'd already learned quite a lot about this hobby. At least I figured I knew enough to ask a few intelligent questions of the assembled scrapbookers.

With some helpful prompting from Ms. Glory, plenty of willing hobbyists were more than delighted to display their photos of grandkids, first grade report cards, old valentines, Sunday school awards, graduation programs, matchbook covers—all neatly grouped and embellished with appropriate stickers and stamps. I was beginning to understand why some people claimed that scrapbooking is addictive and even found myself thinking about the shoeboxes full of Florida memorabilia I'd gathered during my years there. *Maybe someday?*

With Francine and her camera following, I managed to speak briefly with each of the dozen women in the room, hearing the stories of each project. Having moved full circle, I wound up at the table where Penelope Driscoll busily arranged a collage of color snapshots, menus, and ticket stubs. "So there you have it," I said. "A hobby that involves the very finest kind of recycling. Scrapbooking brings new enjoyment of old memories, as well as the fun of creating and sharing remembrances of good times past. This is Lee Barrett reporting for WICH-TV from Glory's Scrapbook Haven in the community center."

I'd no sooner signed off when the expected text from Rhonda arrived. "Wrap it up, kids. Chief Whaley will be doing a presser at 10:45. You've got 15 minutes to get there."

We bid a hasty goodbye to Ms. Glory and her students, and I took an extra moment to thank Penelope for her help. I glanced at her open scrapbook page. One of the color photos showed a young Penelope sitting on a rustic bentwood bench in front of a window. Pete had been right about the lace curtains and the crystal star. They were missing. Everything else matched my visions.

"Come on, Lee! Let's roll!" Francine called, holding the door open for me. "No time to waste."

CHAPTER 21

Francine and I splashed our way back to the mobile unit, my mind still reeling from that brief peek at the sunny day scene of a girl on a bench, wishing there'd been time to ask the woman about it. *Never mind. I can talk to Penelope later and find out where that bench was. Then maybe I'll find out what it means.*

Traveling a tad too fast considering the wet pavement and lowered visibility, and slowing down only when we were within a couple of blocks of the Margin Street police station, we made it before there was any activity on the covered paved area where the lectern and mic were set up. The radio station truck and a couple of Boston TV mobile vans had beat us to the site but so far none of the reporters had yet left the shelter of the vehicles.

The weather had cleared considerably by the time Chief Tom Whaley, resplendent in full dress uniform—gold braid, medals, and all—appeared. Since we hadn't arranged for any umbrella bearers after all, I shed my plastic rain gear, and Francine and

I joined the other reporters in a row in front of the lectern, shielding mics and cameras as best we could, and waited for the promised "breaking news."

Whaley did his usual nervous paper-shuffling, throat-clearing routine before speaking. He hates these press things. Everybody knows it, and most of us kind of sympathize with him because stage fright is such a human trait. Finally, he began.

"I'll make this fast. Don't want you all getting soaked. There has been some significant progress in our investigation of the vehicle recently recovered from one of the abandoned North Shore granite pits." He paused, consulting his notes. "The vehicle, as you may already know, contained human remains. The medical examiner's office has confirmed the identity of the deceased person. Dental records, information from the Massachusetts Registry of Motor Vehicles, and the victim's wallet confirm that the deceased male was Theodore Thorne, aged approximately nineteen at the time of his death. A spent thirty-eight-caliber bullet was found amid debris in the automobile. It appears at this time that the cause of Theodore Thone's death was a gunshot wound causing an isolated frontal rib fracture of the number two rib left side. On April 20, 1974, Theodore Thorne was reported by his parents to Salem PD as missing, believed to be driving a 1971 red Ford Mustang Fastback. Thorne was, at the time, believed to be a runaway, due to family conflict. The 1974 license plate recovered from the vehicle matches the reported plate. After a number of years this matter was assigned to our cold case files. It is now an active murder investigation.

Thank you." Whaley turned away from the mic, as though he thought he might get away without answering questions. *Fat chance of that.*

One of the Boston guys yelled first. "Chief! Have you recovered the weapon? A thirty-eight, you said?"

"No weapon yet. Yes, a thirty-eight."

I waved. "Chief Whaley?"

An undisguised sigh from the podium. "Yes, Ms. Barrett." (In most cases it might be flattering to be known and recognized by the chief, but in my case, not so much.)

"Sir, any suspects? Have you called anyone in for questioning yet?"

The answer surprised me. "We have a list of people we want to talk to. Let me be clear. There are no suspects. We've begun interviewing persons of interest in this matter."

Are Ted Thorne's high school classmates "persons of interest?" I suppose they are. Even Aunt Ibby.

I decided to push my luck. "Follow-up question, sir. What about the person who gave you the tip about the car in the first place? Still anonymous?"

His response was brief. "We're looking into that. Next question?"

The WBZ reporter called out "Was the kid in the car when he got shot?"

Good one. I should have thought of that too.

"We don't think so. Nothing conclusive there yet. Thank you." He backed away again. This time he got away with it. Press conference over.

"This is Lee Barrett outside the Salem Police Station, where Salem Police Chief Tom Whaley has just identified the person whose remains were found in the submerged vintage Mustang recently recovered from an abandoned pit at the old North Shore Granite Works. The deceased was nineteen-year-old Theodore Thorne, who went missing in 1974 and had been presumed to be a runaway. Chief Whaley also revealed that a spent bullet from a thirty-eight-caliber weapon was found amid debris in the car and that the medical examiner has determined that Thorne had been shot. The weapon has not been recovered and there are no suspects. Police are planning to speak with several persons of interest. Stay tuned to WICH-TV for updates on this continuing story."

We climbed back into the mobile unit, damp and cold. Francine turned on the heater and drove back to the TV station. "I don't like thinking about the kid being murdered," she said. "At first I figured if there was a body in the car it was because he'd drowned."

"I know. Me too." I pulled the visor mirror down on my side and groaned. Whatever magic Carmine had wrought on my hair the previous night was gone. Shirley Temple had returned—and not in a good way. I flipped the mirror back up in a hurry. "I guess his poor mother will have to accept that he's dead now, won't she?" *I hope she wasn't alone when she heard about this.*

Back at WICH-TV we found most of the station staff in Rhonda's reception area, all warm and dry, enjoying what looked like a catered picnic. "Come on in, girls!" Buffy Doan beckoned to us. "It's such a dreary day I thought it would be fun to have Panera send over a few lunch goodies for you all. I hope the broccoli cheese soup is still hot. Good heavens, Lee, what have you done to your hair?"

Scott Palmer patted the turquoise seat of the chrome chair beside him. "Sit down, Moon. Looks like you two had quite a morning. That was a surprise, huh? The kid was murdered?"

"Thanks," I said, helping myself to a steak and cheese panini. "Not much doubt about that, I'm afraid. You've done more pressers with the chief than I have, Scott. What do you think about his anonymous tipster answer. Does Whaley know who it is?"

"I don't think he does" Scott looked thoughtful. "Tom's a pretty straight shooter. If he knows and isn't ready to disclose, he would have said something like 'no comment at this time,' instead of 'we're looking into it.'"

"Yep. I get it. You're probably right." *Maybe not. Maybe Whaley knows and maybe Pete does too.*

"The tipster is definitely a person of interest. Bigtime," Scott said. "You should try one of those chocolate chip cookies."

"I think I will. All I've had before this today was a Pop-Tart."

"Still not much of a hand in the kitchen, huh?" He smiled.

"Afraid not." I stood, put my paper plate in the wastebasket, picked up a cookie, and looked at the schedule on the whiteboard behind Rhonda's desk. "Anything there for us this afternoon, Rhonda?"

"I'm sure the senior citizens swim meet at the Y is Scott's, not ours. Right?" Francine said with a broad wink. "Or do you want us to do it, Scotty, while you lay around here eating cookies?"

"You can have it if you want. Old guys in Speedos. Hot stuff."

"No thanks," I said. "We'll stand by here and see what turns up. Thanks for lunch, Mrs. Doan. It was delicious."

Marty and Phil tossed their paper plates away too, joining Francine and me as we checked the schedules on the whiteboard. "Looks like I've got time to wash the leaves on the plastic ficus tree on the *Fun with Gardening* set," Marty announced. "Thanks for lunch, Mrs. D. See you all in the funny papers." Phil, courteous as always, thanked us for the scrapbooking segment for his five o'clock show, and one by one our coworkers went back to work, leaving Rhonda, Francine, and me alone with Buffy and assorted empty food cartons and cookie crumbs. Naturally, we helped with the cleanup.

"Thanks so much, girls," Buffy said, putting the last of the plastic water bottles into the recycling basket. "I couldn't help overhearing what Scott said about Chief Whaley not knowing who that tip came from. He's wrong, you know. Mrs. Whaley is a member of my bridge club and she said that *he* told *her* the information had come from a highly reliable source. 'A person with intimate knowledge of the situation.' That's what she said." She nodded emphatically, amethyst dangle earrings swaying. "So he must know who the informant is, don't you think?"

"It seems reasonable that he might," I agreed. "But since there's a murder involved, and there's a killer out there somewhere, it must be important to protect the person's identity."

"Goodness, you're right." Buffy covered her mouth with both hands. "I should never have said anything about it."

"Wow. A murderer," Francine's voice was a whisper. "That boy died a long time ago. Do you think it's possible there's still a killer in Salem somewhere? Someone who thought the body would never be found?"

Inwardly, I finished the thought. *And now the murderer knows that someone else knew where the car was. And that there was a body in it.*

CHAPTER 22

There was a lot of new information I wanted to record on my index cards. Since Rhonda had nothing scheduled that required my presence at the moment, I took the opportunity to duck downstairs into one of the little cubicles Mr. Doan calls "data ports" where we can close the door, use a company computer, a company phone, gather our thoughts, make notes, get organized. It's one of his better ideas, and I've taken advantage of the neat little hideaway several times. This was such a time.

I put a pile of fresh cards on the left side of the desktop, and the ones containing the notes I had on the case so far on the right. (Okay. I said "case." Call me Nancy.) I'd learned the importance of making notes while the incident or conversation was still fresh in my mind—before the memory began doing tricks—adding and subtracting things.

I began with what Mrs. Doan had just told us. "Maggie Whaley (Chief's wife) told Buffy Doan that her husband had said 'the information' (read 'tip') had come from a 'highly reliable source. A person with intimate knowledge of the situation.'" In parentheses I added, "What does this mean? That the person actually saw something? And what if the murderer is still in Salem?"

That was plenty for one card, I thought. Big important questions but no answers yet. The heading for the next card was brief. Positive ID. I followed that simple declaration with "Chief Whaley released the name and age of the deceased man. Theodore Thorne, aged 19 at time of death."

Next card: "The gun. Chief Whaley said gun used to kill Ted was a .38-caliber weapon. The weapon has not been recovered."

I recorded notes from the chief's presser giving the details he'd released about the license plate, dental records, medical examiner's report, the spent bullet, the victim's fractured rib, the time Ted Thorne was reported missing, the family dysfunction issues, the belief that Ted was a runaway. Carmine's friend had said there were beer cans in the car. Chief didn't mention them. *Why not?*

The scrapbooking class chance meeting with Penelope had added a new dimension to the puzzle. Once again, and for the third time in recent days, a rustic bench had appeared. This time it had shown up in Penelope's scrapbook project, which she intended to share with her classmates. From the stack on the right I pulled my cards referring to the bench in my hall tree mirror vision, my trying-to-remember-details picture, and the real photo in the yearbook. On a fresh card I wrote about the latest real photo, this one in color showing that same bench. I had no details about it yet, but with luck, I'd run into Penelope again at home where she had a meeting with Aunt Ibby planned.

I thought for a moment, then pulled Penelope Driscoll's card. In block letters I wrote: "PENELOPE DRISCOLL NEVER THROWS ANYTHING AWAY." I sat back in the chair, staring at a growing stack of cards that, so far, didn't add up to anything. Why couldn't they be more like River's cards? The tarot cards, whether I understood them or not, always meant *something*.

I thought about the shortened, over-the-phone reading River had done for me. Maybe if I tried to relate the cards she'd read that night to *my* cards, something would click. I didn't have my tarot deck with me, but I found the card I'd headed "Tarot Reading" along with the date. I pulled nine clean cards from the stack and—forsaking any attempt at artwork—began labeling each one in block printing. "The Queen of Wands," I wrote and placed the card faceup on the desk. Next I lettered "Ten of Swords," and put it next to the first card. Then the "Ace of Cups" and so on until all nine of the cards River had told me about were laid out on the desktop like the beginning of a solitaire game.

The Queen of Wands is me. *Hmmm.* Couldn't think of anything to put under that one. Next came the Ten of Swords. Ruin, pain, affliction, tears. I put Ted Thorne's card under that along with the one about his mother and the one about my Red Sox T-shirt vision. The Ace. Beginning of new love. Just for fun, I put the cards for Coach and Penelope under it just because I thought they looked cute together. King of Cups reversed. Powerful man. Without hesitating, I put Steve's card beneath it and the following card, Queen of Swords—beautiful, artificial woman—made me reach for the Betsy Leavitt card. Next came the Star, and I put the card marked "popular table" with seven names on it—for the seven "stars"—beneath it. The Six of Cups promised someone from the past. I left that one empty. The scary one, the Eight of Swords, was next, The blindfolded lady standing in water. Meaning? Fear to move out of a situation. With an indecisive hand, I put the Ibby Russell card under that one. My beloved aunt was still struggling with accepting Ted's death every bit as much as his own mother had.

I pulled my phone from the purse and took a picture of the layout so I wouldn't forget it. I wanted to show it to River and maybe to Pete. It still didn't add up to any real answers, but just the act of organizing this many cards under one heading—Tarot Reading—gave me a little buzz of confidence. I knew that River had photographed the rest of her layout, and maybe when she finished my reading, there'd be places for the cards on diver, hard hats—all the other orphaned cards in the pile.

My phone vibrated. "Hi Rhonda. What's up?"

"Lee, Scott and Old Eddie are both here, so if anything turns up we're covered. I've already sent Francine home. You can clock out whenever you're ready."

I didn't lose any time packing up my belongings, locking the data port, and heading back upstairs. I said good night to Rhonda, thanked Old Eddie for coming in early, and took off for home. With luck, Penelope would be there and I'd know where that bench was—or is.

Penelope's car was parked in the driveway. Good luck so far. I hurried past the garden, barely spoke to the waiting cat on the back steps, and knocked on my aunt's kitchen door. No reply. They were probably in another room. Not surprisingly, the door was unlocked, and I stepped into the kitchen. "Yoo-hoo. It's me, Aunt Ibby," I called.

"Oh, Maralee. We're in the dining room. Come on back."

"Lovely to see you again, dear," Penelope said. "All the girls at scrapbooking are thrilled about being on TV. We can hardly wait to see ourselves in the news."

"It was our pleasure," I told her. "I wish we could have spent more time with you all."

"We understood that you had to leave. Being a reporter is such an exciting career, and Ibby is so proud of you."

"Very true. I am." My aunt beamed.

"I got a chance to see a little of Penelope's scrapbooking project. Fascinating stuff. Do you have it with you?"

"In the car." She sounded apologetic. "All tossed in a box. Not very orderly, but it works for me. Would you like to see what I've done so far, Ibby? It's all about our high school days."

There was the slightest pause before my aunt's bright smile appeared. "I'd love to see it, Penelope. You always were the creative one in the group."

"I'll just run outside and get it, then. Be right

back!" The tiny woman pushed her chair away from the table and scampered away.

"She's so darned cute," I said.

"Yes. Always was. Smart too. I'm sure the scrapbook will be a big hit at the reunion," Aunt Ibby sighed. "Sweet memories. Some bittersweet."

"You're thinking about Ted," I said.

"Yes. But it was a very long time ago. It's hard to think of him as—dead. All these years, I've thought of him as—away, you know?"

"You loved him."

"Oh, yes. We were in love. Young love can be true love. Not everyone knows that." She brushed a hand across her eyes.

Oh wow. Can this be why she never married? Has she been waiting for Ted to come back all these years?

It seemed like a good time to change the subject. "Holding the event at Hamilton Hall is perfect," I said. "Such a gorgeous ballroom."

Her smile returned. "Yes, It's an expensive venue, but Steve generously picked up the tab."

"Good guy," I said. "Must be pretty good at his job, whatever it is. Running for office is expensive these days."

"His parents started the business, the Omigoodness Bakery Shops. Started them right here in Salem years ago." She shook her head. "Still the best darned bagels I ever ate."

"There was one of those shops in Fort Lauderdale when I lived there," I remembered. "Mrs. Doan brings in a bag of them once in a while from the one on Lafayette Street, and there's one at the mall in

Peabody. They're all over the place. Steve Overton owns them all?"

"No. They're franchised. But I'm sure he derives income from all of them."

Penelope appeared in the doorway, almost hidden by the brown corrugated carton in her arms. I hurried to help her, and together we put the box on the table. "Here it is," she said. "I heard you talking about Steve's bagels. Yummy. When it was his turn to host the reunion committee meetings last time, I'll bet we all gained twenty pounds."

"Except Betsy," my aunt said.

"Except Betsy," Penelope echoed. They both laughed, and Penelope pulled the partially completed scrapbook from the box, pushing it across the table to my aunt. "Here's what I've done so far, Ibby. It starts with our freshman year."

"Oh, what fun," Aunt Ibby said. "Maralee, Penelope and I were in middle school together, so we were already friends. We didn't meet the others until we got to high school."

So what year did the bentwood bench appear? Do I have to wait until they get to that page?

I decided to interrupt. Manners be damned. "I'm going to scoot along upstairs and let you two gals enjoy your meeting," I said. "But Penelope, there was one photo I particularly noticed on the page you were working on at Ms. Glory's today. Could I possibly have a peek at that page, and then I'll get out of your way?"

My lapse of etiquette brought the slightly raised eyebrow from my aunt, but her friend seemed happy to oblige. The scrapbook was quickly flipped to its approximate center, and there was the photo of young Penelope seated prettily on that mystifying bench.

I reached across the page and tapped the photo. "Where was that one taken? Do you remember?"

Once again, the two laughed in chorus. "Remember? I remember that day as though it was yesterday," Aunt Ibby declared. "Look how young you were, Penelope. And I always loved that sundress on you."

"It was our sophomore year," her friend said. "Spring break. We all went down to the Thornes' summer place for a picnic. That picture was taken on their front porch."

CHAPTER 23

It took me a moment to figure out how to frame my next question. I knew I'd seen a picture of my aunt and my mother sitting on that same bench—on that same porch, But *that* one had been in a mirror, not in a scrapbook.

"As soon as I saw that picture today at Glory's," I said, "I felt that there was something familiar about it. Could there possibly be a similar snapshot in one of your old albums, Aunt Ibby?" I asked.

"I don't see how there *couldn't* be," Penelope said. "We all spent as much time there as we could, didn't we, Ibby?"

"We did." My aunt smiled a sweet, sad smile. "And yes, to answer your question, I'm sure you've seen pictures of me and your mother on that same porch, sitting on that same bench. I wouldn't be a bit surprised to find that bench is still there."

"This might be a crazy idea," I said. "Would you please look for that picture in your albums, Aunt

Ibby? And would you, too, Penelope? *If* there is such a picture of my mother and my aunt on that bench, and *if* the bench still exists, I want to buy it. I'd frame an enlargement of that picture of the two most important women in my life, and I'd hang it on my living room wall above the actual bench. Do the Thornes still own the place?"

"As far as I know." Penelope flipped the scrapbook's pages back to the beginning and pushed it toward my aunt. "At least Laura Thorne does. Now that her son Ted's gone, I believe she's the only one of the Thornes left. I'll look for that picture, Lee. I love your idea."

"Do you think she'd sell the bench?"

"All you can do is ask," my aunt said.

"Where'd you say this place was?" I asked.

"Not too far," Penelope said. "Over in Essex, near Chebacco Lake, in the forest part. Lots of trees. Very private. And early in the season, like now, there's hardly anybody over there. Mostly summerhouses, you know."

"They let you kids use it? Nice!"

Again the two shared a laugh. "They didn't pay any attention to us. All of us knew they hid the key under the lion statue, and anyway Ted was usually with us and he had his own key," Aunt Ibby said. "We went there whenever we wanted to. Just had to be careful not to make a mess."

"That was in the days before cell phones, dear," Penelope said. "Our parents never knew where we were or how to get in touch with us. I feel sorry for kids today—glued to their phones and those horrid intrusive video cameras everywhere you look. Can't get away with a darn thing, right, Ibby?"

"Hush, Penelope. Don't be giving away all our secrets!" Again, the two dissolved into laughter. It was good to see my aunt enjoying herself. Perhaps she'd accepted Ted's death, I thought. Perhaps she could move on. After a few more minutes I excused myself and, leaving through the living room, climbed the front staircase to my own place. O'Ryan was already there, sitting on the kitchen windowsill.

It felt good to shed damp clothes, and a hot shower was more than welcome. A session with the hair dryer and the straightening brush improved things even more. I put on comfy gray sweats, brought my laptop into the kitchen, broiled a hamburger, toasted a bun, opened a Pepsi, and filled O'Ryan's red bowl with fresh kibble.

The plan was to make the information on the index cards, and some of the thoughts rattling around in my head, into a logical, readable document. Kind of like pulling together a semester's notes for a final paper—except that none of my college dissertations had ever referenced visions, tarot readings, or witch's cats. This paper was for my eyes only. (I was really tempted to title it *The Mystery of the Muddy Mustang* but resisted.)

Once again, I pulled out the cards (which were getting a tad dog-eared by then) and fanned them out on the Lucite table on one side of the laptop, with my hamburger and Pepsi on the other, and got to work.

It was nice, just the cat and me and the gentle ticktock of Kit-Cat Klock's tail counting off the seconds there in my cozy kitchen. I didn't even turn on the TV. Worked right through the five o'clock news and missed the scrapbook segment entirely. I was all the way up to page ten—double-spaced, twelve-point Times New Roman—when my phone buzzed and I learned about what else I'd missed on the five o'clock.

It was Francine. "You watching? Did you see Scott's report?"

"No. I'm working on something. What happened? What'd I miss?"

"They found another piece of evidence in the mud. You know, the mucky stuff in the bottom of the Mustang. One of the detectives was on screen talking about it. Not Pete. One of the other guys. Anyway, it looked like he was in front of that warehouse where they took the car."

"What was it? What did they find?"

Wouldn't you know it? Something breaks in my case and Scott gets to cover it.

"Some kind of jewelry. A necklace I think. Anyway, it's real gold and it's shaped like a piece of a heart. They're back to regular programming now, but I'm sure it'll be on the eleven o'clock. Watch for it."

"I will, for sure. Thanks," I said, reaching for a fresh index card. "Sorry we missed it."

"I'm not," she said. "I was practically mildewed by the time I got home. I don't mind Palmer and Old Eddie doing the honors on this one. Not one bit. See you tomorrow. Wanda says sunny and breezy. No rain."

I wrote on the card just what Francine had told me. A section of a gold necklace shaped like a piece of a heart. *Does that mean part of it is broken off?* If so, they're probably sifting through mud for the broken part. Wait a minute. A piece of a heart is broken off? Heartbroken? Hadn't River mentioned heartbreak in my reading?

I pushed a few of the index cards aside and found the one I'd captioned Ten of Swords. Sure enough. *Ruin and pain, affliction and tears, possible heartbreak.* Coincidence? River says there's no such thing as coincidence. Pete doesn't believe in it, either. But whose heart? Mine's already been broken once—when Johnny died. Why do I fall in love with men in dangerous professions? A race car driver and a cop. Doesn't get much more dangerous than that. I guessed Aunt Ibby's heart was broken when Ted disappeared all those years ago—or maybe it was broken again, when she realized that he wasn't ever coming back.

Trying not to let this new information derail my train of thought, I got back to work. The phone was still on the table. I picked it up and scrolled through recent photos and took another look at my card layout. Maybe another arrangement would make more sense. I moved the laptop aside. This time I used the seven friends—seven stars—as my focus.

By this time O'Ryan's curiosity had kicked in. He left his windowsill perch, climbed onto a chair, then padded across the tabletop. He faced me across the card layout, then picking his way daintily around the cards, he plunked himself down on his haunches directly in front of me. Cats love doing this stuff. Sitting on the newspaper while you're trying to read, walking on the computer keys. "You're in my way, big boy," I scolded. "Move over.

Ignoring my command, he put one paw forward, gently touching the "Ted has his own key" card, tilting it slightly. I reached around him and straightened it. "Mind your own business." I said, trying for a sterner tone. "This isn't a card game."

He said something that sounded like "Mmerratt," gave the same card a definite push toward the Bobby column, twisted his head around, and gave me the golden-eyed cat stare. "I guess you're not playing, are you? Okay. This where you want it?" I put the card under the "Steve gave Bobby a ride home" card. "Anything else?"

There was.

He walked ever so carefully around the card layout to where the rest of them were fanned out, turned his back, and with one swoosh of that long bushy tail, swept the whole pile onto the floor. "You naughty boy! What's the matter with you?" I hurried from my chair, knelt, and began picking up the scattered white oblongs. "Look. They're all mixed up. Bad cat!" It was true. Many of them were facedown on my not-so-immaculate floor. The cat crouched under the table, watching me, looking not at all apologetic. With a sudden move, a yellow paw snaked out, landing on a facedown card, holding it firmly in place. I flipped it over and picked it up. It was the new card. The one I'd just written about—the broken gold heart.

Sometimes O'Ryan is just a cat, playing silly cat games, doing normal cat stuff—eating, napping (a lot of napping) watching birds, chasing squirrels, staring into space, sitting on newspapers. But sometimes he uses his mysterious side—his "I-used-to-be-a-witch's-cat" side—and I've learned to pay close attention to those times. This was clearly one of them.

I put the chosen card on the table at the base of the layout I'd begun, then leaned back in my chair and waited for O'Ryan to make his move. It took a little while. Not having opposable thumbs makes a difference, dexterity-wise. He used a gentle tapping motion to position the card where he wanted it to be, sometimes using his pink nose to push it into place. When he'd finished—and I could tell that he had because he gave the whole arrangement a diffident sniff, then returned to his windowsill, and in a most ungentlemanly posture, proceeded to groom his underside.

The "broken heart" card now lay crosswise over the "bench is on the porch" card, touching the "Ibby" card on one end and the "Ted" card on the other.

Huh?

I studied the tabletop for a long moment. What was witch boy cat trying to tell me? I snapped a quick photo. Okay, Ibby and Ted are connected. I knew that. No secret. But what did the bench on the porch of Ted's parents' summer home have to do with somebody's broken heart? Frustrating. If I'd had a long bushy tail I'd have been tempted to pitch them all back onto the floor.

Instead I gathered the cards together, put a rubber band around them, carried them into my bedroom, and put them into one of the secret compartments in the bureau. I picked up my paper plate and Pepsi bottle, put them into the recycling container, gave the tabletop a couple of squirts of glass cleaner and a quick swipe, and concentrated once more on my manuscript.

Penelope Leavitt says that Mrs. Thorne still owns the summer place near Chebacco Lake. Maybe Pete and I should take a ride over there. O'Ryan thinks it's important. So do I. If Pete doesn't agree maybe Francine and I should go—do a little investigative-reporter field trip. Check out that front porch with its bentwood bench—if it's even still there.

Unbidden, the thought came to me. *Penelope said there's hardly anyone around there this time of year. She also said the key used to be hidden under the lion statue.*

Pete would never go for that! I tried to shake the thought away.

I shrugged and looked over at the cat. Maybe I didn't have to mention it to Pete quite yet. I began to type.

CHAPTER 24

I started over, beginning with the morning when Francine and I had taken a tip from an unreliable source and found a couple of police divers searching for something underwater in an abandoned granite pit. From there on the words just flowed. I realized that I wasn't coming to any profound conclusions, but at least things were assuming some sort of order.

My phone buzzed and I was surprised to see that it was already ten thirty. Caller ID announced Pete. "Hi," I said.

"Hi, yourself. I'm just about to pass Russ Treadwell's ice cream stand. How does a hot fudge sundae sound?"

"Sounds exactly right! You're out late. Working?"

"Old guys' league hockey practice. I'll be aching tomorrow, but it was fun tonight."

"Shall I get the liniment out?"

"No thanks. Ice cream and coffee will do the trick. I didn't wake you, did I?"

"No," I said. "I'm trying to make sense out of all the notes I've made since this car in a granite pit thing started."

"Welcome to the club. So's most of the department. How're you doing with it?" I heard another voice in the background. "Wait a minute. I'll ask her. Do you want nuts and whipped cream?"

"Yes. And a cherry. I haven't come to any conclusions. I keep making connections to Aunt Ibby's classmates though."

"Uh-huh. Well, I'll be along in a few minutes."

"Okay. We can talk about it then."

I sent the manuscript to my printer, put the laptop away, gave the tabletop another swipe with a paper towel, and started the coffee. I turned on the TV, too, hoping Buck Covington would show a photo of the mysterious broken heart on his eleven o'clock broadcast. Pete must know something about that by now. Maybe he'd fill me in on what—if anything—it meant to the investigation. Maybe they'd even found some more of the broken pieces of it.

O'Ryan gave a long stretch—front paws forward, back paws aft, full length—with a big pink-tongued yawn, and stepped down from the windowsill onto a chair—then to the floor, and strolled toward the living room. Pete must be on his way, probably just turning onto Oliver Street. When he got a little closer, the cat would exit the cat door and head downstairs to greet him on the back steps. I'd have a couple of minutes to check my appearance in the oval full-length mirror in my bedroom.

Sweats looked okay and a long pink chiffon scarf kept my hair reasonably neat. I reached for the tube of pink gloss on the bureau, then turned back toward my reflection. But the person in the mirror was no longer me. She looked quite a bit like me—but younger, with red hair a lot like mine. It could be Aunt Ibby, or maybe my mother. She wore a long dress—surely a prom gown—white, full skirted, strapless. There was an orchid corsage on her wrist. Boom. Pete's key turned in the lock. The girl was gone and I was back.

"Better eat this before it melts, babe!" Pete was in the kitchen before I had time to move away from the mirror, to adjust to the reality of where I was in time and space. He came into the room and caught on immediately. "Oh, oh. You seeing things?" He pulled me close. I buried my face in his shoulder and closed my eyes, feeling safety in his arms. "Was it a bad one?"

"No. Not bad. Just . . . startling. They both looked so much like me, you know."

Gently, he steered me back into the kitchen, led me to a chair. "Here. Sit down. Have some ice cream. Who looks like you?"

"I'm sorry." I shook my head. "I'm not making sense, am I? There was a girl in the mirror. Looked like me when I was in high school."

"But it wasn't you?"

"No. Her dress was from the seventies. A prom dress. It was either my aunt or my mother."

"Now I get it." He put both of our sundaes on the

table and handed me a spoon. "Does it mean anything to you? The pretty redhead in a prom dress?"

"Something to do with Aunt Ibby's class reunion, I suppose. Everything lately seems to lead back to that."

"Yes. You're right."

That was a surprise. I thought I was the only one making that connection. "Because Ted was a member of that class?"

"Not just that class. That particular clique. The class president. The two top jocks. The head cheerleader. The valedictorian. The rich kid with the cool car. And Penelope. Haven't figured out where she fits in."

"The popular table in the lunch room." I said. "The seven stars on the tarot card."

"You're losing me, babe," he said, digging into his sundae. "I get the lunch table, but not the card."

"Just something River said." I looked up at the TV. "Not important. Is it eleven o'clock already?"

"Sure is. Want me to turn that off?"

"No. Francine said they found a piece of a necklace in the Mustang. I missed it on the five o'clock broadcast. Have you seen it? The broken heart?"

"Broken heart? You mean the Mizpah benediction necklace from the kid's car?"

I could almost see the light bulb over my head when what he'd said registered. Francine had been talking about one of those two-part heart charms that couples sometimes wear. I recited the Bible passage from memory. "The Lord watch between me and thee while we are absent one from another."

"Right. Genesis, I think. The kid must have been wearing it. Forensics said the bullet nicked it a little when he got shot. There. That's it." He pointed to the TV where a close-up of a man's open palm filled the screen. The anonymous hand held a portion of an inscribed heart. It wasn't broken in the way that I'd first pictured it—shattered and fragmented with raw, jagged edges. There was a neatly staggered line edging the right side of a half-heart shape. A small, uneven dent disfigured the top left curve of the heart.

"Did they find the chain to his half yet?" I asked, eyes still fixed on the screen.

"I don't think so. I imagine it's in the car somewhere though."

I took a mouthful of my sundae and thought about what I was going to say next. The hot fudge had melted into the vanilla ice cream perfectly, and a gentle sprinkle of finely ground nuts crowned the mound of whipped cream. I took my time, savoring taste and texture, then put down my spoon. "The other half of the heart is still on its chain," I said. "I've seen it many times."

Pete nodded. "Your aunt has it?"

"Uh-huh. It's in a jewelry box where she keeps special pieces."

"Did she ever tell you where she got it?"

"She never mentioned it at all and I never asked. Actually, I've always thought that most of the things in that chest had belonged to my mother."

"I'm going to have to ask her about it."

"Of course you are. I'm going to talk to her about

it, too," I promised. "I think she and the other stars are going to help us solve this murder."

He smiled. "Us? Help us?"

"Yep," I said, confidence growing. "You and me, the police chief, a few divers, and the class reunion committee. We're going to solve your cold case."

CHAPTER 25

I wasn't sure whether Pete believed what I'd said about helping him solve the cold case, but at least he didn't laugh or call me Nancy. He just smiled a tiny smile and said, "I guess at this point we can use all the help we can get." He poured us each a cup of decaf and we watched Buck Covington deliver the rest of the news—sans mistakes of course—and finished our sundaes.

Pete had run out of clean clothes at my place, he had hockey gear in his car that needed washing, and he was scheduled for a split shift, so he left for his apartment right after Scott gave the Red Sox scores and Wanda (adorable in a purple satin mini) promised blue skies and green lights for the next day.

I thought about working some more on my writing project but decided that sleep was a better option. I carefully placed the oval mirror in its proper—according to River—feng shui position so that it showed O'Ryan's favorite kitchen window instead of reflecting me in my bed. I tried not to look directly at the glass, preferring no more visions of past, present, or future events; wiped off the last traces of makeup; donned white cotton pajamas; and climbed into bed. O'Ryan joined me there, did his ritual three-times-turn-around, and settled down close beside me. "I love you, cat," I whispered. "Mmmrrup," he replied, purring loudly.

Cuddling with a purring cat is a great sleep aid. I woke early, refreshed and anxious to get downstairs. I planned to talk my aunt out of her current funk and into girl detective mode so she could put her considerable research expertise to work on *our* case. I didn't even bother to make coffee or get dressed, just brushed my teeth and hair, pulled on slippers, and hurried down the front stairs.

Aunt Ibby looked up from her morning *Boston Globe*, not registering the slightest surprise at this early visit by my pajama-clad self. "Good morning, dear. Help yourself to coffee. Fresh banana bread on the counter. It's good with the strawberry jam."

She was correct. I filled my mug and plate and then got right to the point. "Aunt Ibby, I know you've been distracted by all that's been going on lately— your friend Ted's death, all the class reunion business, finding out that Ted was murdered—"

She interrupted. "You think it's time I stopped licking my wounds and started thinking about what I can do to help figure out what happened back in 1974."

"Well, yeah."

"At least I know one thing." She smiled a wry little

smile. "He didn't deliberately stand me up for the senior prom."

"Is that what you thought all these years? That he stood you up?"

"Sure. That's what everybody thought. There I was in my gorgeous prom gown. White. Strapless. He'd sent a corsage. We wore them on our wrists back then. Orchids, no less. The florist delivered it the afternoon of the prom. There was a sweet note inside the box, too, along with a gold necklace." She stopped speaking, leaning on one elbow, fist under her chin, a faraway look in her green eyes. "I still have it. The necklace, I mean. Actually, I still have the note. And the corsage. It's pressed between sheets of waxed paper in the family Bible. Silly old woman."

She hasn't seen the news. She doesn't know yet that Ted was wearing the other half of her necklace when he died. She's reading a Boston paper. They're probably not even carrying the story.

I reached for her hand. "Aunt Ibby," I said. "The police have found Ted's half of the necklace in the car. They say he was wearing it when he died. I'm sorry."

"It's all right." She squeezed my hand. "I always expected that he'd be wearing it—wherever he was. You see, until they found his car, and even after they found it, I believed he was alive. That he'd come back to Salem someday. I think at first, we all believed it. But as time went by, I guess maybe some of the others gave up hope. But not me. I wore my necklace for a while, back in high school. Then one day I put it in my jewelry box and never wore it again."

"I remember seeing it. You planned to wear it again when he came home."

"I was sure he would."

"Because you loved him?"

"Partly that. But mostly it was the cards." She squeezed my hand so hard it hurt. "The damned cards that someone has been sending all these years. Why would anybody do that?"

"Pete said that Ted's mother has cards from him too."

"That doesn't surprise me. Has Pete seen hers? I'd like to see if the dates and postmarks match up with mine."

"So far she hasn't parted with any of them," I said. "Too precious. Maybe she'll turn them over to the police now that—you know."

"I'll give mine to Pete," my aunt spoke sternly. "They're not precious now. Ted didn't send them, that's for sure. Maybe they'll help the police figure this whole thing out."

"Funny how things seem to be coming together," I said. "Pete's been busy with a cold case, which turns out to be the disappearance of a boy and a red Mustang forty-five years ago. Francine and I hear that something's going on at the North Shore pits, and it turns out to be that same red Mustang underwater."

"Same boy, too," Aunt Ibby said, "and he turns out to be the missing member of my class reunion committee."

"There's more, too," I said. "That picture of you and my mother on a bench? The reason I first got interested in it was because I'd seen the bench before. In the hall tree mirror."

"Oh dear. One of those pesky visions. Were we sitting on it then too?"

"No. Ted was."

She grew silent then, got up from the table and poured herself a cup of coffee, paused and looked out the window. "Has Pete checked that cottage out at all?" she asked. "Does he know about the vision?"

"Not exactly," I said. "I planned to tell him about the cottage connection. Seems obvious to me, but he might not think so. I'd even thought about going over there myself. Just to look around, you know?"

"The visions are always important, Maralee. Even when you don't understand them. Isn't that true?"

"It always seems to turn out that way," I agreed.

"I think we need to tell Pete about the cottage." Another long pause. "But since I know exactly where it is, I guess it won't hurt anything if you and I drive over there sometime soon—just to look around."

"Okay then. That's a date." I finished my coffee and stood up to leave. "I'd better get upstairs and dress for work. Glad we had this talk. Between us, we'll figure it all out. Anyway, I already promised Pete I was going to help him solve his cold case."

"It's much more than a cold case now," she said. "We'll help him solve a murder."

"Maybe if I get out early again today," I suggested, "we could take that ride while it's still light outside."

"Maybe," she said. "Betsy's coming over this afternoon. She's all in a snit about something. Says she needs to talk to someone, so I told her I'd be here all day. We didn't set any special time."

"That's okay. It'll keep."

"Been keeping for forty-five years," she said. "A little longer won't matter."

CHAPTER 26

I brought my laptop with me to work just in case I might be able to grab a few minutes to myself in the data port. I wanted to get Aunt Ibby's prom story down on paper—or at least into electronic form. I wondered if Penelope's photo collection included any pictures of my aunt in that strapless white gown. *I'll just bet it does. And I'll bet it looks exactly like it did in my mirror.*

The hoped-for few minutes of downtime didn't seem likely when Francine and I got a look at our schedule. Sometimes Doan likes to restock what he calls "evergreen" topics. Rhonda calls them "greenies." These are short features of local interest that he can use as "fillers" on slow news days. Salem is a never-ending source of these stories. I've done them on a museum exhibit, a candy factory, a fabulous doll-house, dozens of out-of-the-way places viewers might enjoy seeing or learning about. The scrapbooking segment would have worked as one.

"There's going to be an announcement sometime

today about the stuff they've found in that Mustang, but we don't know when it'll be," Rhonda said, waving a copy of our schedule. "Doan doesn't like seeing you two hanging around waiting for something to happen. So here are a few greenies to fill your time today. If I buzz you about the Mustang thing though, drop everything and get your butts over to that warehouse pronto."

First on our list was a women's drum circle over near Jefferson Avenue. Next came a visit to Crow Haven Corner for a session on spell potions and how they're made. Rhonda said we should come back to the station after that one. "Here are information sheets on the first two," she said. "I'll have a sheet on the next one by the time you get back."

Once we were in the van, I read about our first destination, the women's drum circle. "The circle offers equality. There's no beginning and no end. No head and no tail. So the music is cocreated by the participants. An audience can watch as a group consciousness is formed."

The drum circle was congregated in a small, pretty park and had already drawn a small audience when we arrived. The participants as well as the onlookers seemed to be enjoying the improvised music from the drums and the enthusiasm of the smiling performers. I used the material Rhonda had prepared for my introduction, then focused mostly on the sound of the drums and the faces of the drummers. It was, as Rhonda's notes had promised, a group expression, where each individual was somehow in tune with everyone else.

Aunt Ibby's reunion committee was still on my

mind as Rhonda and I returned with our equipment to the van. They'd once been a tight circle of distinctly different individuals, as Pete had pointed out. Yet, even with the disappearance of Ted and the long-distance separation from Bobby, they'd maintained ties with one another. Every five years for nearly half a century, the small group had taken on the task of bringing their classmates together for a festive party. And every five years the chairmanship had changed. No one person was in charge. A collective voice after forty-five years. Remarkable.

Crow Haven has long been a standby evergreen topic for the station. We gathered a quick and easy ten minutes' worth of information and legend on spell potions, how they're made, how they work, and how you can do it yourself. Fascinating and fun for the viewers and for us too.

Francine and I had each been checking our phones frequently, hoping for word about the findings in the muddy Mustang. "They must have sifted through all of it by now," she said. As we drove away from the popular witch shop. "How the heck much mud could a car hold anyway?"

"I suppose it's important that they get as much of the um—remains—as they can, along with any kind of evidence—especially because they're calling it murder."

"I guess." She frowned. "But I just hope they call the presser while we're still on the clock so Scotty doesn't get to do it."

"Amen," I said. "Bad enough he was there for the gold necklace discovery that we missed." We'd just approached Derby Street when my phone vibrated. "Text from Rhonda," I announced, excited.

"Ooh! Maybe we can just change direction and head for the warehouse" She slowed the van, ignoring an annoyed toot of the horn from the car behind us. "What'd she say?"

I read aloud. "Okay on the warehouse presser. Head over there. Detective Rouse will give details. Looks like they're ready to release the body."

Ignoring another blast of a horn, Francine made a quick U-turn (Massachusetts drivers are notoriously impatient with that sort of thing. You get used to it.), and we headed for the Beverly line.

The gal from WESX radio beat us to it this time, but so far no other media vehicles had shown up. We hurried into front-row position facing a wooden lectern set up in front of the chain-link fence. Through an open double-garage door, we both spotted what was left of the Mustang. "Hey, at least they washed it," Francine observed. "But it looks like it's pretty much trashed." She was right. The doors were missing and the hood was sprung in a partly open position.

"I hope for Mrs. Thorne's sake that Rhonda's right." I whispered. "That they're going to release the remains. That they can at least give Ted a decent burial."

"Here comes the detective," Francine said. "Got your mic ready?"

"Sure do." Detective Joyce Rouse was a high school classmate of mine and I was pretty sure I'd get a few questions in. Francine focused her camera on me. "Good afternoon, ladies and gentlemen. I'm Lee

Barrett and I'm on-site in a warehouse district close to the Salem-Beverly line. Here's where the 1971 Mustang, recently recovered from the depths of an abandoned North Shore granite pit, has been stored. The vehicle has been thoroughly searched by police personnel, in order to recover the remains of a man, positively identified as Theodore Thorne, who has been listed as a missing person since 1974. Among the artifacts collected from inside the vehicle, police have found a spent thirty-eight-caliber bullet as well as a gold necklace, one of an apparent pair, which together spell out a familiar Bible verse. Detective Joyce Rouse is approaching the podium and will give a brief statement."

By this time several new media vans had appeared outside the chain-link fence, and reporters had gathered beside and behind me. I aimed my mic in Joyce's direction, and she spoke into one attached to the lectern, looking much more comfortable facing our small press corps than Chief Whaley ever had. She read from a prepared script.

"The investigative, forensic, and medical teams have completed their study of the contents of the automobile recently removed from an abandoned granite pit. Team members agree that all recoverable remains of Theodore Thorne have been obtained and examined carefully, and that they may immediately be released to his family for interment. As there is clear evidence, however, that the death of Theodore Thorne was the result of foul play, the investigation into the matter continues. The Thorne family requests that they be permitted to mourn their loss in private."

Joyce Rouse put the script aside. "The Salem Police Department is regarding the death of this young man as a cold-blooded murder. Police Chief Tom Whaley asks that anyone who has information regarding this matter contact the police department immediately. Your anonymity is assured. Detective Pete Mondello and I will follow up on every call. Even though this crime took place decades ago, the perpetrator may still be in the area, and as the weapon used to kill Mr. Thorne has not been found, his killer may still be armed and dangerous. Thank you all for coming here today. Any questions?"

My hand shot up. Joyce pointed in my direction. "Yes?" Francine turned the camera onto me.

"Lee Barrett, WICH-TV," I said. "Do you know yet where this murder took place? Was it at the granite pit or someplace else?"

"That hasn't been determined, Lee," she said. "But I can tell you this much. We don't think he was shot inside his car. He may have been killed elsewhere and the body placed into the Mustang after his death."

That's new!

She moved on to one of the Boston cable channel guys. "How was that determined?" he asked.

"Position of the wound," she stated. "We know where a rib was impacted by the fatal shot. We also have a garment he was wearing. It's likely he was facing the shooter."

WESX radio was next with a good question, "Have you interviewed any suspects yet?"

"We have not identified any suspects. We have talked with a number of people regarding this case, of course."

WESX followed up. "What kind of people? Family? Neighbors? Friends of his from 1974?"

Joyce nodded. "Certainly. All of those."

I waved my hand. "Lee?"

"Are you getting good cooperation from all those people?"

Slight frown. "Pretty much," she said. "There are still some folks we've not been able to speak with yet."

Nothing unusual there. He must have had lots of friends. Probably spread out all over the country by now. Some might even be dead.

Detective Rouse fielded a few more questions, largely concerning what was to become of the Mustang. Could it be sold for parts? She said that was up to the insurance company, then thanked us all and ducked back inside the fence.

Francine and I packed up our gear and headed for the van. "Good day's work, partner," she said, and we bumped fists. "I'll bet we get off early again. Got plans?"

"Not exactly," I said. "My aunt and I were talking about going for a little drive. You?

"Going to do a little diving," she said. "Hanging around with the divers lately reminded me of how much fun I used to have with those guys."

"Good for you. Maybe I'll try it someday."

We checked in with Rhonda, making sure our transmission had been received okay. It had and Francine was right about our early dismissal. She headed happily to her truck, excited about resuming a sport she clearly loved. I gathered up my purse and laptop, got into my convertible, and drove toward home, excited about taking a ride with my elderly aunt. Go figure.

CHAPTER 27

Aunt Ibby's car was in the garage. There was also a Mercedes in the driveway. Betsy's Mercedes. Aunt Ibby had said Betsy was in a snit about something. I decided that I'd go directly upstairs and wait for her to leave. Interrupting a snit is never a good idea.

O'Ryan greeted me at the door with the usual loving enthusiasm. I picked him up and tiptoed past Aunt Ibby's kitchen door, resisting the strong urge to pause there and listen. I gave myself a mental slap on the wrist for even considering eavesdropping on my aunt and her classmate. Again.

I let myself into my living room and immediately looked out the big bay window toward Oliver Street. The Mercedes was still there. I checked my watch. It was a few minutes after four. We had a good four hours until sunset. That'd be plenty of time to ride over to Chebacco Lake and do a little harmless snooping. I didn't plan to change clothes, but I'd use a few minutes to fill out a couple of index cards with the new information we'd gained from Joyce Rouse.

I pulled the cards from the bureau, carefully and neatly inscribed Joyce's words as I remembered them. Anyway, if I'd missed anything they'd probably rerun the presser on the five o'clock news and I could catch it then—*if* I was still here at five. I hurried to the bay window again, peered around a hanging lantana and my beautiful restored carousel horse, toward the driveway. The Mercedes was still there.

How the heck long can a snit take anyway?

I fed O'Ryan, emptied the dishwasher, and straightened out my underwear drawer. It was nearly five o'clock and Betsy's car was still there. I was about to turn away from the window when she appeared on the pathway below. I instinctively hid behind a jade plant and watched as she approached her car. Even from my third-floor vantage point I saw badly smudged eye makeup. Betsy's stooped shoulders ruined the line of a wonderful Michael Kors suit.

"Okay, she's gone, O'Ryan," I said. I put the laptop on the kitchen table, picked up my purse, and followed the cat downstairs. I knocked on the door, said "It's me," expecting the usual "Come in. It's open." Instead my aunt called. "Just a minute, Maralee. It's locked."

Wow! Pete will be happy. She's taking his advice.

I heard two clicks, as both the lock *and* the dead bolt slid open. I stepped into the kitchen. The cat was already there, via his own door. "I see you're taking Pete's advice to heart," I said. "Good for you."

She was at the sink, rinsing a teacup. "I guess the dead bolt is a bit much, but Betsy's got me so upset I'm feeling a little paranoid."

"I saw her leaving. What's going on?'"

"Oh my dear, sit down. You won't believe it. Want some tea? I think it's still hot."

"Yes. That'll be fine. I'll get it. Sit down and tell me what's wrong with Betsy."

"Oh, the poor soul." She sat down. I sat opposite her at the round table and poured tea for both of us. "She is utterly devastated. I've never seen her so upset."

"Yes. Go on," I prompted.

"I guess you know from the yearbook that Betsy and Bobby were what you might call high school sweethearts"

"Yes, I got that."

"He wanted to marry her. I mean really. He even bought her a tiny diamond ring. But she turned him down. Broke his heart."

"They were too young," I said. "Her parents, his parents, probably everybody objected. Right?"

"True. But the main problem was Bobby had no money, and no immediate prospect of earning much. Betsy is—and always has been—well, high maintenance." She looked down at her teacup. "But that's not the problem now. Seems that Betsy—who's been through two marriages and two divorces—has never forgotten Bobby. Still carrying that old high school torch, so to speak."

"Oh boy. That's what she's so upset about?"

"No. Much worse. Seems she got in touch with him right after the reunion committee meeting. They've been, uh—renewing an old acquaintance, if you know what I mean."

I had to smile at my aunt's reluctance to simply say

that the two were having an affair. "I get the picture," I said, "but they're not kids anymore. They're consenting adults. What's the problem?"

She dropped her voice, as though someone might be listening. "He confided in her. Told her something awful."

"Did she tell you what it was?" I found myself whispering too. I felt silly about that and resumed a normal tone. "What did he tell her?"

"He's dying, Maralee. Bobby Ross is dying, and he's come home to Salem to do it." She quickly wiped away a tear. "She lost him when they were kids and now she's going to lose him again."

"I'm so sorry," I said. "What's wrong? Is it something incurable?"

"Some kind of brain tumor," she said. "He's been to several doctors. They agree. He doesn't have a lot of time left."

"Is Betsy going to continue to—um—see him?"

"Oh yes, she wants him to come live at her house."

"Did he agree?" *I hope he did.*

"He says he has some things to clear up first. Some old debts to pay. He told her he wants to die with a clear conscience." She smiled a shy little smile. "I guess we all want that. I know I do."

"I guess so." I didn't want to think about my aunt dying, so I changed the subject.

"If we're going to take our ride, we'd better get going. We only have a few hours of daylight."

"You're right. Wait 'til I get my purse. My car or yours?"

"Yours, I think. Mine's too darn noticeable."

We didn't lose much time after that. With my aunt at the wheel, it was a short trip to Essex. (She has a bit of a heavy foot on the gas.) With all the windows open and the good-music station playing Pavarotti's "La donna è mobile" full blast, we turned onto the woody road to the lake, and the heady smell of pine trees filled the car.

With the radio turned down, my aunt navigated the twisting road, which turned to dirt after a while. We pulled into a long, well-kept driveway with flowering bushes on either side. A discreet sign read LAKEVIEW COTTAGE. "Looks like Mrs. Thorne is getting ready to move in for the summer," Aunt Ibby said. "See? The lawn's been freshly cut and, look, the summer furniture is on the porch."

"I guess she has a staff that keeps the place up," I said. "It looks lovely." I could already see the bentwood bench beside a window. There was a ceramic pot full of pink petunias beside it.

"That's right." Another of those shy smiles. "We always tried to leave the place as neat as we found it, but we knew that a full cleaning crew would have everything sparkling before his parents ever saw it anyway." We climbed out of the Buick, both of us looking around (in what could only be described as a furtive manner) as though there might be spies hidden behind the tall boxwood hedge.

"Do you think we should have called Mrs. Thorne before we came here?" I asked. "I feel as though we're trespassing."

"I thought of it," she said. "But I hate to call her about buying used furniture while she's in deep mourning. I'm sure she wouldn't mind us being here."

"Aunt Ibby!" I pointed. "Is that the stone lion? Where they hid the key?"

"Sure is. Probably still there."

I'd pictured that lion as much larger—maybe like the ones in front of the New York Public Library. Instead, it was a reclining lion, about a foot tall and a couple of feet long, and it fit nicely on the low brick wall surrounding the porch. "It looks heavy. How did you get the key out from under it?"

"I guess it is kind of heavy, but it only took one of the boys to lift it enough so we could grab the key."

By this time we'd climbed the two steps up to the porch and I had a good look at the bench. It looked just as it had in Penelope's photos and in my visions. It was worn and weather-beaten—in a shabby chic sort of way. I wouldn't even have it refinished. I wanted it more than ever. I also had a clear view of the window. The lace curtains didn't obscure the sparkling crystal star.

"Aunt Ibby," I spoke slowly, not looking away from the window. "Just as a matter of curiosity, were there ever lace curtains in this window when you and your friends came here?"

"No. Not that I can recall. Maybe there weren't any at all. Back then, there were no neighbors nearby. No need for curtains." Long sigh. "Good old days."

"There don't seem to be any nearby now, either."

"Guess not," she agreed. "Are you thinking what I'm thinking?"

"That it wouldn't hurt anything to take a peek inside?"

"If you can lift the lion, I can grab the key."

She remembered exactly where it had been placed—under the lion's extended right paw.

"You just have to get the front of the critter up a little bit so I can grab it." She shrugged. "If it's even still there."

It was. Still in furtive mode, she inserted the key into the lock and opened the door. Simultaneously, we sniffed the air.

"What's that smell?" she asked. "It's familiar."

"Chanel Gabrielle," I said. "I guess we know where Betsy and Bobby have been meeting. This was not a good idea," I whispered, backing away from the threshold.

"Let's leave," she said, pulling the door closed once again.

So we both chickened out at the very start of our illicit trip down my aunt's memory lane—and my search for the origin of some visions. She locked the door. I lifted the lion again while she slipped the key back into its accustomed spot. I pulled out my phone and snapped a quick picture of the bench in front of the lace-curtained window and we (furtively) got back into the Buick and backed out of the well-kept driveway—scattering a few pebbles as we spun out on the gravel road.

"I think this is one adventure I won't share with Pete right away," I said. "It was borderline breaking and entering, I suppose, except we didn't actually enter. But I did want to see if that bench was still there. Oh, I hope Mrs. Thorne will sell it to me—and that you or Penelope will find that picture of you and my mother."

"I'm sure we'll find it. I've been so busy I haven't

had a chance to dig out those albums." She glanced at the rearview mirror. "Hope no one saw us sneaking around. But you know what? I was astonished that so much of the place hadn't changed. I just got a quick peek, but the clock on the mantel of the stone fireplace is just as I remembered it. I wasn't surprised about the bench, though. Those things never wear out. It's probably more than a hundred years old. Ted told me once that his great-grandfather Thorne made it."

"I hope Betsy never finds out that we know she and Bobby have been meeting there," I said.

"I'll certainly never tell. She'd think we were snooping on her. Bad enough that just a few days ago she and I had a little disagreement about being in each other's business."

Must have been the conversation I overheard in the back hall.

"Oh?" I said, still curious about what that had been about—but not wanting to admit to listening through the kitchen door.

"Oh, what a tangled web we weave . . ."

She tightened her grip on the wheel. "It was silly, really. She apologized today for what she'd said."

I waited for her to continue. Long pause. *What did she say?*

"It was nothing, really. Nothing at all."

Obviously, I wasn't going to get an answer. None of my business anyway. I had a few questions for Pete—without referring to the recent snooping excursion I'd just made with my aunt. I wanted to tell him about the lace curtains and the crystal star that verified my vision too. I even had photo evidence I couldn't share with him. This whole thing had been a really bad idea.

There was still some daylight left when we reached home, and our cat was waiting for us on the back steps. He didn't run toward us with his usual happy-cat greetings, just lay there, head erect, facing us, tail curled around his rump, right paw extended.

Exactly like the stone lion.

CHAPTER 28

O'Ryan held his king-of-beasts pose exactly long enough to be sure we noticed, then scooted inside through his cat door. We dutifully followed. Aunt Ibby fished in her purse for her keys, then—almost ceremoniously—unlocked her kitchen door. We went inside, and she, just as carefully, relocked it.

"Can't be too careful," she said. "Pete is right about that." She covered her mouth with one hand. "Guess we just proved that, didn't we? It was much too easy to get in there."

"I know. And obviously, we're not the only people who know how to do it," I said. "How many more, besides you and your reunion committee, know where that key is?"

"Good Lord, I have no idea. I'm sure some of Ted's parents' friends might know about it—and what if some of us have brought other people over there during the past forty-odd years?" The green eyes widened. "It's a perfect place for—you know—

whatever Betsy and Bobby are doing. Such a thing had never occurred to me before!"

I smiled and gave her a hug. "Of course it wouldn't occur to *you*, my darling aunt, but what about your classmates? Let's start with Steve Overton. Tell me about him." I opened the refrigerator. "But first, can I heat up this macaroni and cheese casserole? I'm starving."

"Sounds good. Turn on the oven and I'll throw together a salad." She pulled a wooden salad bowl from a cabinet and began assembling a colorful assortment of fresh veggies on the butcher-block counter. "Steve Overton," she mused. "Class president. Successful businessman. Inherited the Omigoodness Bakeries from his parents and has grown it into a national chain." She giggled. "I wonder if he'll use a bagel for the first letter of his last name in his political ads like he did when he ran for class president."

"Did he really?" I could picture it. A bagel makes a wonderful letter *O*.

"Sure did. He got a lot of mileage out of those bagels. Bribed everyone with them. We all teased him about it. 'A vote in every bagel.' He used to get to school early and hand them out while they were still warm. Who wouldn't vote for him after that?"

"He won easily, I suppose."

"The other kid didn't have a chance. I don't even remember who it was." She sprinkled grated Parmesan cheese onto the salad, tossing it expertly, and put the bowl onto the table. I stood beside the stove, waiting for the timer to announce that the mac and cheese was ready.

"So, was he a good class president?"

Thoughtful pause. "You know, that's hard to answer. He didn't personally do much. But everything seemed to get done. I guess you could say Steve was very good at delegating duties."

"That's a useful talent," I said.

"Right. Penelope was Steve's main communicator. She'd say something like 'Ibby, Steve would like you to take charge of preparing the class history. You're so good with words he wouldn't trust anybody else to do it.'"

"So naturally, you did it."

"Sure. I was flattered."

"Did you get credit for it?" I thought I knew what her answer would be.

"Not exactly. But everybody knew it was my work," she declared.

I didn't comment on the unfairness of that. The timer bell rang and I pulled the golden deliciousness from the oven, carried it to the table, and sat opposite my aunt. "We used to wonder sometimes if Penelope was actually the brains behind it all," she continued. "Many times we all heard him say, 'Penelope. Take care of that, will you, sweetheart?' And she always did."

So that's where Penelope fits in at the popular table. She could be counted on to do Steve's bidding.

"Gee. Maybe he should hire her to be his campaign manager," I suggested, halfway seriously.

"He's probably considered it." She put a hefty portion of mac and cheese onto my plate. "Here. Have some salad too. Your eating habits are disturbing. Penelope isn't the only person Steve could manipulate.

I even wrote his acceptance speech for him when he was elected class president."

"Was he a good student?" I helped myself to salad, topping it off with homemade blue cheese dressing.

"As and Bs. The occasional gentlemanly C or D. He was better than average."

"Sounds like the kind that got his girlfriends to do his homework," I said, remembering "helping" some high school boyfriends that way myself.

"Not just girlfriends. For instance, Warren—Coach—was a whiz at chemistry. I was best at English. Betsy could read and write Spanish—her mother came from Honduras. Bobby loved math. Sometimes, at exam time, if the weather was nice, we'd all get together at Ted's cottage and have a cram session. We were all good at something. We liked helping each other."

"What about Ted? His specialty?"

Big smile. "Ted was rich, good-looking, had a cool car and the key to a great cottage. He didn't need anything else."

"And Steve probably brought the bagels." I offered.

"Exactly," she said. "Good times."

We finished our impromptu but well-organized meal, topped it off with Grape-Nuts pudding and whipped cream, and washed dishes together as we had done so many times over the years. We didn't discuss our late-afternoon excursion at all, and I hoped that O'Ryan wouldn't repeat his stone lion impersonation anytime soon. It was nearly eight o'clock when I headed up the front stairs to my apartment. O'Ryan chose to stay with my aunt, who had promised to start reading a new Sofie Kelly Magical Cats Mystery book to him.

I took a fast shower, put on a lime green cotton beach coverup that doubled as a nightshirt, pulled my wet hair into a messy bun, and headed for the laptop on the kitchen table. I still hadn't put Aunt Ibby's prom story into words, and now I had the Bobby and Betsy saga to add to my growing manuscript. I didn't confide our intrusion into the Thornes' cottage even to this most personal account, but did add the information about the lace curtains and the crystal star without giving any attribution to the (guilty) source. I knew Pete would visit the place anyway in the course of the investigation, and he'd see the window for himself. I condensed Aunt Ibby's information about her classmates, simply listing the seven by first names and putting each one's special talent beside his or her name. I leaned back in my chair, read over what I'd written, and hit the print button, listening to the printer in the bedroom add the new words to my manuscript, which was leading—where? I still didn't know the answer to that but felt that at least I was moving in a forward direction.

Before closing the laptop, I checked my email. This is something I know I should do more often. It was, as usual, mostly cluttered with not-quite-spam junk mail. I scrolled through ads, notices, and names of people I didn't know until River North's name popped up. I opened the message. "Hi Lee. I finished that reading. Nothing too exciting there, and probably nothing to worry about. Here's a condensed version. Ten of Pentacles: Established family of wealth. Inheritance. Six of Pentacles: Charity. Gifts. The Fool:

A choice is offered. Four of Cups: Discontent, reevaluation. That's all I've got. Call if you have questions. Love ya, River."

I printed that too. I guessed the "established family of wealth" would most likely mean the Thornes, but the Omigoodness Bakery chain might fit the established family category, too, and Steve had inherited it. How about "a choice is offered?" Was that for Bobby and Betsy? Would Bobby choose to spend his last days with her? Gifts might mean the necklace Aunt Ibby got on prom night. Discontent and reevaluation might mean anything. Or nothing at all. I closed the laptop, carried it into the bedroom, picked up the newly printed pages, and added them to the growing document. The whole stack fit neatly into a Gianni Bini shoebox, which I put on the closet's top shelf. Hidden in plain sight.

As I turned to go back to the kitchen, I checked myself out in the oval mirror in its swivel-tilt cherry-wood stand. Pete hadn't said anything about coming over, but sometimes it's a spur-of-the-moment thing. The green cover-up looked okay, and the color was good with my eyes. My hair was no messier than usual, and Pete's used to seeing me without makeup. I began to turn away from my reflection, then stopped.

The vision in the mirror was one of those sneaky "developing Polaroid" ones, slowly coming into focus and impossible to ignore. So I stood there, just watching as the scene—made up at first of uneven gray shapes—morphed into a stone fireplace. A clock appeared on the mantelpiece and the room took on color. Beside the clock was a framed picture of a man and a woman. Coach and Penelope? Looked like them. It faded so rapidly I couldn't be sure. Last to develop was a clear image of a man, his face contorted in rage. I didn't know that man, but I knew that what he held in his hand was a gun.

Then the picture was gone. I sat on the edge of my bed. This was a bad one. I knew I was safe, there in my pretty bedroom. I was fully aware that what I had seen was not real, but a trick of my mind. Even so, I was terrified. The scene was unmistakably a room in the summer cottage. Who was the man? What had enraged him, and who was being threatened with that gun?

The visions, I've learned, can show me the past, the present, or the future. I'd experienced all three. Had I witnessed something that had happened long ago or was it yet to happen? Most frightening was the possibility that it was happening now. I needed to tell someone. I needed to tell Pete.

He answered on the first ring. "Pete, I . . . uh . . . just saw something. In the mirror." My voice quavered.

"Okay, babe. Slow down. Tell me what it is."

I described the room and the man with the gun. "It was a revolver. Not a gun like yours. I've seen pictures of the room before," I said. "It's the Thornes' summer place. I don't know who the man is. You know I can't tell when these things I see have already happened or will happen. What if it's happening now?"

"Okay. Listen. I'll call Essex PD and ask for a cruiser to go by and check the place. Will that make you feel better?"

"Yes," I said. "Thank you. Oh, Pete, the man is so angry. What if he's going to shoot someone?"

What if he already has?

"It'll be all right, Lee. Don't worry. I'll come by when I finish up here. Okay? Around eleven?"

"Yes, please."

I felt a little better after talking to Pete. I was glad I was *able* to tell him about the visions. It hadn't always been that way. Then I had another frightening thought. What if Betsy and Bobby were there in the house and the Essex cops broke in on them?

What have I done?

I looked at the clock. It was still early. I ran down the front stairs. Aunt Ibby's bedroom door was open. She and O'Ryan looked up, startled when I knocked and then burst in. She put down her book, took off her reading glasses. "What's wrong, dear?

I told her what I'd done. "Should you call Betsy? Warn her?"

"Maralee. We aren't supposed to know she's been there—if in fact she was. We smelled her perfume, but maybe it wasn't even hers She's not the only person in the world to wear Chanel Gabrielle." She already had her phone in her hand. "Maybe it was the cleaning lady."

At around a hundred fifty an ounce?

Sweet, innocent voice. "Hello, Betts? Ibby. I've been concerned about you. Are you feeling better? That's good. Say, my niece and I took a ride over to Chebacco Lake this afternoon, and we drove by the old cottage. Maralee wanted to see if that bentwood bench was still there. She wants to buy it. She has a thing for antiques." Little laugh. "Yes. Just like her aunt. But, Betts, her boyfriend is a policeman, you know? And he told her that the Essex police are having one of their cruisers drive by the place at night. Know anything about that?" She nodded, listening. O'Ryan appeared to listen, too, his ears straight up, golden eyes focused on my aunt. "Oh, I'll bet you're right. I was just wondering. I'm turning into a nosy old biddy. Have a good evening, dear. Glad you're feeling better."

She replaced the phone on her bedside table. "Betsy says probably Mrs. Thorne has asked them to check, since she'll be moving to the summerhouse soon. So she and Bobby obviously aren't there—and probably won't dare to go back."

"Dodged a bullet there, didn't we?" I said, immediately regretting the unfortunate cliché. "I'm sorry, but the vision was so real."

"I understand," she said, "Maybe we'd better do as Pete always tells us and stop snooping into things that are none of our business."

I breathed a long sigh of relief. "You are so right! No more Nancy Drew for me. Visions or no visions. I could have put poor Betsy and Bobby in a terrible position. As if they didn't have trouble enough with him being so sick and all." I held up my right hand. "I'll leave it all up to the police. I mean it."

"Good." She picked up her book, and O'Ryan snuggled up beside her. She peered at me over the rim of her reading glasses. "But then how are we going to figure out who that angry man is?"

CHAPTER 29

Pete arrived a few minutes before eleven with a concerned expression and two chocolate shakes. "Everything's quiet over Essex way," he said. "The officer walked around the property, shone his flashlight into the windows. Nothing seemed out of order." He held me close. "You sounded so worried on the phone. I wish I could protect you from seeing things like you do."

"I'm sorry I bothered you about it. And the Essex officer too. But it was very real. Very scary."

"I understand. I want you to always call me when you're frightened by anything. Even things in a mirror." He ruffled my hair and smiled. "You look so darned cute."

"I love you," I said. "I'm glad there was nothing bad going on at the cottage."

"Nope. All clear. The officer did note that the gravel driveway looked as though someone had spun their tires leaving." He handed me my shake. "Probably the lawn guy or the cleaning crew in a hurry to go home."

I sipped my chocolate shake and answered with a noncommittal "Uh-huh." Pete was scheduled for another split shift the next day, so we made tentative plans to have lunch together unless something hugely newsworthy interrupted one or both of us. We watched the eleven o'clock news on the kitchen TV. Buck Covington led with my coverage of Detective Rouse's press conference and added that Ted Thorne's remains had been released to his mother, and that plans for his burial, followed by a celebration of his life, would be announced soon.

"Celebration of his much-too-short life," Pete mumbled. "He was barely out of his childhood."

"Aunt Ibby says you can have those cards she thought were from him," I said. "Has his mother offered to give hers up yet?"

"Yep. We already have them. We've checked the dates. The cards stopped shortly after Mr. Thorne died."

"Really? Aunt Ibby didn't mention that."

"She may not have noticed," he said. "One of the classmates said that they all believed Ted would come home after his father passed."

"Yes I heard that too. I gather the man wasn't mourned a great deal."

So the police have started interviewing the classmates.

Pete shook his head. "Nobody had much good to say about him, except that he was a good provider. Other than that, he apparently was a mean, angry SOB."

The Angry Man. He had a gun.

We'd finished our shakes and the news was over. We cuddled for a bit, then Pete said a reluctant good night and let himself out just as O'Ryan came in. The cat, barely acknowledging me, hopped onto my bed, turned around three times, and flopped down right in the middle of the comforter. Bed seemed like a good idea, but I knew I wasn't quite ready for sleep yet.

Could the angry man in my vision be Mr. Thorne? There had to be plenty of photos of such a prominent citizen. I vowed to check online in the morning. I was sure I'd recognize that face. And what about the gun? Poor young Ted had died of a bullet wound. The bullet had come from a .38-caliber gun. Was it a revolver? Had the gun been fired by his own father? I rolled over onto my side and pulled the covers over my head. *That's just too hideous to even think about. Fathers don't murder their kids.* My online criminology course had taught me that indeed they sometimes do. I hoped for Mrs. Thorne's sake that in this case it wasn't true.

My thoughts turned to Betsy and Bobby. If the police interviewed them, they'd have to tell the truth about Bobby's condition. Maybe I should have told Pete what Aunt Ibby had told me. Maybe I should have told him that the lead-footed driver who'd sprayed gravel all over the Thornes' neat driveway was my aunt. Maybe I should have told him I'd looked inside the cottage door . . .

I fell asleep itemizing my litany of maybes.

I woke up vowing to come clean about all of it when Pete and I met later in the day for lunch. The decision made me feel better right away. It wasn't as though I'd actually *lied* to him. But I felt as guilty as though I had.

Wanda's prediction of blue skies was right on, with

the temperature so pleasant I was almost tempted to put the top down. With a to-go cup of coffee in the drink holder and a strawberry Pop-Tart on a paper napkin balanced on the center console, I made good time on the short commute to work, noting the early signs of summer. There was already a line of tour buses in front of the Witch Museum, and the tulips were in bloom on the common. I found myself humming as I pulled into the parking lot beside the WICH-TV building. Francine's truck wasn't there yet, but Steve Overton's Jaguar was. It would be hard to miss it. OVERTON FOR CONGRESS stickers decorated the rear window, and an American flag was affixed to the driver's side mirror.

I wasn't exactly surprised. He'd told me, after all, that he'd be seeing me often because of his planned advertising schedule. I seemed to be seeing more of my aunt's classmates these days than I ever saw of my own.

I locked the Vette and walked past the Jag, noting that the *O* in Overton was not in the shape of a bagel and making a mental bet with myself that there'd be a box of the real things on Rhonda's desk. I punched my code into the electronic keypad on the downstairs studio door and, reluctantly, stepped out of the sunshine and salty sea air into the cool darkness inside. I clattered up the metal stairs to the second floor, not surprised to see a small crowd gathered in Rhonda's reception area.

"Hi, Lee. Come on in." Scott Palmer called. "Look, we've got coffee and bagels and Danish and everything. A real feast."

Carol J. Perry

"I see," I said. Plates of food and canisters of coffee were spread the entire length of the curved counter surrounding Rhonda's workstation. Even the towering arrangement of artificial iris had been moved aside to accommodate the bounty. "Quite a treat. What's the occasion?" *As if I don't know.*

"Good morning, Ms. Barrett," Steve Overton moved from behind a group of the tech guys and extended his hand. "How good to see you again. As I mentioned, I'll be doing a lot of advertising on this fine station. Bruce tells me that you've become quite a star in the short time you've been here."

Bruce Doan said THAT? About ME? I found it hard to believe but thanked Overton anyway. "I enjoy my work here very much," I said. "I'm sure our production department will do a fine job on your commercials."

"Counting on it," he said. "I've been talking to Ms. McCarthy, bouncing a few ideas around."

"Marty will take good care of you," I promised, picking up a bagel and a pat of cream cheese, and wrapping them in a red, white, and blue paper napkin "Nice to see you again. Excuse me now. Need to get to work." I moved as close as I could to get within earshot of Rhonda. "Schedule?" I mouthed.

She nodded, reaching across a delicious-smelling mound of cinnamon bagels and handing me several sheets of paper, stapled together. "Here you go," she said, "Good luck."

Francine appeared then outside the glass door. I held it open for her. "I'll wait for you in the parking lot." I waved the sheaf of papers. "Grab some goodies and let's gets started. Looks like a busy one."

Once outside, I headed for a green bench beside the seawall. The bench bore a brass plaque inscribed "In loving memory of Ariel Constellation." It marked the spot where the onetime WICH-TV call-in psychic had died. Most people think the station put it there, but it was actually a gift from Ariel's coven. On such a nice day it was a pleasant place to sit—overlooking the blue, blue water of the harbor, munching on a whole wheat bagel with cream cheese. I began to read the first page of our assignment sheet.

Aha! A protest march. Nice way to start the day. I'd heard Aunt Ibby talking about the movement of some of Salem's valued historical records from the Salem-based Peabody Essex Museum to a storage facility over in Rowley, of all places—allegedly making them more difficult to access and less secure. Seemed worth protesting. Rhonda had given me a brief background on the controversy, and I was sure interviews with a couple of protesters would fill in any gaps.

I was about to read the next page when a masculine voice spoke my name. "Ms. Barrett? I hope I'm not intruding, but I wanted to speak to you confidentially for just a moment." It was Steve Overton. "May I join you?" he asked, while already sliding onto the bench beside me.

I plunked the printed schedule down between us. "How can I help you, Mr. Overton?"

"Steve," he corrected with a bright smile.

"How can I help you?" I repeated, hoping this old man wasn't making a clumsy pass.

"I'm concerned about Ibby," he said, replacing the smile with downcast features. "How is she taking all this?"

"Taking it?"

"Yes. Poor Ted's death," he said. "They were very close, you know, and we were all so hopeful that he'd come back to us—maybe for the very reunion we've been planning.

He's really worried about my aunt.

"She's doing well, Steve," I said, feeling embarrassed because of what I'd thought. "At first, she didn't want to believe it was Ted, but she's come to accept it. It's kind of you to be concerned."

"I am," he said. "I hope the others have rallied around her. I'm so busy with the campaign, you know." He gave a helpless gesture. "I wish I could be more active with the committee. Does she see the others?"

"Yes. Penelope's been at the house working on badges, and Betsy was there just yesterday," I reported, not going into detail. "I'm sure she'll be just fine. They all will."

"Haven't Bobby or Coach been around to see her?"

"Not that I know of," I said. "It's been just the girls."

"I see. Of course there's the funeral and the memorial service for all of us to endure." He stood up. "But, I'm keeping you from your work. Please give Ibby my love. I'll try to make the next meeting."

"I'll tell her I saw you," I said.

"I'm sure you and I will see each other often during the campaign," he said. "I plan on doing plenty of TV advertising, and much of it will be produced right here at WICH-TV." He gave a little bow and headed for the Jag.

"Bye," I said, and looked again at the blue, blue ocean, and wondered what the heck that was all about. I didn't have much time to think further about

Aunt Ibby's reunion committee. Francine arrived at my bench with her copy of the schedule in one hand and a bagel in the other. "Let's get this show on the road," she said. "Doan says that Mrs. Doan is heading up the protest in front of the museum and she wants to be sure it gets good coverage."

The protest wasn't as big as I'd thought it might be, and it was assuredly nonviolent. The protesters, mostly middle-aged, well-dressed women, marched back and forth across the street from the museum. There were a couple of men and a few students among them, and Mrs. Doan in purple linen carried a SAVE OUR HISTORY sign. Not great TV by Doan's standards, and we were the only media there. We gave it our best shot and, hopefully, convinced some of our audience that saving a city's history can be important.

The second assignment involved a Habitat for Humanity project in Peabody—one of those heart-warming segments everybody likes. It's fun covering good news where people are caring for people. That one brought us up to lunchtime. I was anxious to call Pete—to tell him about what I, along with my aunt, had been up to. I was prepared for a mini-lecture on minding my own business and a few remarks about "the snoop sisters." We deserved it. I decided against telling Pete we'd opened the cottage door. After all, we hadn't gone inside—not one single step.

I ducked into the data port to call Pete, and to check online for a photo of Gerard Thorne. A report of Gerard Thorne's appointment to the board of directors of a prestigious private school appeared immediately. There was an accompanying photo. Even when he was smiling, Mr. Thorne looked angry.

Pete answered with a cheerful "Hi, babe. Hoped that was you. Ready for lunch?"

"I am," I said. "Maybe I'll have a salad. There was a serious bagelfest at the station this morning."

"Overton?"

"Sure thing. Don't know much about his politics yet, but his bagels get my vote."

"Mine too. We got a big box of them over here yesterday." He laughed. "Chief told him not to send any more. Might look like a bribe."

"I'm sure you guys ate all the evidence," I said. "Pete, you know the vision I told you about? The one with the man and the revolver?"

"Of course." Cop voice. " It didn't come back again, did it?"

"No, thank goodness. But I know who he is. It's Gerard Thorne."

Long pause. "Hmm. Interesting. Well, if you're ready, I'll be over in a few minutes to pick you up."

"I'll be outside by Ariel's bench. Okay?"

"Okay. And Lee, could you tell what kind of a revolver it was?"

I thought about the vision. Squeezed my eyes shut, then opened them. "I'm sorry. They all look pretty much alike, don't they?"

"Pretty much," he said. "Never mind. I'm leaving now. See you in a few."

"See you," I echoed. I gathered up my gear, locked the data port, and went upstairs to return the key to Rhonda.

Once outside in the springtime sunshine again, I thought about how I was going to tell Pete about

Aunt Ibby being responsible for the gravel mess in the Thornes' driveway and about Bobby being terminally ill. I sure wasn't going to tell him about what was going on between Betsy and Bobby. None of my business how and where they met. And after all, come to think of it, why couldn't the cleaning lady use Chanel Gabrielle?

CHAPTER 30

There were already a couple of tourists sitting on Ariel's bench, so I walked out to the front of the building to meet Pete. I didn't like keeping secrets from him. It would be a relief to tell him the truth—at least most of it.

He pulled up to the curb and reached across the console to open the door for me. "Red Line Café okay?" I happily agreed. They have wonderful salads and about fifty different kinds of coffee. The Essex Street sidewalk people watching there is excellent too. (The "red line" refers to Salem's Heritage Trail, where a painted red line guides visitors to historic sites and destinations.)

We found seats near the big front window. I waited until my chicken Caesar salad and Pete's BLT panini had been served before I mentioned what had been on my mind since the previous night. "There's some stuff I need to get off my chest," I told him. "First, I don't know whether it's important for you to know this or not, but Bobby Ross came home to Salem to die. He has an inoperable brain tumor."

Pete nodded, but didn't say anything. I continued. "One of the visions showed my aunt and my mother sitting on an old bentwood bench. It turned out that Penelope has that same picture in a scrapbook she's making. She said the bench was on the porch of Ted's parents' summer place." Pete began to look puzzled. "I needed to find out if the bench still existed. So Aunt Ibby and I took a little ride over to Chebacco Lake, and that bench is on the porch of that cottage right now. I was going to see if Mrs. Thorne would sell it to me."

"You want to buy a beat-up old bench? Why?" he asked with a totally puzzled look.

"Don't you see? I'll have an enlargement of the photo of my aunt and my mother nicely framed with that actual bench right below it."

"Oh. I guess, if you like it . . ." Pete's not a fan of shabby chic. He still makes fun of my cute kitchen footstool with the chipped blue paint that I once grabbed from a neighbor's trash.

"I do. I *love* it. Naturally, I'm not going to bother Mrs. Thorne right now about it. But here's what I need to tell you. When we left the place, Aunt Ibby kind of spun her tires a little, and I think that's where the scattered gravel came from."

"And you didn't think to mention any of this earlier?" Patient cop voice.

"Bobby Ross being so sick? Or my aunt's heavy foot on the gas?"

"Both, really, though we already knew about Ross.

Too bad." He looked down at the table. "Young guy like that. He hasn't had it easy. Blowing out his knee and messing up any big-league chances he had, now this. No wonder he drinks too much."

"Who told you about it? About the tumor?" I was curious.

"He did. He was one of the first of Thorne's friends we've talked to. Now, about your aunt's driving." He put down his sandwich and frowned. "Why didn't you say something when I told you what the Essex officer had said about it?"

I took a deep breath. "I'd never throw my aunt under the proverbial bus, even for you. And a few rocks didn't seem like a big deal to me. But if the police and Mrs. Thorne are concerned, and if the lawn man or the cleaning lady might be blamed, I'm telling you this—in confidence."

He nodded. "Makes sense. The gravel, not the old piece of junk furniture on the porch."

"I'm glad you understand. I should have known you would. But tell me, you've been interviewing Ted Thorne's classmates?"

"Are you snooping? "

"Of course."

"Okay, Nancy Drew. We talked to Mr. Whipple yesterday."

"Mr. Whipple?"

"Coach."

"Oh, of course. You know, it seems as though I keep running into my aunt's classmates lately, but I haven't seen the coach since the evening of the reunion meeting." *Except in my mirror. Should I have mentioned the framed picture beside the clock on the mantel? Is it really there? Or was that a picture from Penelope's scrapbook?*

"Interesting guy," Pete said, then looked at his watch. That's usually a signal that a conversation is over. "Guess we'd both better be getting back to work."

"One more thing," I said. "Were there beer cans in the car?"

"Yes."

"But you haven't released that information. Why not?"

He shrugged. "We try to hold some things back, things the killer would know. How'd you find out?"

"My hairdresser, Carmine. He heard it at the gym. He said everybody knows about it."

Pete sighed. "Sometimes holding things back doesn't work."

We split the check as we often do and exited onto Essex Street where signs of a robust tourist season were already in evidence. Witch shops, boutiques, cafés, gift shops, art galleries fronted the old main street with colorful window displays. A few costumed types strolled among the shoppers, adding to the festive atmosphere.

Pete drove back to the station without further mention of the current happenings, even though I prodded a bit. "Was Coach helpful at all?"

"Every bit helps," Pete said.

"Have you seen Penelope's scrapbooks?"

"She has quite a collection, I understand." He made a sweeping gesture with one hand. "Big collection."

"Want to come over after work?" I asked.

"It'll be late again. After eleven."

"We can watch River. The movie is *Dead Silence*."

"Creepy puppets?"

"I think so"

"It's a date." He leaned across the console and kissed my cheek. "Love you."

I entered the brass-fronted elevator and smiled all the way up to the second floor. Francine was already there. "Easy one this afternoon," she said. "We get to do the Salem Trolley Tour with the tourists. Maybe we'll finish early again." Her tone was hopeful. "Got another date with my diver buddies."

"A beautiful day for it," I said, and it was. We parked the mobile van and joined a happy group of visitors aboard the replica turn-of-the-century trolley. Even those of us who live here enjoy a fresh drive-by view of the House of the Seven Gables, the Pirate Museum, the dungeon where they kept the witches, all accompanied by a guide's narration. One storefront stood out to me from the other buildings we passed. Red, white, and blue bunting was draped over the doorway, and a large gold American eagle dominated the display window. There was a huge, gold letter *O* covering almost all of the front of the place. The *O* wasn't shaped like a bagel, but there was no doubt about whose headquarters it was. There was no doubt about the identity of the couple who'd just stepped from the bright blue door. The man was so tall, and the woman so tiny, there was almost a comical aspect to their appearance. They each wore a blue baseball cap with a red *O* over the visor. The two waved red, white, and blue signs at our passing open-sided vehicle, and most of the passengers waved back.

Penelope and Coach! They must be part of the Overton campaign team.

Why wouldn't they be? They've been friends for over forty years. Still, something troubled me about the two—such an unlikely pair—just as it had when they'd appeared at our front door together on the night of the reunion committee meeting, and again when they'd appeared together in the mirror vision.

Francine had been filming the scenery and recording the guide's narrative since we'd started. Now and then, when the trolley stopped for a photo op at a place of particular interest, I took the opportunity to interview a passenger or two on their impressions of my home city. I'm still often surprised when visitors comment enthusiastically about things we native Salemites take for granted, like beautiful doorways, brick sidewalks, old graveyards. When the tour ended and we returned to the Trolley Depot, Francine and I were satisfied that viewers would enjoy the segment.

Once back in the van I asked Francine if she'd filmed the Overton headquarters. She had. "I wonder if Mr. Doan will want to cut it," I said. "Other candidates might want equal time."

"I doubt that he'd cut it," she said. "Rhonda says Overton is buying a lot of advertising. But maybe we should run it by the boss, just to be sure." I was interested to see it myself, curious to get a closer look at Penelope and Coach. *Why?* I asked myself. *Those two are probably the least interesting people on the whole reunion committee.*

We arranged to meet Marty with her production

crew. Mr. Doan joined us and we watched the editing process together. "That shot of the Overton headquarters has to go," he said. "The other candidates will be screaming for equal time. Anyway, any advertising Overton gets from us, he's gonna have to pay for. Cash up front." The questionable portion was swiftly deleted, including the glimpse of the smiling and waving Penelope and Coach. I was still on the clock until five and had over an hour to fill. I asked Rhonda for the key to the data port. "I'll be right downstairs if you need me," I said.

"What do you do down there anyway?" Rhonda took the key from the locked top drawer.

"I'm doing a little research on a few things for next time I wear my investigative-reporter hat," I told her—which was mostly true—even if I had no idea where my notes were leading me. I accepted the key and hurried down the metal stairway. I'd left my laptop at home and chose not to confide my thoughts to the company computer, so I carried a yellow legal pad and pen. I could transcribe my scribbling later. After all, I'd have until eleven o'clock tonight to make whatever sense I could of today's observations.

I closed the glass door behind me and stared at the key in my hand. Keys. Keys had been on my mind lately. Pete's repeated reminders to my aunt to lock her doors. The key beneath the stone lion at the Thornes' cottage. I scribbled the word "keys" on my pad. Something to think about.

I wrote down, as accurately as I could remember, the conversation I'd had with Pete at the Red Line, and how I'd admitted that I'd delayed telling him about the trip to Chebacco Lake and about Bobby

Ross's failing health. He'd definitely dodged my question about Coach, but I was used to him keeping police business to himself. I guess he was used to me keeping details of the visions to *myself*. Fair is fair.

I'd identified the armed man in my vision. It was surely Gerard Thorne. I wrote that down. I made a brief note about the conversation I'd had with Steve Overton on Ariel's bench. He'd expressed concern about my aunt and he'd asked if any of the others had been around to see her. That was about it. (I didn't record my mistaken thought about his intentions.) Should I note that I'd seen Coach and Penelope from the trolley? I debated for a few seconds. It was trivial, but I wrote it down anyway, including the fact that Mr. Doan had deleted the footage.

I stared at the pad, experiencing the feeling that I'd forgotten something important. It was like the moment in the grocery store when you know there's something else you need, but you can't remember exactly what it is.

A knock on the glass door behind me interrupted my mind-searching. I wheeled around in my chair. Scott Palmer, one hand shading his eyes, peered in at me. I pulled the unlocked door open. (So much for remembering keys!) "Hi Scott. What's up?"

"Rhonda just got a call about kids sneaking into the old granite pits. Guess all your coverage inspired a few to want to try jumping off those cliffs. You and Francine are off in about half an hour. Old Eddie and I can take it if you want. Your call."

I thought about it. "Why don't you guys take it? I know Francine has plans."

"Okay. We're on it. You're already all over the five

o'clock," he announced. "Archer's using both the museum protesters and the Habitat for Humanity pieces. Maybe I'll get something good for the eleven."

"I'm sure you will," I said. "I'll be watching." I picked up my purse, pad, and pen, locked the data port, and followed Scott upstairs. Francine and Rhonda were watching a competitor's channel on Rhonda's monitor, meaning the boss had left the building. I handed the key to Rhonda.

"All locked up and ready to leave," I said. "Francine, Scott and Old Eddie are going to take over. See you in the morning."

Francine gave a happy thumbs-up and hurried out the door—on her way to join a group of divers who knew what they were doing as Scott set out to find some young divers who surely didn't.

I hoped Aunt Ibby would be home when I got there. I was anxious to tell her that Gerard Thorne was the man in the vision. I was less anxious to say that the reason I'd looked him up was because I'd entertained the possibility that this reputedly bad-tempered person could have killed his own son. If my aunt had remained friendly with Ted's mother all these years, had her relationship with his late father possibly been cordial, too?

The Buick was in the garage, the cat was on the back steps—not, thankfully, pretending to be a lion. I heard music from inside (John Denver) and knocked on her kitchen door. "It's me," I called. "You busy?"

"Just a minute, Maralee," she answered. "It's locked." After a couple of clicks, the door swung open. She wiped her hands on a red-and-blue striped apron marked "Crazy Cat Lady."

"Come in, dear. How was your day?"

I gave her a quick rundown of the places Francine and I had been, then launched right into the topic that was on my mind. "The angry man in the vision is Gerard Thorne," I said.

She nodded. "You think he might have shot Ted?"

"It occurred to me, yes."

"I'm hesitant to say it, but sadly, it is possible. He had a dreadful temper. I hope it's not so. Poor Laura."

"I've already told Pete about the vision, and who the man is."

"Forty-five years makes for an extremely cold case, I should think. Gerard died more than ten years ago, so *he* can't be questioned."

"Pete can't base an investigation on one of my visions anyway," I said. "They don't always mean what they seem to mean at first, so that makes them all the harder to decipher."

She faced me and I recognized her "wise old owl" face. "But maybe Pete can find out if Gerard Thorne had a gun," she said, one eyebrow raised. "I'll just bet he can."

I caught on. "You're right. If he *did* have a gun, maybe Pete can find out what kind it was!"

"I suppose it won't be too hard. All he'd have to do is ask Laura. She'd know if her husband had a gun."

"It may even have been registered somewhere," I suggested.

"Maybe." She sounded doubtful. "People weren't so aware of gun safety back then as they are now."

"I told him about the vision anyway. He can do whatever he thinks is right about it."

"Good solution. I'll be interested to see your ride on the trolley. Do you know when it'll be on?"

"It was still in production when I left. A couple of your classmates almost made it onto the news, but Mr. Doan deleted them."

"He did? Who was it?" She frowned. "And why did they get scrubbed?"

"Coach Whipple and Penelope," I told her. "They were in front of a Steve Overton campaign office waving at the trolley. I guess they're on the campaign team. Doan said if we ran it the other candidates might want equal time."

"That makes sense," she said. "Funny. Penelope didn't mention campaigning when she was here."

"She had a hat with an *O* on it. So did Coach. Maybe they'd just bought the hats to help a classmate out."

"I'll bet that's it," my aunt said. "I should take a ride on the trolley one of these days. Haven't done it in years."

"You'll enjoy it. I did." I pulled the door open. "Coming, O'Ryan?"

The cat followed me out into the hall, then led the way up the twisty stairway to the third floor. I tossed the yellow legal pad onto the kitchen table and hurried to the bedroom to retrieve the laptop, anxious to transcribe my notes. Sometimes my handwriting is so messy I was afraid if I delayed I wouldn't be able to read it.

O'Ryan sat on the windowsill, watching me. I followed my notes, making fragments of words into sentences, adding details here and there. I included the conversation I'd had with my aunt about Gerard Thorne and the possibility that he'd owned a gun.

I read over what I'd written, then hit the print button. I turned to face the cat as the printer in the next room hummed. "What do you think, O'Ryan?"

He held his head high, ears erect, and put his right paw forward. The damned lion was back.

CHAPTER 31

By the time Pete arrived, I'd put the manuscript away and changed into leopard-print pajamas. The kitchen TV was tuned to WICH-TV, where Buck Covington read the national news—flawlessly, of course. Pete carried a dry cleaner's bag and a small suitcase, indicating that his supply of clean clothes had been replenished, and headed for the bedroom.

"Scott Palmer was heading over to the granite pits when I left work," I said, following him and making room in the closet for his additions. "Seems some kids were trying out the high-diving experience that their parents used to enjoy. I wonder if Buck will show it."

"It'll just encourage more of them to try it, I suppose," he said. Little half smile. "But it never killed anybody."

"Not that we know of," I agreed as we returned to the kitchen. "Caused some bloodshed though. Wally in production likes to show off the scar he got doing it."

"Sounds attractive." He pointed to the TV. "Look, there's Scott in front of a granite pit." He turned up the sound.

"Several youngsters were apprehended this afternoon here on the North Shore granite pits property." Scott stood beside a NO TRESPASSING sign. "Although the area is plainly posted, the temptation to scale the heights of the granite bluffs and to jump into the deep water far below apparently still holds appeal for area youth. The young men involved were prevented from carrying out their plans by the local sheriff's department and were released to the custody of their parents with a stern warning."

"Uh-oh. The kids must have been rounded up before Scott and Old Eddie arrived," I said. "No story there. He'll probably have to go to video of the car being pulled out." I'd no sooner spoken the words when Francine's shot of the dripping Mustang emerging from the water loomed on the screen. Scott began a condensed recitation of the recent happenings at the pits, with a stern warning to area kids who might want to try the jump. "Scott Palmer here at the site of the recent discovery of a long-missing vehicle and the scene of possible danger to daredevil area kids. Now, back to Buck Covington at the studio."

Buck, with earnest expression and network announcer tone, gazed into the camera. "In a related story, Salem police have released a photo of what they believe may possibly be the type of weapon used in the shooting death of Ted Thorne, whose remains were found recently in a submerged vehicle at the North Shore Granite pits." A photo of a revolver filled the screen.

"That's the gun," I exclaimed.

Pete nodded. "Thorne had a gun just like that. We haven't found the gun yet, but we know he had one."

I poured coffee for both of us. "I didn't want to think that Ted's own father could have shot him." I waved at the screen. "What made you suspect he was the killer?"

Pete looked surprised. "He's not a suspect. We don't have a suspect yet. We only have a possible type of weapon. Mrs. Thorne says her husband once owned a .38-caliber revolver like the one Buck just showed. So far that's the only weapon associated with the victim, and we don't know where it is."

I was embarrassed that I'd jumped to such a horrible conclusion. "Oh, Pete. I'm ashamed of myself. In my mind I'd already convicted Gerard Thorne of killing his son just because of a dumb vision. I should have known the man wouldn't shoot his own child, even if he had a bad temper."

"We don't know that he didn't, Lee. We only know that he once owned a gun that could have killed the boy. That's all. We have to be impartial."

Will I ever learn to think like a cop?

"You're so fair, Pete," I said. "I have to stop jumping to conclusions. Especially since my conclusions are based on things no one else can see."

"You're special, no doubt." Big, sweet smile. "But, think about it. When you see things, they usually mean *something*. Even if it's not what it first looks like."

"You're right." Imaginary light bulb over my head. "I guess what I need to do is think about why Mr. Thorne showed me his gun. If that was his gun. If he didn't kill Ted."

"That's the way."

"He looked very angry." I thought about the man's face. "Maybe he was angry *because* his son was murdered."

Pete nodded. "Go on."

"Maybe—just maybe—he's not just angry because his son was murdered, but maybe—just maybe—Ted was murdered with his father's gun! Is that possible?"

"Of course it's possible. But we can't jump to that conclusion, either. You see how it works?"

"I'm beginning to," I said. "Now I'll have to begin analyzing the other visions too."

"Don't overthink it all, babe. I'll help if I can. Okay? What kind of ice cream do we have in the freezer?"

I welcomed the change of subject. "Chocolate chip," I said, and got out bowls and spoons while Pete wielded the ice cream scoop. Funny how a late-night bowl of ice cream can chase away discussion of visions, cliff-jumping kids, and long-ago murder. We washed the dishes, then Pete and I snuggled together on my big bed watching River's creepy movie.

O'Ryan joined us during the mid-movie break while River did a tarot reading for a caller promising a sum of money from a surprising source and good news from a distant relative. The cat gave me a good-night lick on the chin, turned around three times, and lay down at the foot of the bed.

"Got anything for breakfast, or shall we go out in the morning?" Pete asked.

"Pop-Tarts," I reported. "Strawberry."

"My favorite," he said. "Good night."

As I listened to the even breathing of the man I loved, and the gentle cat snores issuing from the foot of the bed, I thought about recent visions besides the Gerard-Thorne-with-a-gun one. What kind of impartial message could I read into the falling car? Ted Thorne wearing a Red Sox T-shirt and sitting on the bentwood bench? Coach and Penelope in a picture frame?

Falling car. Wait a minute. A car doesn't fall all by itself. Something causes it to fall. A bad driver, an earthquake, an unfortunate bump in the road—not in this case. It was pushed.

Who pushed the Mustang?

The boy on the bench. We know who the boy is. Ted Thorne. We know where the bench is. At the Thornes' summer cottage. Ted is wearing the Red Sox shirt he wore when he died. Okay. The boy in the shirt on the bench at the cottage.

Was the boy killed at the cottage?

A framed picture of Coach and Penelope. The picture is over the fireplace at the cottage. It fades away quickly. This one seems almost too easy.

Are Coach and Penelope being framed?

Great. Three more questions. No real answers.

CHAPTER 32

The questions were still on my mind when I awoke in the morning. Pete, as usual, had the coffee brewing before I'd climbed out of bed. O'Ryan sniffed at his empty red bowl, gave me a judgmental stare, and headed through the cat door for the undoubtedly greener pastures downstairs.

"I've been thinking about what we talked about last night," I said, and one by one, as completely as I could recall them, I told Pete about my late-night analyses of the recent visions. "I'm afraid all I've done is create three more questions," I admitted. "What do you think?"

He was silent as he poured coffee into our matching New Hampshire Speedway mugs (treasured souvenirs of the first weekend we'd spent together). His expression was serious—almost cop faced, I thought. "You've given me something to think about, babe. The first one, the idea that the car was pushed off the cliff, was what we've assumed from the start. But the other two—those seem to lead in a new direction. Our investigation hasn't given us any solid indication about the actual scene of the murder. The family summer home? Interesting. And the very idea that Penelope and Coach could somehow be framed? That one is completely off the wall." A wry smile. "No pun intended. What makes you think they could be?"

"I don't *think* that," I said. "I don't plan these things, you know. But the word 'frame' is an obvious tip-off. Isn't it?"

"It seems to be," he agreed, "but it isn't anything I can hang a serious police investigation on."

"You'll keep it in mind anyway, won't you? Those two have enough problems already."

"They do. I'll keep all three questions in mind. I take you seriously, Lee. Always." He touched my hand. "You know none of this fits into any standard investigation process. I don't exactly know what to do with it."

"Neither do I. One Pop-Tart or two?"

"Two please. One for here and one to go, okay? I'm working a normal shift today. Nine to five. You too?"

"Me too, unless something important turns up."

"Same here. Maybe it'll be a nice quiet, dull day for both of us."

"Not *too* dull. I'm in the breaking-news business, remember?" I said, looking up at Kit-Cat Klock. "Time to get ready for a not-too-dull day." I finished my coffee and headed down to my old second-floor bedroom to shower and dress. "Talk to you later."

"Want to do something tonight? Dinner? Movie? Walk on the beach?" He raised his coffee mug. "All of the above?"

"Sounds good."

I was still smiling when I backed my car out of the garage and started for work. Pete and I hadn't had a real "date" in quite a while, and I looked forward to the promised evening. As soon as I reached the WICH-TV building on Derby Street I saw that Francine's truck was in her usual spot and the mobile van was in front of the station in the "ready to roll" position.

Looks like something's going on already. This isn't a sign of a quiet, dull day. I parked, then dashed across the lot to the street-side front door, taking the stairway instead of the slow elevator to the second floor. Francine and Mr. Doan stood next to Rhonda's desk, looking at the giant monitor screen. I joined them.

"What's happening?" I didn't have to ask twice. The answer was on the TV. Phil Archer's voice issued from the speakers as a picture of a young Bobby wearing hockey gear loomed on the big screen.

"Salem High School's class of 1974 has lost yet another member, this time due to an apparent suicide. The body of Robert Ross, onetime UMass hockey great, was discovered less than an hour ago at the home of Salem socialite and model Betsy Leavitt. Ms. Leavitt is also a member of the class of 1974, as was the late Ted Thorne, whose remains were found just a week ago in a long-submerged vehicle. Mr. Ross recently arrived in Salem from his home in San Francisco. He was apparently a houseguest at the Leavitt home. No information as to the exact cause of his death, except that it appears to have been self-inflicted. We have no further information on this tragedy at this time. Stay tuned to WICH-TV for more news as it happens."

"Bobby Ross?" I was incredulous. "I know him. I was talking about him just this morning."

"You know him?" Bruce Doan picked up on my words right away. "Got any inside information we can use?"

"What? No? I don't—didn't actually *know* him. Met him a couple of times recently. That's all." I turned away from the screen. "My aunt graduated with that class too."

"Well, there's your angle," Doan announced. "Get together with your aunt and see what you can find out about him. Why did he off himself? Especially at somebody else's house. That's just wrong."

"Oh, Mr. Doan. I don't know. My aunt will be terribly upset about this. Losing another friend. I can't question her!"

"Listen, Barrett," he growled. "You're a newsman now. Remember? Newswoman if you like. Do your job. Get on it right now." He turned his back and yanked open his office door. "Now!" he barked.

Francine and I looked at each other, then at Rhonda. "Got any script for this one?" I asked.

Rhonda, ever efficient even under impossible circumstances, handed me a handwritten note. "I haven't had a chance to type it yet, but here's Leavitt's address. At least you can get a shot of the place where it happened. This is shaping up to be a Class of Seventy-four story, don't you think so?"

"Yeah," Francine agreed. "Two bodies in one week. And don't forget. The Overton guy was a classmate too. Maybe he'll have a comment."

"Good idea, Francine." Rhonda offered a high five

across the counter. "He'll want to talk for sure. What a publicity hound."

I didn't remark on that observation, true as it was, still concerned about what my aunt's reaction to this news might be. I needed to call her, and certainly not to pry for information about Bobby. It was likely that I was the only one in the room who knew that Bobby had been close to death anyway. Why would he choose to kill himself at Betsy's home? It didn't make sense.

"Francine, want to go down and get the van started? I need to make a quick phone call and I'll be right out."

"On my way," she said. "Listen, I have to take my truck in for service right after work and my diving gear is still in it. Mind if I stash it in your trunk? I'll pick it up Monday when they bring my truck back."

"Sure." I tossed her my keys, then held my hand out to Rhonda. "Data port key please?" I needed some privacy for this call.

Once inside the little room, I called my aunt. She picked up right away. "Oh, Maralee. You've heard?"

"Yes," I said. "Are you all right?"

"Such a dreadful shock. I'm mostly worried about Betsy. I've tried to reach her, but she's not answering any of her phones." Her voice quavered ever so slightly. "It's hard to believe Bobby would do this. Betsy told me that they'd rediscovered their love. That they planned to spend whatever time he had left together."

"Have you talked to any of the others? Penelope, Coach, and Mr. Overton??"

"Steve called. I was too upset to talk. He was on his way over to Betsy's."

"Does he know that Bobby was terminal?"

"Yes."

I opened the data port door and started up the stairs once more. "Francine and I are on the way there too. Mr. Doan wants a shot of the place where this happened."

"Oh, poor Betsy. As soon as I reach her, I'm going to insist that she stay here with us for a while," she said. "She doesn't need all the attention from the press. Including you, my dear."

I joined Francine in the van, regretting the assignment we'd been handed, but determined to learn everything we could about this latest death. When we pulled into the long driveway leading to the Leavitt estate, both of us gave an involuntary "Wow." The house, which Penelope had confided to Aunt Ibby was part of Betsy's most recent divorce settlement, was both enormous and beautiful. Bobby could have lived out his days quite comfortably there, I was sure.

Ours was the only media vehicle so far, but there were two police cars on-site. I didn't see any sign of the medical examiner's van, so I assumed they'd already done their work and left. Francine was setting up a tripod, preparing for a fixed shot of me with the gorgeous house in the background, when Pete appeared in the doorway—one of those famous beautiful entranceways tourists admire.

"No yellow tape this time," Francine whispered. "Why so many cops?"

I wondered that myself and hoped Pete would

provide some answers. He walked toward us, holding up one hand. Was that a greeting hand? Or a back-off hand?

"Hi, girls. Things are happening fast this morning."

"Can you tell us the latest about what's going on here, Pete?" I reached into the van for my mic. "How did Bobby Ross die?"

"No mic yet, Lee." Cop voice. "It was an apparent self-inflicted gunshot wound."

"The weapon?" I asked, picturing Gerard Thorne in my mind, almost anticipating the answer.

"A .38-caliber revolver. I sent it to ballistics."

"Do you think it's the same gun?"

"It's just a gun." Cop face. Cop voice.

I didn't even pretend surprise. "How is Betsy holding up?"

"Not too well, I'm afraid."

"Can you make a brief statement on camera?" I asked. "I won't ask questions."

"Okay."

I signaled to Francine to begin filming and stood beside Pete. "Good morning, ladies and gentlemen. I'm Lee Barrett, here at the scene of the most recent tragedy to befall a member of Salem High School's class of 1974. Bobby Ross was a well-known high school and college athlete, and news of his suicide this morning follows news of the death of his classmate Ted Thorne, whose remains were discovered during the past week. Salem Police Detective Pete Mondello is with us here at the home of yet another classmate, where Bobby Ross apparently took his own life. Detective, what can you tell us about Mr. Ross's death?"

"Thank you, Ms. Barrett. At approximately seven o'clock this morning, a 911 operator received a call from the owner of the home behind us, reporting the death of a man on her property. Police responded and discovered the body of Robert Ross on an outdoor patio at the rear of the house, deceased with an apparent self-inflicted gunshot wound. The weapon has been recovered. That's all we have just now."

I had to bite my tongue to keep from asking some obvious questions, but I'd promised. "Thank you, Detective." I said, knowing Mr. Doan wasn't going to be satisfied with such scant information. I decided to pad it a little.

"Bobby Ross was a member of the class reunion committee who were hard at work planning for their forty-fifth class reunion to be celebrated this summer."

Francine waved from behind the camera and pointed to the driveway. Steve had arrived. "Yet another member of the Class of Seventy-four has just arrived here," I said. "Well-known congressional hopeful Steve Overton was a member of the reunion committee too. We'll see if he'll have a few words to share about his friend and classmate, Bobby Ross."

Steve's Jaguar with its red, white, and blue stickers, window flag flying, rolled up the driveway and into the carport. Steve stepped out of the passenger side door. *Who's the woman driving?*

My silent question was answered immediately when Penelope rolled down the driver's side window, spoke briefly to Steve, then backed down the driveway and out of the yard. Steve looked around and, spotting me in front of the mobile van with its giant

WICH-TV letters, waved and hurried toward me. I walked to meet him, mic extended. "Mr. Overton, Lee Barrett, WICH-TV. This is another sad day for you, I'm sure. Do you have a few words for our audience?"

He reached for the mic and faced the camera. "I'm sure I speak for all of our classmates, Bobby's and mine, when I say we are devastated by this awful news. Bobby had been away from Salem for many years, and there'd been a joyous welcome for him when he came home." He bowed his head. "He confided in a few of us the sad fact that he'd come home to die." He brushed an arm across his eyes. "He had an inoperable tumor." He handed me the mic. "Sorry. That's all."

I tried to hide my surprise at the abrupt announcement. "Thank you, Mr. Overton," I said, but the man had already retreated to the carport, where someone had opened a door and admitted him to the house. *Betsy?*

"Ladies and gentlemen, we've just learned from a classmate that Bobby Ross, whose body was discovered here during the early hours this morning, was suffering from a terminal illness and may have taken his own life." I signed off then, telling the audience that WICH-TV would continue to follow the story as facts emerged. Mr. Doan would be satisfied with Steve's surprising announcement for now anyway, and I could try to find out if my crazy, vision-based suspicion about the suicide weapon could possibly be correct.

Did the same revolver kill both Ted Thorne and Bobby Ross, forty-five years apart?

"Let's pack up the gear for now, Francine," I said. "I'm going to try to talk to Betsy, but I'm certainly not going to shove a microphone in her face under these circumstances."

"Scott Palmer would," she said softly, folding the tripod and returning it to its case.

"I know," I said. "Maybe I don't have the killer instinct it takes for this job."

CHAPTER 33

I walked into the carport and knocked on the same door Steve had used. A uniformed officer answered. "Yes, ma'am?"

"I'm Lee Barrett. A—uh—friend of Ms. Leavitt. Would you ask her if she'll see me for a moment?"

I heard Betsy's voice from the next room. "Lee? Come in, please. Have you come to take me to Ibby's house? She called me. Said she'd pick me up."

I walked past the officer into a sunny kitchen. He touched his cap and went outside. Betsy sat in a rocking chair beside a window, looking very small. Steve sat on a stool beside her, holding her hand. I knelt on the floor in front of her. "I'm sure she's on her way then," I said. "I know you'll be comfortable there."

"I've offered Betsy my condo in Marblehead," Steve said. "Twenty-four-hour security. She'll be safe." He glared in my direction. "From intrusion by the press." His point was unmistakable.

"Steve, you're so kind." Tears coursed down Betsy's face. "You've always taken care of others." She looked at me. "Do you know how many charities this dear man supports?"

Steve shook his head, began to protest. "It's nothing."

"It's true. Bobby told me about them. And about how you've helped him and so many others over the years. You're a true friend."

"Then you'll accept my offer. I promise you'll be comfortable there." He stood up, pulling her to her feet. "Pack up a few things. I'll have Penelope pull my car up."

Betsy extricated her hands from his. "Don't misunderstand, Steve. I've accepted Ibby's offer. I don't want to be alone now. I'll be fine at her house. The household staff can take care of this place. I'm sure Ibby'll be here any minute." She moved toward a doorway behind her. "I need to go and pack. Excuse me." Betsy-like, she whirled through a doorway behind her, leaving me with a clearly annoyed Steve.

He pulled a phone from his pocket, scowled in my direction, turned away, and spoke in a muffled tone. "Penelope? Pull up into the carport now. What? No. She isn't coming. Hurry up." He faced me, a smile replacing the scowl. "Not your fault, Ms. Barrett. Not at all. I'm sure you'll respect her privacy. Take good care of our darling Betsy." He bowed a tiny bow and left the kitchen. I heard the purr-growl of the sweet Jaguar engine. I watched from the doorway as it backed away. The Buick appeared at the foot of the driveway just as the Jag whizzed past.

I waved to my aunt, motioning for her to pull into the carport. The same officer who'd admitted me to Betsy's kitchen held up one hand and motioned for her to stop. The law won. She stopped. Pete appeared then, approaching the driver's side window. It was already open and I saw my aunt poke her head out. I couldn't hear a word spoken between them, but I knew both of them well enough to imagine the conversation.

Pete stepped back. The Buick moved slowly toward me and stopped close to the kitchen door. "Come on inside," I said. "Betsy's packing. She's going home with you."

"I told Pete I was going to take her with me," she said. "He needs to talk to her soon about Bobby's death. I'm so sorry Bobby chose that way out. Betsy wanted so much for them to have some time together."

I didn't mention the gun. After all, as Pete said. It's just a gun. There must be hundreds of .38-caliber guns in Salem. If Gerard Thorne hadn't appeared with his in my vision, it would never have occurred to me that both men could have been killed with the same one.

"Was that Penelope driving Steve's car?" my aunt asked as she followed me inside. "Sure looked like her."

"It was," I said. "Maybe she needed a job. Betsy says that Steve does a lot of charity work. Good deeds. Seems he'd been helping Bobby out for a long time. Other people too."

"I didn't know that but I'm not surprised. The Omigoodness Bakeries have always sponsored fundraising drives for good causes. Their logo is still on the library's bookmobile because of their generosity."

"Bernie the Bagel Beagle." I smiled, remembering

the cartoon dog logo. "Do they still have the guy in the dog suit out in front of the store waving to the cars?"

"Haven't seen Bernie in years. He was cute. Steve's parents used to make him wear the dog suit whenever they opened a new franchise." She giggled. "Oh, how he hated it. As soon as Steve took over as CEO of Omigoodness, Bernie disappeared."

Betsy, red-eyed but stylish as ever in Versace, pulling a Gucci-tapestry wheeled suitcase, joined us. "Oh Ibby, you are too kind. I just can't bear staying here another minute. I was so sure Bobby and I . . ." The tears began again. I took the suitcase from Betsy, and my aunt pulled her into a quick embrace, "Come along then, Betts," she said, steering her friend toward the door. "We'll be off."

I held the passenger door of the Buick open for Betsy, then lifted the suitcase into the backseat. "See you at home later," I said, and waved as they drove away. I looked around for Francine and the mobile unit, and started down the driveway to where they waited. One of the police cars had already left, but a forensics team in a marked white van had taken its place. I recognized the Ford E-450 vehicle. I'd never seen the inside, but Pete had said it was climate-controlled with a full electronics suite and its own generator.

Can yellow tape be far behind?

"Can you grab a shot of that white van before we leave?" I asked Francine. "Before the cops throw us out?"

She didn't waste time asking questions, just grabbed her handheld camera and zoomed in on the big Ford van. She got the shot just as white-uniformed team members emerged, heading toward the rear of the house, probably, I guessed, to the patio where Bobby's life had ended.

We were back inside our vehicle and on our way out of Betsy's big, beautiful yard before the first few feet of POLICE LINE DO NOT CROSS yellow tape was stretched across the entrance.

"What just happened?" Francine glanced at the rearview mirror. "Did I miss something?"

"We both did. Let's ride around the block, then come back and do a stand-up in front of that police line. I don't know exactly what we missed, but Doan is going to want to know that something's going on in there. Something we didn't know about an hour ago."

She turned into a nearby driveway and wheeled the van around. "Something about the dead guy that was on the patio?"

"Must be." We pulled up beside the now-off-limits entrance to the Leavitt estate. An officer Francine and I had met a few times before stood behind several feet behind the tape. "Hi, Ms. Barrett, Francine," he said. "Can't let you in this time."

"What's going on, Jimmy?" Francine asked.

"Tell you the truth, girls," he said. "I don't know. Far as I can tell, it was just a suicide. Happens every day. Too bad, but it happens every day." He moved out of camera range, continuing to watch us.

I picked a spot in front of the tape and Francine began recording. "As we reported earlier, a suicide has occurred at this address, where police identified former local athlete Bobby Ross as the victim of a self-inflicted gunshot wound. Since that time, however, police have cordoned off the premises and a team of forensic scientists are on scene as we speak. Also, we have information that a .38-caliber weapon has been turned over to the county ballistics unit for examination. Stay tuned to WICH-TV for further breaking news."

I signed off with my name, and we climbed back into the van. "That'll wrap it up for now, I guess. Not likely we'll get anything from those guys. Let's head back to the barn and I'll make a few phone calls. See what more I can dig up on the victim."

"Poor guy," Francine said. "Hey, maybe there's some kind of a curse on that high school class. We ought to ask River. She knows a lot of witches."

I let the witch comment pass and breathed a silent prayer that no more bad things would happen to Salem High's class of 1974. "Don't even think that," I said, concerned about my precious Aunt Ibby. My first phone call would be to her, with a gentle reminder to lock her doors.

CHAPTER 34

According to Rhonda, our reporting efforts had
been well received by Doan, at least well enough that
he'd left his office and gone to a Chamber of Com-
merce luncheon. I went to the data port to begin
making some telephone calls and taking some notes.
The first call was to my aunt.

"Is Betsy getting settled in?" I asked. "She must be
devastated. Did Bobby have any family in Salem or in
San Francisco that will have to be notified?"

"I'm trying to get her to take a nap. Right now
she's out in the garden picking some pole beans for
dinner. Wants to be helpful. She says it takes her
mind off her troubles. Bobby was married once and
divorced a long time ago. I hate to say it, but they say
it was because of his drinking. I remember that he
was raised by his grandmother and she's gone." Aunt
Ibby sighed. "I haven't spoken to Betts about final
arrangements for him. I'm sure several of us can pitch
in for that."

"Aunt Ibby, there's something going on back at Betsy's house." I told her about the ramped-up police presence. "Keep your doors locked and don't tell anybody that she's with you. Pete and Steve Overton know where she is, of course, and Penelope, I guess, but Betsy's in no condition to be hounded by media people. Including me."

"Pete's already called. He's coming over later to talk to her. Steve called, too, but she didn't want to speak to him yet. I'll remember to lock the doors the minute she comes in. Don't forget your keys."

My next call was to Coach. He and Bobby had been the sports stars of the group. I guess they belonged because of the hero status high school athletes attain. Betsy had extraordinary beauty and the automatic adoration awarded cheerleaders. Aunt Ibby had brains and breeding. Steve had street smarts, money, and, yes, free bagels. Ted was superrich and gorgeous. Penelope—I had yet to figure out where she fit in. But right now I wanted to learn more about Bobby. Since he and Coach hadn't been known for academic excellence, or money, had they ever felt that they were simply "token jocks" at the popular table? I was betting they had, and that Coach Whipple might have some special insight into what made Bobby tick. Some little something that the others had never seen.

"Hello, Coach? This is Lee Barrett. Ibby Russell's niece. We met at her house. Remember?"

"I certainly remember you, sweetheart. I saw you on TV today. That red hair sure is pretty."

"Thank you." *I was on TV talking about two dead*

friends of yours and you want to talk about my hair?" You and Bobby were high school pals. I wonder if you'd share some of your thoughts about him."

"For your TV news show?"

"Yes. Of course." *It's not my show, but why bring that up?* "You two were the sports heroes of the group. Did you keep in touch after high school?" My pen was poised over the yellow pad.

"We did, for quite a while. We both had sports scholarships, you know? Bobby went to UMass, me to BC. We both used to come home to Salem for holidays, summer vacations. Bobby usually stayed at my place."

"He didn't go home?"

"Didn't have one. His grandma died and their place was a rental."

"Did the others in the group know that? That he was homeless?"

"Sure, I guess so." A little chuckle. "But Bobby had always liked staying with me. Ever since we were kids. He wasn't crazy about Steve, and Ted could be kind of intimidating. All that money, you know? Bobby never complained about anything though. He'd go along to get along. Know what I mean?"

I wrote as fast as I could, wishing I'd made time to take a shorthand course somewhere along the line. "He was good company then?"

"Right. Except for sometimes when he was drunk."

"Has he been staying with you this time?"

"You mean before he moved in over at Betsy's place? No. He was going to, but Steve loaned him a condo in Marblehead." Another chuckle. "It came complete with a liquor cabinet too."

That explains his condition when he arrived for the reunion committee meeting. And seriously, I hope Steve wasn't going to put Betsy into the same condo where Bobby had been staying.

"Not too good for somebody with a drinking problem," I said. "I hope he wasn't driving."

"Nope. Lost his license years ago. The booze wrecked his marriage and got him booted out of college too."

That was a surprise. "I heard he lost his scholarship because he injured his knee playing hockey."

"Yeah, well, you get on ice skates roaring drunk and start fights, you get hurt. Hurt bad." He paused. "A shame really. If he'd ever stayed straight, he could have gone pro."

"Betsy had such high hopes that she could help make his last days comfortable. Losing him, after they'd just found each other again—she's taking it hard."

"I'll bet. He wanted to marry her right out of high school, you know," he said. "Spent every cent he had to buy her a ring."

"They were so young," I said. "Besides that, perhaps Betsy realized that he couldn't possibly afford her."

He laughed aloud. "Know what she told him?"

"What?"

"She told him she loved him, too, but she was damned if she was going to go through life as Betsy Ross!"

"That must have been hard for him to take."

"Yep. Sure was. He didn't talk about it much. After he lost his scholarship, he hooked up with some hippie chick and lit out for California." His tone had turned serious. "He married her but it didn't last. He admitted it was because of the booze. Listen, sweetheart. Maybe old Bobby is better off dead, know what I mean?"

I didn't have an answer for that. "Thank you for talking with me, Coach," I said. "I'm sure you'll be notified when the—uh—final arrangements are made."

Next on my list of phone calls was Penelope. Busy Penelope. Would she be at Glory's Scrapbook Haven? Waving at traffic from Overton headquarters? Or driving Steve's Jaguar? I tapped in her mobile number. I'd already mentally rehearsed the way I'd begin the conversation.

"Oh, Penelope, It's Lee Barrett. I'm so glad I caught you. I have a favor to ask, but first let me say how sorry I am about the loss of another of your classmates. What a shame."

"Thank you, Lee. We're all shocked, naturally. Steve said that you and Ibby are taking care of Betsy. That's good." Her voice brightened. "Now, what can I do for you? A favor, you say?"

"Yes. It's about the picture of my mother and Aunt Ibby. The one on the bench at the Thornes' cottage?"

"Yes. I remember you asked about it before and I've even found the negative for you. I know a really good photo finisher. Not everyone works with the old negatives anymore. Everything is digital these days. Shall I have some prints made for you?"

"I'm thinking of getting an enlargement made." I explained my plan for trying to buy the bench from Mrs. Thorne and hanging the photo above it. "The bench is still there on the porch of the Thornes' cottage," I said. "Can you believe it?"

"That's a lovely idea, Lee," she said. "It makes me happy when people preserve old things. I guess you've heard that I have a reputation for *never* throwing anything away."

"I have heard that," I admitted. "I have a fondness for things vintage, myself. The next time you come to the house for a reunion committee meeting, I'll show you my apartment if you have time. I know you stay busy. Saw you and Coach waving signs in front of the Overton headquarters. It's so nice of you two to help a classmate out like that."

"I'd love to see your apartment," she said. "By the way, Warren and I aren't exactly volunteers. Steve pays for our time. He's the one who's helping us out. Savings only go so far, you know."

"From what I've seen, your group has stayed pretty tight all these years. Coach . . . uh, Warren . . . told me how he'd taken Bobby in, back when he had no home to go to, and now Betsy is staying with Aunt Ibby and Steve is helping you out. That's so nice." I paused, hoping she'd offer something new—something to help me connect the dots. She did.

"You're right about us staying tight. All for one and one for all, as they say." Little giggle. "We sure missed Teddy when he ran off—I mean, we all *thought* he'd run off. He was the one who'd brought us all together in the first place. Everybody loved Ted."

Clearly not everybody. Somebody shot him.

"He was certainly a handsome kid, and with all that money and the cool car and the great summer place, I'm sure he attracted lots of friends," I said. "He must have seen something very special in each of you."

"You think so? Never thought about it that way. We know he saw something special in Ibby, of course. True love. I mean—until he stood her up for the senior

prom. Wow! Was she ever steamed." Another giggle.
"You know what they say about a redhead's temper.
Oops. Excuse me. You are one. Sorry."

"It's okay. I guess that would make anybody angry."

"Did you know they'd been nominated for prom
king and queen? So, she got queen, and the runner-
up for king was Bobby, of all people." She made a
phew sound. "And him, drunk. Stepping all over her
feet and the hem of her dress when they tried to
dance together. She left right after that. Who could
blame her? Threw the crown in the trash on the way
out the door. I still have it."

"You have it?"

"Sure. I'd never throw anything that nice away.
My grandkids think it was mine. I never bothered to
tell them different." Sad little laugh. "Imagine that.
Me. Queen of the prom. Fat chance of that. Ibby was
the pretty one. The smart one. The one with the best
boyfriend. Oh well, she really deserved everything
she got. Everybody loved Ibby."

I'd no sooner said "thanks," and "goodbye" to
Penelope when my phone buzzed. "Rhonda's got an
assignment for us," Francine said. "You through with
your phone calls?"

"For now," I said. "I'll be right up." I wished I'd had
time to write down every bit of the information I'd
picked up from my two calls. But my notes were fairly
legible, and this time I was sure I'd be able to remember whatever I hadn't scribbled onto paper.

Our assignment looked like a pleasant one. No
muddy cars, human remains, or guns. Instead we'd
be giving our viewers a mini-tour of some Salem
gardens. We started out with the gardens at the

House of the Seven Gables. We could smell lilacs
before we'd even parked the mobile unit. From there
we went to the gorgeous Ropes Memorial Garden on
Essex Street, then for some more practical plantings,
we visited four of the city's community gardens, where
some four hundred families share gardening plots,
raising their own vegetables, herbs, and flowers. We
wound up at a plant sale fund-raiser on the Salem
Common.

"This was really fun, wasn't it?" Francine was enthusiastic. It was early afternoon when we packed up
the cameras and mics, along with assorted hanging
baskets, herb bowls, and houseplants we'd each
picked up along the way. "I love flowers," she said as
we drove back to Derby Street. "They remind me of
happy things. Weddings, Valentine's Day, violets, and
Johnny-jump-ups in my Gramma's backyard. Don't
you love 'em?"

"Sure do," I said. But my thoughts had turned,
unbidden, to a withered corsage pressed in a family
Bible, and to teenaged Ibby's humiliation and hurt
and anger.

I willed the unhappy thoughts away and told
Francine about the bouquet of orange blossoms I'd
carried when I married Johnny Barrett, and about
how Pete Mondello and I take a boat ride to Misery
Island every summer to plant purple pansies on a
little gray dog's grave.

CHAPTER 35

Those memories calmed me, brought me back to the present, helped me focus on the job at hand—and that job was to entertain, to interest, and to educate the viewers of WICH-TV. That meant giving my very best whether the topic was flower gardens, shelter pets, or murder. I thought back to the beginning of the mystery of Ted Thorne's death and that deep, watery grave.

Exactly what was the beginning? For me, it was the muddy car breaking the surface of the freshwater pool. *Wait a minute. This isn't about me.* It's about how that Mustang, with its sad cargo, got down there in the first place.

No! It's about how we knew it was there! I'd barely focused on that at all. A tip, Pete had said. The chief got an anonymous tip, one that he'd found credible enough to spend department money on an expensive retrieval exercise.

I almost smacked myself on the forehead. I'd never even asked Pete or the chief himself what kind of tip it was. Phone? Tweet? Email? Snail mail? Letters cut from magazines and pasted on colored paper? What?

Francine and I transferred our newly purchased greenery to our own vehicles and weren't even all the way up to the second floor via the clunky elevator, when I called Pete. "Pete," I said, "can you tell me what kind of tip the chief got about the sunken car? Verbal, written, text?"

"Sure. It was a letter. Typewritten. Very detailed. Unsigned."

"Did you see it?"

"Yes."

"You didn't tell me."

"No. Chief wanted to keep it quiet until the document examiners got through with it."

"Document examiners?"

"Yep. They use ultraviolet light. Infrared. Electrostatic detection devices. High-tech stuff. Learned a lot."

"Then I can use what you just said? That it was a typewritten letter?"

"Yes. Quite likely from an old Olympia manual machine"

"Will you tell me what it says?"

"Can't do that yet, babe. Off the record, it's possible that the writer was involved in disposing of Thorne's body, if not in his actual death. We're working on that angle," he said. "That's all I can give you right now."

We got out of the elevator and I stopped in the hall to continue the conversation while Francine went on into the office. The idea that the tipster could have been a killer was a chilling one. I thought of the varied postmarks on the "Ted" letters, the ones Mrs. Thorne and my aunt had received. "Do you know where the letter was mailed?"

"It has a Salem postmark."

"How about video of whoever mailed it?"

He laughed. "This isn't a television show, babe. There really aren't cameras on every mailbox in town."

I sighed. Investigating a cold case/missing person/murder isn't easy. I didn't envy Pete's job. "Okay, thanks anyway," I said. "Anything on that gun yet?"

"Not yet. They take their time. We still on for tonight?"

"Yes. Around seven?"

I joined Francine at Rhonda's reception desk. Both of them had eyes fixed on the screen above the desk. "What's going on?" I asked. Rhonda pointed. "Looks like Scott Palmer got to your houseguest."

The scene was familiar. It was Aunt Ibby's garden where a tearful Betsy with a partly full basket of green beans faced Scott and the camera across the wrought-iron garden fence. "Did you find Bobby Ross's body, Ms. Leavitt?" Scott practically shouted the question. Her answer was unintelligible, but she nodded her head yes.

Scott persisted. "Do you know why he did it, Ms. Leavitt?"

There was such pain on her face, beautiful despite the tears, it was hard to watch. "It wasn't Bobby's fault," she sobbed. "None of this was his fault at all." She dropped the basket, scattering beans, and ran toward the back door and safety. The cruel camera followed as she stumbled blindly up the steps and into the house. O'Ryan appeared through the cat door and approached the garden. The camera focused on the cat while Scott began his sign-off. "This is Scott Palmer reporting from outside a private residence on Winter Street. This has been an exclusive WICH-TV interview with famed model Betsy Leavitt, at whose home the lifeless body of onetime local high school athlete Bobby Ross was discovered this morning. Ms. Leavitt confirmed that she was the one who discovered the body. Suicide is indicated."

While Scott spoke, O'Ryan had crept closer. With a graceful leap, the cat landed on the fence's top rail. Then with a loud yowl, he stretched out a sheathed paw, smacked the reporter on the side of the head, jumped down, and retreated through the cat door. Scott recovered his composure as well as he could under the circumstances and hastily signed off.

O'Ryan never did like Scott.

"That was just cold," Rhonda said. "The poor woman."

I agreed. "There was no need to ambush her. We thought she'd be safe there from that kind of media abuse."

"I wish the cat had given him a good scratch," Francine said. "Do you think you should go home, Lee? See if your aunt and Ms. Leavitt are okay?"

"I think I should."

"Go ahead," Rhonda said, "and give O'Ryan a special treat."

My car smelled of rosemary and spearmint and basil. That made the trip home almost pleasant. I parked in the garage and, after gathering up my plants, locked the car, locked the garage door, and hurried along the path between the house and the garden. O'Ryan waited for me on the back steps. I unlocked that door and went inside, paused to put the plants on the potting table in the laundry room, and tapped on my aunt's kitchen door. "Aunt Ibby, it's me," I called.

"Just a minute, Maralee. It's locked. I'm coming."

I bent and picked up the cat, who purred happily. "Good boy," I whispered into his ear. "If anyone ever deserved a good smack upside the head it's Scott Palmer."

My aunt quickly ushered me inside, looking back and forth in the hall behind me, pushing the door shut and locking it. "Poor Betsy is terrified," she stage-whispered. "Did you see what Scott did to her out there? Nobody from the TV station followed you home did they?"

"Of course not. Scott did that on his own. What a creep. He knows where we live and must have figured that she'd come outdoors eventually." I looked around the kitchen. "Where is she?"

"Upstairs in the guest room. I made her some chamomile tea. I hope she's finally taking a nap. She found his body, you know."

A gunshot wound to the head. I shuddered. "It must have been horrible. Did she hear the shot?"

"She heard something during the night, but she didn't think about a gun. Who does? You think of a car backfiring or fireworks or something like that." She sat down at the table. "There was just the one sound. Boom! Then everything was quiet. She went back to sleep. Didn't find him until this morning."

"Did she have any clue that he was—that something like this could happen?"

"She says no. She's quite vehement about that. Sit down, will you, dear?" She motioned to the chair opposite hers. "Some things just aren't adding up."

"Like what? The man was dying. Why wouldn't he be despondent?" I sat and faced her.

"Like, where did he get a gun? Betsy didn't have one and all Bobby brought with him was an overnight bag." She leaned forward, both elbows on the table, chin propped on her fists. "I'm telling you, Maralee, something isn't right about this. Did Pete tell you anything more about that gun?"

"It's a revolver. A thirty-eight. The ballistics people have it."

"The same kind of gun that killed Ted?"

I shrugged. "There are lots of guns that fire those same bullets, and that—what happened to Ted—that was forty-five years ago."

I don't want them to be connected. That would be too terrible.

"There was a note. Betsy found a note."

"A note? From Bobby?"

"She took it. It was on the table beside the—beside Bobby. Wait a minute. I'll make us some tea." She stood and walked to the sink. She filled the teakettle, her back to me. "Betsy didn't give the note to the police. I told her she should."

"What does it say?"

"I don't know. She says it's hers and she doesn't have to show it to anybody."

I thought about that. "I suppose it's a suicide note. It was probably addressed to her. It's not a crime to kill yourself. Maybe she *doesn't* have to show it to anybody."

She put tea bags into two cups. "Pete thinks something's not right, too, doesn't he? Why else is the yellow tape around Betsy's house?"

I couldn't answer that. "I talked to Pete about another note today," I told her. "The tip the chief got about the sunken car. That was in a note."

"Yes. I knew that."

"You did? How did you know?"

"Oh, somebody mentioned it I guess. On TV? At the library?" She poured the hot water into our cups. "I remember now. I think Penelope said something about it when we were making copies of the yearbook pictures. It was a typewritten note. Very hard to trace."

CHAPTER 36

I sipped my tea. My aunt sipped hers. The kitchen was quiet. I broke the silence. "I suppose quite a few people knew about the tipster's note. It'd be hard to keep a thing like that entirely quiet. Things leak."

"Yes," Aunt Ibby agreed. "They do. There could even be copies of the thing floating around." She cocked her head to one side the way she does sometimes when she's thinking. "I suppose Pete might know about that. I mean, if they sent the original away for the experts to study, they must have kept a copy or two for themselves. You think?"

"I'm sure they did. But how would somebody like Penelope get to see it? I'll bet she heard it from someone else, same as you heard it from her."

"She spends some time with Warren Whipple," she said. "Could he be a 'leaker'?"

"I talked to him just today," I said. "Talked to her, too, as a matter of fact. Coach and Bobby had kept in touch over the years. He was quite philosophical about Bobby's death, though. Said maybe he was better off dead. Coach blamed all of Bobby's troubles on alcohol."

"You know, Maralee, I've been thinking about that very thing. It wasn't until right after Ted disappeared that Bobby's heavy drinking began." Her brow furrowed. "I'm sure he drank a few beers now and then. They all did. But none of us ever saw him drunk until the night of our senior prom. That was right after Ted went missing."

"Penelope talked about that, too," I said. "You never told me you were prom queen."

"Penelope talks entirely too much." Her cheeks colored slightly.

"Penelope said he stepped on your feet and your dress. No wonder you were angry with him."

"I was. I stomped out of the place like a drama queen instead of a prom queen." She finished her tea. "Very unladylike. I'm sorry I did that."

"Penelope saved your crown. Did you know?"

"No! Really? How sweet. Penelope never liked to see anything go to waste. Does she still have it?"

"Her grandkids think she won it."

"Good. She probably should have. Everybody liked her."

"That's what she said about you," I replayed Penelope's words in my mind. "You were 'the pretty one. The smart one. The one with the best boyfriend.' And everybody loved you."

Had there been a touch of envy in those words? Maybe more than a touch?

"Penelope is so generous," she said. "She's putting a lot of work into the scrapbook for the reunion, rounding up all those old pictures and clippings and all. I'm sure it'll be a masterpiece."

"I'm sure it will," I agreed. "She's located the negative of the picture of you and my mother. She's even going to recommend her photo finisher so it'll be perfect."

"That's just like her. Always putting others first. Speaking of the picture, I haven't had the heart to call Laura Thorne about the bench yet." She carried our cups to the sink. "I can't imagine how heartbroken she must be after learning about what really happened to her boy. But at least she has some closure. For the first time in decades she'll know where he is. There'll be a service and he'll be laid to rest next to his father."

The angry-faced father with a gun.

"Have plans been announced yet?"

"Not yet, but it'll probably be soon. Then there's poor dead Bobby to deal with." She softly tsk-tsked. "We'll have to wait for them to release the body. I'm going to ask the committee to pitch in for his final arrangements."

"Betsy may want to do it by herself. She loved him," I said.

"He was one of us. We'll all be involved." I knew that determined voice. The committee—what was left of it—would be involved. *Two of the seven stars are already missing.*

"Steve will be furious about Scott Palmer tracking Betsy down the way he did. He wanted her to go to a condo he owns where she'd be safe from media creeps like Scott. And from me too, I guess."

Long sigh. "Yes, that was unfortunate. As if the poor

woman wasn't stressed enough after what she's been through this day—to have a camera stuck in her face and impudent, rude questions."

"O'Ryan took care of Scott pretty well, don't you think?"

"O'Ryan? What do you mean?"

I realized that Aunt Ibby had stopped watching the telecast when Betsy ran into the house. I told her about the well-placed cat paw and we laughed together. "Rhonda told me to reward him with a special treat," I said. "Do you have some of his favorites?"

She opened a cabinet and pulled down a fresh box of soft-centered crunchies and put a generous handful into his red bowl. "So Steve offered Betsy one of his condos? She told me Bobby had been staying in one."

"Coach told me that too. It's in Marblehead. Complete with a full liquor cabinet."

"Uh-oh. 'Lead us not into temptation—'"

"'And deliver us from evil,'" I added to the old prayer. "I wonder if Bobby had been drinking last night when he—uh—died."

"I'm sure the medical examiner has determined that by now. The world will know all about it soon enough. Leaks, you know."

"I'm sure you're right. I need to get upstairs and write down what's happened today. I'm trying hard to journal everything about the case."

My aunt smiled at my use of the word "case," but didn't comment on it. "Good idea, Maralee. Meticulous note keeping is a necessary habit for a reporter if she's striving for accuracy."

"That's me," I said, opening the door to the hall. "I brought home a few herb plants for us to share.

They're on the potting table. I'll check in with you later. Pete and I have a movie date tonight."

O'Ryan followed me into the hall, then stood looking from the kitchen to the stairway and back. "Make up your mind, cat," I told him. "There are treats upstairs too." He trotted ahead of me, and together we climbed the twisty staircase.

I tossed the yellow pad and my phone onto the kitchen table and retrieved the laptop from my bedroom. I planned to transcribe my data port notes, then add to them the things I'd just learned since I'd come home from work little more than an hour ago. Things were moving fast.

And leading . . . where?

Never mind. I was getting more confident that it'd all make sense—eventually. I rewarded O'Ryan with a couple more of the crunchy treats, then got to work. By five o'clock I'd sent a dozen more pages to the bedroom printer. O'Ryan followed me into the room and appeared to be interested when I pulled the Gianni Bini shoebox from the top shelf and added the new pages to the stack. "Look at this, cat," I said. "If all this was a *real* mystery book, I'd be almost ready to go to press with it."

Not a real mystery book—but it's all shaping up to be a real mystery. Maybe more than one!

O'Ryan didn't seem at all impressed with my literary efforts but sat in the exact middle of the bed and did his golden-eyes cat-staring thing, which borders on the hypnotic. "Okay. Cut that out," I said. "Are you trying to tell me something?"

He blinked, then moved to the edge of the bed, stuck out one big paw, and spun the oval mirror in my direction. "I'm going to have to look, aren't I?" I muttered. "What is it this time?"

I delayed it for a minute, putting the shoebox ever so carefully back onto the top shelf. I knew though, eventually, I'd have to see what was in the mirror. I sat on the edge of the bed and faced it.

Surprise! I saw myself. I realized in seconds though that this wasn't a true reflection of me. It was an image of my mother. She was in her early thirties just like me. She wore jeans and a plaid shirt, similar to, but not matching, the jeans and shirt I wore. She raised her hand, extending her open palm toward me. I put my hand on the mirror, touching the image of her hand. "I love you, Mama," I said aloud. She smiled. I watched her lips as she formed the words, "I love you, Maralee." She began to fade away. "Don't go," I said. "Please." She put her fingers to her lips and blew me a kiss. Then she was gone.

I began to cry. O'Ryan came over to where I sat and crawled onto my lap, reaching up to lick my tears. I held him close, burying my face in soft fur. We stayed together like that for a long moment, until I felt a warmth, a calmness, a kind of lightness. "I'm okay now, O'Ryan," I said. "That was the best, most wonderful vision I've ever had."

CHAPTER 37

Pete arrived at seven, bearing, of all things, a gardenia corsage. "Lady was on the corner selling them. Two bucks. First date we've had in a while, so I thought, why not?"

What a guy!

I pinned the sweet-smelling blossom to the lapel of my NASCAR jacket. Our first destination was Cinema Salem. This time we'd have to flip a coin, choosing between Pete's choice, *Deadpool 2*, and mine, *The Book Club*. I picked heads. We always use the same quarter, and it was Pete's turn to flip. "Tails. You lose," he practically gloated. I did a fake pout but didn't really mind. I like Josh Brolin anyway.

We held hands in the dark and shared a big bucket of buttery popcorn. It was around nine thirty when we left the theater. "What do you think?" Pete asked. "Seafood? Italian? Chinese? Thai?" Salem has such a wide variety of restaurants, in every price range, decor, and national origin, it's much harder to pick a place to eat than it is to choose a movie. We settled on fried clam rolls and Pepsi at Dube's on Jefferson Avenue, not far from the police station.

"Mind if we stop by my office on the way home?" he asked. "I want to check on a couple of things." I didn't mind a bit. The front counter officer knew me, so I was comfortable sitting in the lobby, chatting with him while Pete went down the long corridor to his office.

I recognized that he was wearing his cop face as soon as he reappeared in the lobby. He took my arm and propelled me toward the door, with a brisk "See ya later" to the desk cop "We may have a little problem," he said as soon as we were inside his car. "I had a text from the Essex PD."

"Not about the gravel in the driveway again!" I almost snorted. "Don't they have anything more important to worry about over there?"

"Yeah. They do." Cop voice. "One of the cleaning guys reported to Mrs. Thorne that it looked as though someone had been sleeping in one of the beds. She called the Essex PD. They checked it out. Did a little print dusting and Bobby Ross's prints turned up. Any ideas about that?"

I had a pretty good idea that Bobby and Betsy had been there together, but I wasn't about to give Betsy any more grief than she already had. I remembered what Coach had told me about Bobby being homeless from time to time, and I repeated what he'd told me to Pete. "Ted Thorne's friends knew where the key to the cottage was hidden," I said. "If Bobby needed a place to sleep, he could have opened the front door and walked right in."

"How do you know that—and where is the key?" he asked. Normal voice this time.

"Aunt Ibby told me about it, and it's under the front paw of the stone lion on the wall."

"Good job, Lee. You'd make a good cop."

"So you keep telling me, but no thanks!"

"Mind if I call Essex right now and give them that information?" He already had the phone in his hand.

"Go for it," I said. Finding Bobby's prints couldn't hurt him now, I reasoned. Pete relayed what I'd said and put the phone away. I leaned back in my seat, inhaling the lovely smell of my gardenia, which by then had fragranced the whole car. "It smells so good in here," I said "Better than those little pine tree things. My car smelled good today too. Francine and I bought potted plants."

I could tell he wasn't listening. Cop face frown. "Lee, do all the people on the reunion committee know about that key?"

"I suppose so," I said.

"Men and women both?"

"Sure. Why wouldn't they?"

"Now you know and I know and how many others do you suppose know about it?"

"I have no idea. It's an old cottage. I suppose Mr. and Mrs. Thorne told friends about it too."

"Right," he said. "There've probably been a hundred people in and out of there over the years. So Bobby's prints don't mean much of anything, really. And we can't ask him about it."

"Nope. Can't ask him." *Oh boy. You could ask Betsy. Or Aunt Ibby. Or me.*

Pete parked on the Winter Street side of the house. He walked around the car and helped me out. Such a gentleman! He walked with me to the front door, waited while I unlocked it, gave the waiting cat a pat on the head, kissed me good night, and ran down the steps. With a tiny little toot of the horn, he drove out of sight.

I stepped from the foyer into Aunt Ibby's living room. The lights were out in there, but I could see light from the kitchen. I tiptoed across the room and peeked around the corner. Alexa was playing a John Denver tune softly and my aunt sat alone at the round table. "That you, Maralee?" my aunt called. "Come on in."

"I'm glad you're up," I said. "I had the most beautiful vision just before Pete arrived. I wanted to share it with you."

"A beautiful vision? That's not something I've heard you say before." She patted the seat of the chair beside her. "Tell me about it."

I took off my jacket, hung my purse on the back of a chair, and remembered to unpin the slightly wilting white flower. "Look. Pete gave me a gardenia." I held it close to my face and inhaled deeply. "I love this smell."

"Umm. It's delightful," she said. "Now tell me what you saw?"

"It was O'Ryan's idea for me to look at the mirror in my room." I pointed to the cat, who'd followed me to the kitchen and now sat in front of the refrigerator, grooming his whiskers and ignoring us. I told her how the picture had come slowly into focus and how at first I'd thought I was seeing my own reflection. "It was Mama," I said. "It was really her. I touched her hand and I told her I love her." I felt tears welling up again. "She told me she loves me, and she blew me a kiss."

Aunt Ibby smiled, then shook her head. "That gardenia means more than you know," she said. "Carrie loved their fragrance too. She wore Jungle Gardenia perfume all the time. Isn't it a lovely coincidence that you'd see her in your mirror, and Pete would give you a gardenia on the same day?"

"Pete doesn't believe in coincidences," I said. "Neither does River."

"Maybe it isn't one, then," my aunt mused. "I'd like to believe it isn't."

O'Ryan moved away from the refrigerator just then, posing pointer-like, facing the living room. Within seconds, Betsy appeared in the doorway wearing a pale blue silk robe. "I thought I heard music. Hello, Lee. Hello, Ibby. I've had a good nap." She joined us at the table. It was one of those moments when I hadn't the slightest idea of what to say. She'd just lost a loved one, then been ambushed by the press. What's an appropriate comment?

"I'm glad you were able to rest, Betts," my aunt said. "Can I get you a bite to eat? Tea? Coffee?"

"Coffee would be great, dear," she said. "Nothing to eat, though. I have a shoot next Monday. Can't afford to gain an ounce."

I was astonished. Here I was close to tears over a

vision in a mirror and a two-dollar flower, and she sounded perfectly normal after all she'd been through. I couldn't do anything about the loss of Bobby, but I felt as though I should apologize for Scott's insensitivity.

"Ms. Leavitt—Betsy," I stammered, "I'm so sorry about the way Scott Palmer behaved today. He's a colleague, but I want you to know that he doesn't represent all of us at WICH-TV."

"Thank you, Lee. I do appreciate your concern, but Lord knows I've had television cameras shoved in my face for years." She patted her hair. Silvery little giggle. "Though I usually looked better. I should have handled it more gracefully. Perhaps you'll tell Scott I'll give him a proper interview some other time."

I had no comment ready for that, either. "I'll make the coffee, Aunt Ibby," I said. "Don't get up." I filled Mr. Coffee with water, measured hazelnut decaf into the basket, and marveled at some people's ability to compartmentalize. I killed some time filling a chintz-patterned cream pitcher with half-and-half, putting packets of both sugar and Sweet'N Low into the companion sugar bowl, and placing them onto a tray along with three matching coffee cups. I added a few biscotti just in case, then poured the coffee.

"Thank you, dear," my aunt said as I put the tray on the table. I resumed my seat as O'Ryan hopped up onto a vacant chair, fixing the golden-eyed cat stare on Betsy. She stared right back. "Look. He's going to try to outstare me," she said. "I play this game with my little tiger cat, Pixie. I love cats."

Big point for Betsy. She loves cats, and O'Ryan seems to like her.

"Is Pixie at your house, Betsy?" I asked. "I'll be glad to go and get her tomorrow if you'd like. We have a carrier, and O'Ryan doesn't mind having cat company at all."

"Would you? Could you?" She stopped the staring contest, clapped her hands together like a little girl, then frowned. "But will the police let you in?"

"Maralee's beau is a police detective, Betsy," Aunt Ibby announced. "She may be able to pull some strings."

So it was decided. In the morning I'd ask for permission to pick up Pixie the cat. I finished my coffee, picked up my purse, put my jacket over my shoulders, picked up my wilting gardenia, and taking a biscotti with me, said good night to my aunt and her old friend and went upstairs, O'Ryan tagging along behind. I'd wanted to tell my aunt that I'd told Pete about the hidden key and about Bobby's prints being on the bed, but it didn't seem like something I should talk about in front of Betsy. I could do it later.

It was too late to work on the laptop, but I still had a stack of index cards in my purse. I wrote on one, "My mother appeared in a vision. She says she loves me and blew me a kiss." I added a note. "She always wore Jungle Gardenia perfume." On the next card I wrote that the Essex Police had found Bobby's prints in the bedroom of the cottage. On another, though it didn't seem particularly relevant to anything, I wrote, "Betsy Leavitt says she loves cats and has one named Pixie. I have volunteered to ask permission to go into Betsy's house for the purpose of rescuing Pixie."

So it was decided. I wasn't sure, of course, that I'd actually *get* permission to go into a house surrounded with police tape, but if I couldn't go in, I'd find some other way to bring cat and mistress together. I know I'd hate to be separated from O'Ryan if I was as stressed as I knew Betsy must be—despite her everything-is-normal front.

CHAPTER 38

I called Pete first thing in the morning and asked. He said no. Actually he said hell, no. But he told me to bring the cat carrier over to Betsy's place and he'd get Pixie for me. I wanted to get the cat transporting over with before my regular 9:00 a.m. check-in time at WICH-TV, so Pete agreed to meet me in front of the Leavitt estate at eight.

With the cat carrier on the passenger seat, a to-go cup of coffee in the holder, and my last Pop-Tart along with a stale biscotti balanced on the dash, I was parked at the curb a few minutes before eight. I walked to the end of the driveway where I had a good view of the house and yard. Something new had been added. In the spot where the high-tech forensics vehicle had been the day before was another white van, one I'd seen before. A little too often before. Subtle black lettering on the side spelled out CRIME SCENE INVESTIGATION.

I saw Pete then, on the front steps of the house. He held a small, squirming tiger cat in his arms. As he walked toward me, I dashed back to the Vette, picked up the carrier, ducked under the tape, and met him halfway up the driveway. "Just pop her right in here, Pete," I said, holding the carrier door open. "Did she scratch you?"

With the cat safely stashed, he held up one scraped hand. "She did. Just a little. Poor thing is frightened. She'll be glad to get out of here. People running around all over the place." He lifted the carrier with one hand and took my arm with the other, leading me toward the street. "You'd better be on your way too."

"You know I'm going to call the news department the minute I leave here, so you might as well tell me what's going on. CSI all of a sudden? What happened?"

I lifted the yellow tape and we both scooted under. "We got the report from ballistics," he said. "The gun that killed Ross is the same one that killed the Thorne kid."

I was pretty sure I knew the answer to my next question before I asked it. "Do you know whose gun it was?"

"It was registered more than forty years ago to Gerard Thorne."

I was still puzzled. "The angry man. But how does that make this a crime scene? Gerard Thorne didn't kill Bobby Ross."

"No. He didn't." I opened my car door and Pete deposited the carrier with its meowing occupant carefully onto the passenger seat. "But somebody did." He turned and ducked back under the tape. "See you later."

"You sure will! I have to deliver Pixie," I climbed

into my front seat, "but I'm calling Francine to pick me up and we'll be back here in no time." He didn't answer.

I did what I'd said I'd do. I texted Francine. "Pick me up in front of my house. CSI at Leavitt's." I drove a little too fast. Had the Vette secured in the garage and the caged cat inside Aunt Ibby's kitchen within fifteen minutes. "Here's Pixie," I announced to my startled aunt. "Gotta run."

"Wait a minute," she followed me through the living room and into the foyer. "Betsy showed me the note. We don't think Bobby shot himself."

"Pete doesn't think so, either." I heard an impatient toot of a horn. "Francine's waiting. I'll call you."

"But Maralee!" She stood in the front doorway as I ran down the steps. "It's important!"

"I'll call you," I repeated, and jumped into the van. "Let's roll," I told Francine. "CSI is at Betsy's, and Pete thinks Bobby didn't shoot himself. And the gun is the same one that killed Ted Thorne."

"Boy, I wish we had a siren on this buggy," Francine stopped for a red light, tapping her foot, revving the engine. She grew quiet, concentrating on her driving for several miles. "You mean . . ." she spoke slowly. "You mean maybe whoever shot the Thorne kid is still here? Right here in Salem?"

"This is crazy, I know. But the gun was registered to Gerard Thorne."

"He's dead, too," she said. "Everybody's dead."

"Not everybody," I said as we parked behind a WBZ-TV mobile unit from Boston in front of Betsy's house. "Crap! I thought we'd be first."

The Boston guy was already getting into position

for a stand-up, and he'd picked the best spot, right where the tape crossed the driveway with a good shot of the house and the CSI vehicle. "Let me out," I said. "I want to hear what he's got. I'm pretty sure we've got a better backstory."

I was right. Boston only had the fact that an apparent suicide victim, whose body had been discovered at this address, may have actually been shot by a second party. He gave some Wikipedia-type information about Bobby's brief hockey career and mentioned that Bobby had been a classmate of Ted Thorne. He threw in a few sentences about the Mustang recovery but didn't say anything about the gun.

I heard an urgent *pssst* from Francine. She motioned me back to the van. "Grab your hand mic and I'll take the small camera," she whispered. "Follow me. I've found a better view around back."

I did as she said, following her down a narrow, dusty service road, the kind trash pickup trucks and delivery vehicles use in upscale neighborhoods like this one. There was a skinny piece of tape across the line of trees marking the property line there, too, but if you poked a camera between a couple of trees, the view of the house was unobstructed. There were a couple of police cars back there, including Pete's Crown Vic along with a biohazard cleanup truck. Best of all, there was a patio. Without curtains, or screens, or venetian blinds. Just nice big windows. Not a darned thing obstructed our view of what was going on inside that room.

There was no show prep script from Rhonda for this, so I'd just have to wing it. There wasn't any room for a typical stand-up, either. We decided to take a shot of me in front of the trees, then I'd do a voice-over while Francine focused her camera with zoom lens on the patio windows. I'd peek through the foliage as well as I could and describe whatever I saw.

I used what I call a "golf course voice," speaking in the low tones golf announcers use when they don't want to disturb the golfer. "Ladies and gentlemen, Lee Barrett here, close to the scene of what had yesterday been called a suicide. The lifeless body of Bobby Ross, onetime Salem High School ice hockey star, was discovered on the patio of a friend's home—the victim of a gunshot. A confidential source has informed WICH-TV that the weapon found here was also used in the murder of Ted Thorne, whose body was recently retrieved from a local granite pit. We'll watch together, as police continue their investigation into this puzzling chain of events." I stepped to one side and Francine swiftly moved the camera to the vantage point between the trees. I pushed some branches and leaves aside, peered toward the house, and wished I'd brought binoculars.

I'd never given a great deal of thought to the cleanup process of a crime scene. Maybe I should have. I only hoped this segment wouldn't air during anyone's mealtime. Fortunately, the patio had several windows, and Francine quickly moved her focus to the one farthest away from what I'd described with few words. "Workers in hazmat suits" and "blood spatter pattern." This next scene was a little easier to describe. "We can see several officers gathered around a tabletop," I said, recognizing one of them as a handwriting expert I'd met before. *Betsy already swiped the suicide note. What are they looking at?* "There are apparently a number of experts on scene," I said, filling airtime the best I could, since I had no idea what was actually going on. "They'll be studying various aspects of the case, utilizing the latest technologies available to the police department. Stay tuned to WICH-TV throughout the day and evening, as we bring you the latest developments in this ongoing investigation." I signaled Francine to stop filming. "We didn't get a lot, but Doan will at least be pleased with the blood spatters." We ran along the unpaved alley back to our waiting mobile unit. As I put my mic away, I thought about what we'd just witnessed through Betsy's patio windows.

If Bobby didn't commit suicide, the note Betsy took can't be a suicide note, can it? Is that what Aunt Ibby was trying to tell me?

CHAPTER 39

I called my aunt. "I'm sorry I ran out like that. You were trying to tell me something?"

"I'm glad you called. Betsy and I think she'd better give this note to the police after all. Maralee, Bobby didn't shoot himself no matter what the note says."

"What does it say?"

"Oh, it's a goodbye note all right, but it's an 'I'm dying' note, not an 'I'll going to kill myself' note. We'd take it down to the police station right now, but she's afraid to go outdoors after what happened in the garden."

"I don't blame her. Look. I'll tell Pete. He'll know how to handle it."

"Good idea. Betts says to thank you for bringing Pixie here. She's a dear little thing. O'Ryan took to her right away. They're playing together like kittens. What was going on that made you take off in such a hurry this morning anyway?"

"Somehow the police have figured out the same

thing you and Betsy did. It's not a suicide. The crime scene crew was there at the Leavitt place. The cleanup crew too. And Aunt Ibby, there's no easy way to tell you this—the gun was the same one that killed Ted."

She didn't speak.

"It was Mr. Thorne's gun."

She gasped. "But, how? I mean, I'd thought it might be possible—even though it seems unspeakable— I'd thought Gerard Thorne might have killed Ted. But he couldn't have killed Bobby."

"Someone knew where the gun was, then," I said, thinking aloud. "When you were all kids, did you even know Mr. Thorne *had* a gun?"

"I sure didn't. We didn't talk about guns back then—except about the military, of course. Not like now."

We'd arrived at the TV station by then and Francine hurried ahead of me to the downstairs studio. I paused beside the van and looked around, dropping my voice.

"I'll call Pete about what you said. We're back at the station now. There's something I wanted to tell you last night. I had to tell Pete about the hidden key because Mrs. Thorne had the Essex police check the place. They found Bobby's prints in there."

Another gasp. "Were Betsy's prints there, too?"

"Guess not. We don't know for sure that she ever was there, do we?"

"No. Of course we don't. It was just perfume, for heaven's sake. Could have been the cleaning lady."

"I'll call Pete and tell him about the note. Anything

else going on that I should know about?" I asked. "Things are moving so fast lately."

"You're right. There's another meeting of the reunion committee scheduled for Saturday evening," she said. "Under the circumstances I'm not sure what to do about that."

"I'd say do it. You and Betsy are both already there and—well—'the show must go on.'"

"You're right," she said. "We still have a lot to accomplish in a short time. I'll call Warren and Penelope and Steve and remind them about it."

I hurried up the metal stairs and into the office where Scott and Francine leaned against Rhonda's counter, watching the big monitor. I heard my own voice in the hushed golf course tone describing the scene as I saw it through the trees.

"Oh, yuck," Rhonda squealed. "Was that real blood on the wall?"

"Afraid so," I said. "Sorry. We didn't know what we were going to see when we started shooting."

"No problem. Doan will love that part."

"Right," Scott said, not looking at me. "You know Doan's motto. 'If it bleeds, it leads.'"

"The interesting part is the handwriting expert being there." I pointed to the screen. "See? He's the guy in the tan sport jacket. I heard that there was no suicide note, but he's sure examining something."

Rhonda moved closer to the screen. "He's looking at a phone book. Yellow pages."

"You're right," Francine agreed. "Wonder what he's looking up."

"Not open," I said. "He's looking at the cover."

Scott tried to look wise. "They do that to look for

imprints. Like if somebody was writing a note with their paper on top of that phone book, the cover is soft enough so sometimes the cops can read what was on the note."

"You saw that on *Monk*. Or maybe *Father Brown*," Francine said.

"Probably both," Rhonda offered. "And about a dozen more."

"I'll bet it still works though," I said, reluctantly agreeing with Scott.

"Did you know I was in your yard while you were off, Moon?" he asked me. "I interviewed Bobby Ross's lady friend."

"You ambushed my aunt's houseguest, Scott. Made her cry."

Francine snickered. "And royally pissed off a cat."

"Just doing my job," he said. "That woman knows more than she's telling."

He may be right about that. Still, it was a crummy way to do it.

Scott ignored the cat remark "So they found a gun, huh? And they think it's the one that killed Ted Thorne? Did you see the it?"

"No, of course not. I suppose the ballistics people have it." (I really had seen it—in a mirror—but I wasn't about to share that.)

"Seems like a simple case to me," Scott said. "Bobby Ross killed the Thorne kid back in the day, then his conscience got to eatin' at him so he offed himself. Simple."

I didn't comment. I'd been thinking the same thing at first, but recent events made it clear this was much more complicated.

CHAPTER 40

The rest of our schedule looked comparatively uneventful, except that Mr. Doan wanted to talk to me about when I might have a new investigative report ready. Thinking fast, I promised that I was gathering material about the Salem High School class of 1974—and how they were coping with the mysterious deaths of two of their classmates. "Not ready for prime time yet," I told him, "but I have pages of material already."

His response was brief. "Hurry up about it then. I'll get Palmer to help you if you can't handle it yourself."

Was that a threat or a promise?

"No need, thanks. I have sort of an inside track, Mr. Doan. My aunt heads up the reunion committee and they meet at my house." I managed a confident smile. "Actually, I'll see them all on Saturday night."

"Perfect. That's the day after tomorrow. I'll get Rhonda to schedule your report for next week sometime. Francine can record the meeting. You need a lighting and sound crew over there?"

"Uh—I don't think so. I'm sure Francine can handle all of it and Marty will edit."

Great. *Great!* How was I supposed to pull this off? First, I'd better let my aunt know about it. I was pretty sure she'd be okay with having the camera there, but what about the others? Steve wouldn't be a problem. The more face time the better for a congressional hopeful. Betsy was the consummate TV pro. No worries there. Penelope had handled the interview at the scrapbook class well enough, and Coach surely had been interviewed on camera a million times during his career. I began to relax. If no one objected to being filmed, this could turn out to be pretty good for all of us.

I called Aunt Ibby, and after a moment's hesitation about what to serve for refreshments, she okayed the idea and promised to get in touch with the others. Francine liked it right away, and Marty, as usual, pronounced it "a piece of cake." We'd start with the nitty-gritty of planning a reunion—the invitations, the venue, the music, the caterers, the budget—and somehow work in the reality of dealing with the deaths of classmates. After forty-five years, in the natural order of things, there'd be old friends missing. But the deaths of Bobby and Ted didn't fit the natural order of things—which made *this* class reunion newsworthy.

When Pete called to see if I had time for a drive-through lunch, I ran it all by him. "What do you think?" I asked. "It could be a pretty interesting piece if we can pull it off. We'll have to condense a two- or three-hour meeting into a ten-minute segment, but I think it'll draw some viewers."

"I like it," he said. "Meet you out front in five."

He was right on time. I climbed into the Crown Vic. "So you like the idea?"

"Yeah. I'd sit in on the meeting if I could, but if I can get a print of the unedited tape, that'll be just as good."

"You'd have to clear that with Mr. Doan, I guess, but I don't see why not. Reporting on a reunion committee meeting isn't any different than covering a city hall meeting or a protest march. It's informational news." I looked at him. Cop face. "Why would you want to see it?"

He gave a little shrug of his shoulders, ordered our burgers and sodas through the speaker, then faced me. "Everyone on that committee knew both of the victims more than casually. It was a tight little group."

"That's true. Are you saying that you suspect one of them could have something to do with murder? Was there something written on that phone book?"

He frowned. "You saw us? How?"

"It was fair," I said, raising my right hand. "We were on city land, peeking through the bushes. Not even crossing the police tape. Was there something imprinted on the cover of the book?"

"No, Nancy Drew. There wasn't. You watch too much television." He smiled. "There was no imprint. Just a capital *T*."

"That's how the cards Aunt Ibby and Ted's mom got were signed. Just a capital *T*. You think Bobby sent those cards?"

"Maybe. Or maybe he was just doodling. The man drank. Drank a lot. Anyway, I'm not saying any of the group had anything to do with the deaths. But I'd like to watch the proceedings tonight. Something might come up during their conversations that could be useful, that's all. Body language can be helpful too." He handed me the burgers and put the drinks into the cup holders. "Want to eat on the Common?"

We found a parking space on the east side of the Common, walked across Washington Street, and scored one of the new benches. Relaxing in a lush green oasis in the middle of your favorite city with a much-loved man on a fine spring day can be as good as a week's vacation someplace else. Throw in a good old American cheeseburger and a sugary drink and all's right with the world.

For the better part of an hour we watched kids playing Frisbee, little girls jumping rope—*Cinderella, dressed in yella, ran upstairs to kiss a fella*—laughed at the antics of squirrels, tossed bread crumbs to cooing pigeons, talked about the movie we'd just seen and Pete's nephews' upcoming Pee Wee Hockey tournament, and even made plans to go on a whale-watching trip soon. Not a single word was spoken about a submerged car or an angry man in a mirror or a blood-spattered wall or a key hidden under a stone lion.

Pete dropped me off back at the station with a quick kiss. "I'll call you later, babe. Guess you're busy Saturday night, but maybe we can do something Sunday."

The Saturday-night reminder pushed my brain back into investigative-reporter mode. I'd need to think up some questions, or at least select some topics that would lead the conversation toward the areas I wanted to hear discussed. Not easy. I'd learned that in some of my earlier reporting ventures. A reporter has to press for relevant information without being too pushy (à la Scott Palmer). I knew that Mr. Doan wouldn't mind if I made someone cry ("the women like it"), or even instigated a fistfight ("holds audience attention"). I preferred not to do either and focused on figuring out the best way to show interaction among all seven members of the group—living or dead—then and now.

Why were Steve and Betsy cool toward one another? Was Penelope jealous of my aunt? *How* jealous? Exactly how furious had Aunt Ibby been when she thought Ted had stood her up? Why had Bobby, a promising young athlete with a bright future, suddenly tossed it all away like an angry prom queen's crown? Why were both Coach Whipple and Penelope on Overton's payroll? If Bobby's last note wasn't about suicide, what was it about? I'd have to play it by ear and try to keep them on the track I wanted them to stick to. If nothing else, it should be an interesting piece and might even turn out to somehow be helpful to Pete.

I scribbled those questions onto an index card and stuck it in my purse. I was sure I'd think of more, but I had plenty of cards left. Francine and I did a short piece with a pleasant group of senior ladies at the Brookhouse on Derby Street who'd formed a mystery book club. They were reading their way through Sue Grafton's alphabet books, and the discussion was about *B is for Burglar,* where someone was camping out illegally in someone else's apartment. I grabbed a card and scribbled "How often did Bobby 'camp out' at the Thornes' cottage?"

Next we did an outdoor stand-up at the Burying Point Cemetery on Charter Street, which naturally made me think of final services for the two departed classmates. I took a couple of seconds to write— "Funerals. When? Where?" An afterthought struck me once we were back in the van and headed for the station, "Who will pay for Bobby's funeral?" I wrote. "Or did he have money stashed somewhere?"

By the time I got home to the Winter Street house a little after five o'clock, I had my game plan for the reunion spot pretty well set in my mind. I could already visualize my aunt, Penelope, Betsy, Steve, and Coach at the dining room table. It was the lunchroom's "popular table"—minus two. I could use that. A good visual. I'd open with a shot of Penelope's lunchtime photo of the group, then fade to the five in my aunt's dining room. Saturday was two days away. Plenty of time to work out the details—to think up some more leading questions—and probably to help my aunt decide on what to serve for refreshments.

In a pinch, we know where we can get some excellent bagels.

CHAPTER 41

By the time Saturday morning rolled around I was satisfied that everything was in place for a good piece of investigative reporting. All of the reunion committee had promised to attend. Doan had agreed easily to let Pete have an unedited copy of the whole meeting, and I'd memorized a list of questions I could ask if the proceedings grew boring, or if there was a moment of the dreaded "dead air."

The dining room table had been polished to within an inch of its mahogany life, and a sweet stack of Virgilio's cannoli reposed in my aunt's refrigerator. All three of the women involved had spent Friday together getting their hair styled and nails manicured. (Pedicures too, of course, though it was doubtful that any feet would be displayed.) I'd seen Bobby's note to Betsy, and she'd turned it over to Pete. It was brief and looked as though it had been hastily scrawled with a medium-point black marker. The man was dying and he had some regrets about his life. The only mystery to me was why had somebody killed him when he was close to death anyway? A suicide note? A getting ready to die note? What's the difference?

The note was straightforward on the surface of it, but cryptic at the same time.

> *Every stupid minute of my whole stupid life since high school has been a big fat accident. All of it was an accident. Nobody means to do stupid stuff like that. I want everybody to know it wasn't anybody's fault. You get drunk. You mess up. It's what you do afterward that makes a difference. We did the wrong thing. But now, I think I've done my best to make some of it right. Mothers deserve the truth.*

> *Bobby Ross*

It makes sense for a man to think of his mother when he's dying, even though Bobby's mother hadn't even raised him. Who was the "We" in "We did the wrong thing?" Did it have to do with his relationship with Betsy? Maybe the group would be able to shed some light on it all. Or maybe it would be best to keep quiet about the note—let the police handle it. I decided that was definitely the best course to take.

Since all the "girls" had gone for the full beauty treatment, I booked an afternoon appointment with Carmine to do my face and hair. After all, I reasoned, this would be an important investigative report—a good chunk of time on the nightly news. I decided on a simple pink silk sheath with three-quarter sleeves and a V neckline—a little deeper than usual, but nothing to rival Wanda's wardrobe.

I arrived at the station a little before two and hurried past the darkened sets to the dressing/makeup room. Carmine was already there. After the usual discussion about my unruly red hair, peppered with product recommendations to tame it, he got to work. I relaxed in the chair while Carmine lathered, massaged, rinsed, tinted, rinsed—luxury!

Carmine, as always, was chatty. "I've been watching the news about that car they found with the dead guy and the bullet and all. Then the other one—the old hockey player. Both of them in the same high school class and both of them shot with the same gun. Weird, huh?" He didn't wait for a response. "I mean, somebody held onto that old revolver for a long time. You heard anything new about it? Did the old guy shoot himself or not?"

"It'll be on the news anyway, so I don't mind talking about it. Bobby Ross, that's the hockey player, left a note. I've seen the note. It's mostly an apology about his life, I'd say. He mentions drinking and doing stupid stuff. Something about his mother deserving the truth. He was dying anyway, you know? So suicide seems strange, doesn't it?" Carmine toweled my hair and led me to the styling chair in front of the mirror. "The police say it wasn't suicide," I continued. "They think somebody shot him."

He wielded the hair dryer. "Jealous girlfriend? Somebody he owed money to? Hey, maybe *he* shot the first kid—the one with the nice car—and kept the gun all these years."

"Bobby was at a friend's house when he got shot.

She says he brought only a small suitcase and she helped him unpack it. No gun."

He stopped, mid-blow-dry. "*She* says? He was staying with a girlfriend?

"Yes. Betsy Leavitt. It was in the papers. They were classmates."

Carmine resumed drying. "Well then. It's her. The jealous girlfriend. Probably killed the first one too." He gave the dryer a little tug. "Women!"

"I don't think so," I told him. "She brought him to her house to make his last days as pleasant as possible. They were—close."

"Not the girlfriend? Then it's money. Is he rich?" He heated the straightening brush. "Or does he owe somebody something? Big-time?"

"Not rich. The opposite really, I'd say." I studied myself in the mirror. "I have no idea what kind of debt he had. We've been trying to figure out how to cover his funeral expenses. No family that we know of."

"A real loser, huh?" His reflection in the mirror grew somber. "Bummer. Hey! Here's an idea. He found out who killed the first guy so he was black-mailing the one who did it. Maybe the poor sufferin' bastard wanted to pay for his own funeral."

"That's an interesting theory, Carmine," I said, and it truly was. "I've given up trying to figure it all out. I'm going to try to stop worrying about it and just let the police handle it."

"That's all we can do, I guess." He smoothed something sweet-smelling from a pink bottle onto my curls, guided the heated brush gently, magically giving me the hair I wish I'd been born with. He spent another half hour doing makeup, and I left the dressing room, with my step and my wallet both a little lighter, feeling like a new woman and headed for home.

Coach, Penelope, and Steve were due to arrive at five o'clock, and Aunt Ibby hoped to have the meeting over within a couple of hours. "It'll still be light out," she said, "Those of us of a certain age don't like driving after dark. I've ordered pizza for you and me and Betsy to be delivered at nine. Francine is welcome too. I ordered extra-large."

My efficient aunt had prepared a meeting agenda, with headings for each topic, "Call meeting to order, Moment of silence for absent classmates, Report on invitations, Report on caterer, Decide on a theme, Preview class scrapbook," and so on. I was especially interested in seeing the scrapbook. Penelope had told Aunt Ibby that it wasn't entirely finished, but that it was "presentable." I hoped the "popular table" picture was included.

Francine arrived at four thirty with an adjustable light stand, halogen lights, tripod, both lavaliere and handheld mics, and video cameras, and got right to work setting up in the dining room. Beautifully groomed and stylishly dressed, Aunt Ibby and Betsy joined us, watching the process with interest, then finding their seats for the meeting. Aunt Ibby, wearing a royal blue linen tunic with slim white pants, sat at the head of the table facing the camera. A slim gold chain peeked from the neckline, and I wondered if she was wearing the half-heart pendant Ted had given her. Betsy, in a simple but fabulous bright red Valentino midi, sat at her right. Once again, I drew door-answering duty. Sorely tempted to hang a sheet over the hall tree mirror, I settled for sitting on the attached bench with my back to the offending surface. O'Ryan sat silently on the bottom step of the front staircase, watching and keeping me company.

Steve was the first to arrive. I opened the front door, then looked behind him, expecting to see Penelope parking the Jaguar. Steve was alone, though, and he'd parked the Jag under a streetlight, which nicely illuminated the red, white, and blue stickers on the rear window. "Mr. Overton, come right in," I said. "My aunt and Betsy are in the dining room. I think you know the way."

"I do indeed." He beamed. "Please call me Steve. It's good to see you again, Lee. You look particularly lovely this evening."

"Thank you," I said. He didn't move, just looked at me expectantly.

"Thank you, Steve?"

"That's better." He walked through the living room arch toward the dining room and his waiting classmates.

Coach and Penelope arrived together at precisely five. Coach carried the scrapbook under his arm—I recognized the shape. I'd seen several of them at Glory's Scrapbook Haven. Penelope carried two long boxes. "You're right on time," I said. "The others are already in the dining room. I'll go in with you. We're not expecting anyone else." I followed the two—one tall and the other so tiny. They looked cute together, though, just as though he was carrying her books home from school. I dared a backward glance at the mirror. Nothing there except the reflection of the front staircase and the yellow cat on the bottom step.

The classmates greeted one another, I introduced

Francine to those who hadn't met her before. My
aunt sat at the head of the table, Francine with the
cameras at the opposite end. Steve was seated with
Betsy on his left and Penelope on his right. Coach
and I sat across from the three, leaving an empty
space where Bobby would have been. Awkward, but it
couldn't be helped. I gave a fast rundown of how this
would work. Half an hour of them doing whatever
was on the schedule while I did some voice-over. We'd
break for refreshments, then another half hour and
windup. Piece of cake. Francine fitted each of the
classmates with lavaliere mics—tiny things that clip
to a lapel or collar and do a good job, especially for
interviews. I chose to use my usual handheld mic.
(Call me vain, but I think the old-fashioned stick mic
makes me look more like a real reporter!)

CHAPTER 42

Aunt Ibby got right down to business, tapping on the table with a pencil, calling the meeting to order. "Welcome, everyone, to this very special meeting of our committee. We don't usually have members of the press with us, but we're sharing our reunion plans this evening with the audience of WICH-TV. My name is Isobel Russell. I was a member of the Salem High School Class of 1974." She proceeded to introduce the others. I was last. "My niece, Maralee Barrett, is here to help you get to know us. This is our forty-fifth reunion. By this time, every high school class has lost some of their number. We are unique only in the particularly tragic way we've lost two of ours. Let's bow our heads together in loving memory of Bobby Ross and Ted Thorne."

My aunt was well aware of Bruce Doan's dread of dead air. The memorial moment was short indeed, and the meeting proceeded, this time with conversation about the status of invitations muted while I did a voice-over. "The necessary business of organizing a reunion, gathering classmates from all over the country together every five years is particularly difficult this time. Mailing lists must be updated, an appropriate venue secured, music and entertainment booked, caterer selected. And all the while the committee is mourning the loss of two of their number. Yes, ladies and gentlemen, Ted Thorne and Bobby Ross were part of this select little group."

I paused as Francine focused on the committee at work. They were doing a fairly good job of not looking at the camera. Francine muted their mics. I continued my voice-over while the committee passed around the proposed buffet menu for the reunion dinner. "Ted Thorne disappeared in his almost-new red Mustang forty-five years ago. Everyone thought he'd run away from an unhappy home life, an abusive father. Every five years, they thought—believed—he'd be back. Indeed, his mother and his girlfriend said they'd received cards from him over the years. About ten years back, the cards stopped—right after Ted's father died. They thought for sure Ted would come home then."

I dropped my voice. "Ted Thorne came home last week. Not in the way they'd expected." I knew this was where Marty would insert the video of the muddy car being pulled from the pit. *Perfect.* I continued, "There was a meeting here earlier this month. Bobby Ross was here." Francine focused on the empty chair. *Good girl!* "Bobby and Steve were going to get together and order the invitations," I intoned. "Penelope, the unofficial historian of the group, volunteered to put together a scrapbook of their high school days. We'll share a look at those photos and remembrances a little later tonight." Francine focused on the scrapbook, which lay open on the table in front of Penelope. It was upside down from where I sat, but I could see a photo of a group of people on the front porch that had become so familiar to me in recent days. There were boys and girls both—kids on the low wall, on the bench, on the steps, even one boy leaning against the stone lion. Was everyone there? One, two, three—yes, there were seven.

The lapel mics were turned up again, as the group discussed the pros and cons of white or ivory stock for the invitation, and the merits of offering two choices of entrée or three.

I consulted my copy of the meeting agenda. "The group is about to discuss the theme of their upcoming event," I announced. "Let's listen in, shall we?" Francine turned the lapel mics up once again.

Coach was the first to speak. "I've had a chance to look over Penny's scrapbook," he said. "It's full of great photos . . . and she has plenty more material. There's another basket full of her stuff out in my car. How about using big blowups of the old photos, some of hers and some from the yearbook—and plastering them all over the place?"

"I like that," Betsy said. "Good one, Warren."

"I agree," my aunt said. "Any other suggestions?"

Steve raised his hand. "I was going to suggest a senior prom theme, with emphasis on the 'senior' part. You know, crepe paper streamers and seventies music like the old days, but with gag prizes like canes and walkers." The idea was immediately met with boos and other vocal disapproval noises. Steve laughed, holding both hands in the air. "Okay. You're right. It stinks. Let's go with Coach's idea."

"Motion?" my aunt asked in true *Robert's Rules of Order* fashion.

"So moved," Betsy said.

Steve seconded the motion and it was unanimously approved. Penelope's smile was broad and contagious. It was clear to me that the rest of the meeting would be devoted to studying the scrapbook-in-progress. It seemed like a logical time to break for refreshments.

All of us took off our microphones and were free to move around. Coach and Penelope went out to his car to get the promised "basket of stuff." Aunt Ibby and I went to the kitchen and arranged the silver tea service and the platter of cannoli onto Grandma Forbes's antique tea cart. Francine called Marty to discuss some editing ideas, while Steve and Betsy remained in their seats with their heads together, apparently deep in conversation.

What's up with that?

I thought about the several index cards I'd put under the "Betsy" heading, beginning with the notation at the first reunion committee meeting about how cool the relationship between the class president and the head cheerleader seemed to be. I remembered, too, the angry conversation I'd overheard between Betsy and my aunt, yet now they seemed to be as close as sisters. Apparently, they'd all made up their differences. None of my business anyway.

Once the table had been cleared of teacups and dessert dishes, my aunt once again called the meeting to order. Penelope's scrapbook and the accompanying basket—which was literally full of material—took center position. Penelope turned the pages, one by one, and at the same time turned the book so that it faced the opposite side of the table. With all the committee members' mics open, the chorus of "Ooh" and "Ahhh" and "Do you remember . . ." made for good audio. I'd turned my mic off, in favor of listening to the others. Marty was going to have a ball with this report, I was sure, and so was I. And most likely, Mr. Doan was going to like it too. So far, a win-win.

I was seated beside Coach, facing Steve, Penelope, and Betsy. While we were focused on the artistry of the scrapbook, which had been put together with clever embellishments like little stick-on pom-poms on a cheerleader page, and a newspaper clipping about a big win on a football game page, I noticed that Steve had pulled the basket toward himself and was quietly rifling through the contents—not just rifling through, but occasionally slipping a photo *under* the basket. Positioned as I was, I couldn't very well look over his shoulder and see what was going on. I pushed my chair back and stood up. "Does anybody beside me want coffee?" I said. "I'm going to start a pot."

Coach wanted coffee, and so did Betsy. "Be right back," I said, and headed for the kitchen, passing behind Steve's chair just as he pulled a 5 × 7 color print from the jumble of photos. I reached over his shoulder and pulled it from his hand. "Look what Steve's found, everybody! How cute is this? Is that you Penelope? You must have been at a homework party. Remember those?" I handed it across the table. "This one has to be in the scrapbook."

And Pete needs to see it first.

The photo showed a young Penelope seated at a table beside a stone fireplace. Her expression was one of concentration as her hands played across a vintage avocado green Olympia manual typewriter.

If the bentwood bench and the mantel clock and the stone lion are all still at the Thornes' summer cottage after all these years, is the Olympia typewriter still there? Did someone type the tipster letter to the police on that same machine? Was Steve pulling that picture from the pile to hide it—or to help the police?

I continued on my way to the kitchen, wondering how I was going to get a look at the rest of the pictures he'd stashed. I considered spilling coffee on the basket but quickly dismissed that idea since the theme of the reunion now depended on Penelope's old photos and I'd be in a world of trouble with the whole group.

I'd made the coffee and pulled three mugs from the cabinet when Pixie dashed into the kitchen, followed by a playful O'Ryan. They made a couple of circuits of the room, in and out between counter and table and chairs, then with Pixie in the lead, raced into the dining room. I put the three mugs, sugar, and creamer on a tray, and followed the cats. Pixie, ears flattened, leaped into her mistress's lap and from there, up onto the table, looking down at O'Ryan. Francine was capturing all the action and was, I was sure, loving every second of the sudden cat-induced turmoil, complete with a few strident boy-cat yowls from O'Ryan. Steve, clearly not a cat lover, had abandoned his place at the table, purloined prints and all, and had taken a position behind the empty chair next to Coach. Aunt Ibby moved from her spot at the head of the table, and not even trying to be stealthy, lifted the basket and picked up the small stack of photos. Carrying them in one hand, she wordlessly left the dining room.

O'Ryan, taking advantage of Steve's newly vacated chair, climbed onto it and faced a smirking Pixie. (Yes, cats can smirk. Especially tiger cats. They do it all the time.) Amid laughter and cat noises, Betsy attempted to restore order in the room. She lifted Pixie from the table and scolded O'Ryan gently. "Excuse me, everybody, while I put this naughty girl in my room." She cuddled the little cat, and with O'Ryan following somewhat meekly, walked in the same direction my aunt had taken moments before.

Francine shot me a questioning look. I gave a fast hand-twirl, signaling her to keep filming. Marty could straighten it all out later. Meanwhile, interesting things might be happening here. I delivered the coffees, taking extra care to protect the scrapbook and basket from possible spills. I picked up my hand mic and addressed Penelope. "Have you gathered the pictures and mementos into particular categories?" I asked, hoping to get things back on track. "Like the football games? The proms? Spring break?"

"Not exactly. It's more like spring, summer, fall, and winter, with the sports and the parties shown in whatever season they really happened." This information drew all eyes back to the book, and the people back to their original seats. "See?" Penelope said. "Here's one of the drama club doing *A Christmas Carol.* That goes in the winter section."

"This is going to be a pretty fat scrapbook," Coach said. "Nobody's going to want to leave anything out."

"Maybe it'll have to be two volumes." My aunt spoke from the living room doorway. "There seems to be plenty of wonderful material." She laughed softly, putting one hand to her throat, her touch highlighting a new addition: the Mizpah necklace I'd wondered about. "That is, if some people don't keep snitching all the unflattering pictures of themselves."

She put the handful of photos in front of Steve. He colored slightly and joined in the laughter. "Can't have the competition getting hold of pictures of me with spinach in my teeth!" The awkward moment passed, and the group resumed the friendly banter that old snapshots produce in any setting.

Betsy appeared at the living room doorway and quietly rejoined us at the table. "Is the kitty all settled down?" I asked.

"She's sound asleep on the bed in the beautiful guestroom Ibby has so kindly provided for me."

"It's my pleasure, Betsy," my aunt said. "Ours is a friendship of very long standing."

Coach reached across the table, touching Penelope's hand. "All of us have been friends a real long time. All of us. And we've got to talk about what we're going to do about a funeral for Bobby." He pulled his hand back. "Trust me. That man didn't have a pot to pee in. I know."

The question about Bobby's funeral and final resting place had been one of the ones I'd planned to ask anyway. Better that one of them raised it. The rest of them were ready to comment. Steve was first. "It would be my honor to pay for Bobby's funeral," he said.

Betsy waved a dismissive and perfectly manicured hand. "Oh, Steve. We all know you have money. So do I. This should be something the whole class can participate in, not just our little clique. We can put the necessary cash up front, of course, then maybe add a line to the invitations asking all of our classmates for a donation in addition to the price of the dinner."

"I like that, Betsy," my aunt said. "And although Laura Thorne has no need for us to help with Ted's arrangements, maybe we can fund a scholarship in his name."

Francine tapped her watch, reminding me that our two hours was almost up.

I picked up my mic. "Perhaps the viewers of WICH-TV would like to contribute, too," I said. "Thank you all so very much for sharing your reunion plans with all of us. We share your sorrow at the loss of those classmates who have passed, and especially the two you've honored here tonight. We commend all of you on this committee for your hard work and dedication. The forty-fifth reunion of the Salem High School class of 1974 promises to be the best one ever. I'm Lee Barrett."

CHAPTER 43

No one seemed to be in a hurry to leave. Everyone, including me, wanted to linger over the scrapbook. It was a true work of art, even though Penelope insisted that it was "nowhere near finished." I especially wanted to get another look at that photo of Penelope typing. More than a look. I wanted to snap a quick picture of it and send it to Pete, pronto.

"If it's going to grow to two volumes, Penelope, maybe I can help," Betsy offered. "I'm not an artist by any means, but I'd love to learn how to do it." She looked down at the table. "I could use some distraction right now."

"Sure you could do it," Penelope said. "Just meet me at Glory's Scrapbook Haven Monday morning. Lee can tell you. It's fun."

Steve appeared to be making an attempt to organize the items remaining in the basket, muttering, "Summer, winter, fall," separating photos, game-day programs, and yellowed clippings into four piles.

He looked up. "Ibby, did you return all those bad photos of me? I wouldn't want an opponent to get any of them."

"No worries, Steve," she said. "They aren't that bad, but you do what you want to with them. Penelope doesn't need them for the scrapbook anyway, do you Penelope?"

"You kidding? Steve was a big wheel." She laughed. "We have more pictures of him than anybody. We won't miss a few, especially if he had spinach in his teeth."

Steve stuffed the photos into an inside pocket of his sport coat. "I'll take great pleasure in burning them."

"They're probably some of the out-of-focus ones I used to take with Penelope's camera." Coach pantomimed holding a camera to his eye and clicking the shutter. "Not a good photographer, but then, she can't play basketball!!" Penelope stuck her tongue out at him and continued turning the pages of the scrapbook while my aunt and Betsy watched over her shoulder.

Francine had finished packing the camera equipment, the lights, and mics, and I helped her carry it all out to her truck. "I'll go by the station and drop this off," she said. "Marty'll be there. She's doing River's show but she might have time to start work on this. Cutting it down to ten or fifteen minutes won't be easy, but she's the best. Doan's going to want your investigative piece ASAP."

"I think it's going to be okay," I said. "The element of a good mystery is there, along with a group of senior citizens planning a special party for their classmates in spite of the bad things happening around them."

She climbed into the driver's seat. "You aren't kidding. It's nice how they're planning to honor their friends, though, isn't it? And that photo collection is awesome."

I agreed with her on both counts and returned to the house, where O'Ryan waited in the foyer, having watched Francine and me from the tall windows beside the front door. "Okay, cat," I said. "Let's go grab that picture with the typewriter in it. Thanks for the cat race distraction earlier. I wonder what Aunt Ibby found in the ones she grabbed." He began to follow me but paused in front of the hall tree, looking from the mirror to me and back. I picked him up. "Uh-uh, let's not go there right now." I carried him through the living room and back into the dining room.

"Have you got a special category for schoolwork, Penelope?" I asked. "That cute picture of you doing your homework ought to be in it."

"Coach thinks so too." With a shy smile she handed me the picture. "It's not very good. He just likes it because he's the one who took it."

"Let me look at it under a better light." I carried the photo to the kitchen, holding it toward the overhead lamp. "Looks good to me," I said loudly. I set it on the table, looked around to be sure no one was watching from the next room and took one picture, hit *send*, and it was on its way to Pete.

None of the remaining guests seemed anxious to leave, so I made another pot of coffee. Coach and Penelope held up photos and laughed together.

They were such a cute couple. My aunt and Steve sat together, quietly discussing the most discreet wording for requesting donations on the reunion invitations. Betsy and I talked about our cats. After a while, though, she excused herself. "I think I'll go upstairs and check on Pixie," she said. "Maybe I'll take a little nap before dinner."

Her shoulders slumped as she walked toward the foyer. Betsy knew how to put on a brave front, but she was clearly sad. I resisted the urge to give her a hug. "Pizza will be here at nine," I said. "Have a good rest."

With Betsy gone, that left me as the odd man out, sitting alone in the chair at the head of the table. Penelope and Coach sat, heads together, laughing, talking, My aunt and Steve were on the other side, silent. Aunt Ibby, pen in hand, made notes on a legal pad. Steve had pushed his chair back a little and seemed to be staring at her. She looked particularly lovely tonight, I thought. Royal blue was a good color for her. She knew it. Her hair, still red—with admittedly a little help from a rinse—her complexion smooth, with only the slightest suggestion of wrinkles. (No wonder Pete sometimes asks me if I'll be as good-looking as Aunt Ibby when I get old.) I looked again at Steve. Was that look adoration? Was he having more than friendly thoughts about my aunt? *Why not? Old people need love too.* I thought again of Betsy, upstairs with her little cat, mourning the loss of Bobby.

Penelope glanced out the window, then at her watch. "Getting dark," she said. "This has been such fun, but I need to be on my way. Warren, will you help me gather all this stuff up?"

"Sure," he said, and the two carefully slipped the scrapbook into a canvas bag and put the sorted photos into shoebox-shaped cases with subject dividers between categories. *So efficient!*

I realized then for the first time that it was no wonder Penelope was a valued member of the clique. She'd probably been the one who'd insisted that the others study for exams, that they remembered to celebrate each other's birthdays, even that Ted had gas for his car. It didn't matter that she wasn't a class officer, wasn't a cheerleader, wasn't beautiful or especially smart. Everybody should have a friend like Penelope. The seven were blessed to have had her. So were the ones who were left.

"Penelope," Steve said, still not taking his eyes away from my aunt, "why don't you just take my car? You have the spare set of keys, don't you? I'm not through here, and I'll grab a ride with Coach. That okay with you, Coach?" He didn't wait for an answer. "Penny, you can pick me up in the morning. I'll call you."

I could tell that it wasn't okay with Coach, who wanted to go home with Penelope. But, I remembered, Coach was on the Overton payroll. So was Penelope. My phone buzzed. Pete. I excused myself, walking out to the foyer before I answered.

"Thanks for the picture, Lee," he said. "Good eye. That's the correct model Olympia machine. Looks like it was in the Thornes' cottage."

"I'm sure it was," I said, "and Mrs. Thorne has kept so much of the old furnishings there, maybe the typewriter is there too."

"We'll be checking it out in the morning. It's a long shot, but worth looking. You'd make a good cop."

"Yeah, yeah," I said. "I know. We're having pizza later if you want to come over."

"Can't do it, babe," he said. "Marie and Donny invited me over for barbeque." (Yes, Pete's brother-in-law and sister are Donny and Marie.) "Good night. Love you."

"Love you, too" I said. The cat, once again, paused in front of the mirror. I looked. Swirling colors, flashing lights, then the vision. O'Ryan by then had hopped up onto the seat, pink nose pressed against the glass. And no wonder. It was Aunt Ibby's aquarium fitted neatly between books on a shelf in our study, just as it should be. I looked more closely. The fish swam in their slow-motion fashion. But instead of gliding into the turreted castle and over the treasure chest, they swam in and out of the open windows of a little red Mustang.

CHAPTER 44

It was not an easy vision to erase from my mind. But I had to, and quickly. Coach and Penelope entered the foyer. Coach now carried the basket as well as the canvas-bagged scrapbook; Penelope had a box under each arm. "Here, let me hold the door for you. Good night, Penelope. Just ring the bell when you want to come back in, Coach," I said, realizing that they might want a few minutes of relative privacy before Penelope drove off in the Jaguar.

Things were still quiet in the dining room when O'Ryan and I returned. My aunt handed me a page from the legal pad. "Take a look at this, will you, dear? See if it strikes the right tone between inviting someone to a party and asking for money for a funeral."

I took the paper. "Not an easy task," I said. Not surprisingly, she'd nailed it. Not too light, and not dark at all. "It's just right, Aunt Ibby. Don't you think so, Mr. Overton?"

"Steve," he insisted. "And yes, of course it's perfect."

Again, the long look in her direction. This time, she caught it, and looked away, her cheeks coloring slightly.

The doorbell chimed "The Impossible Dream." "That'll be Coach coming back inside." I retraced my steps, this time not looking at the mirror, and admitted a downcast Coach.

"You about through yet, Steve?" he asked. "Getting dark out there."

"Oh, come on. You're not afraid to drive in the dark, are you?" Steve's tone was condescending, sarcastic. Not at all the way he'd spoken to me or to my aunt or to Betsy or to Penelope. Or even to Bobby when they'd been here at the last meeting.

That attitude's not going to get you elected to anything, Mr. Overton.

My aunt spoke up, with a smile. "Well, gentlemen, I'm afraid I'm going to have to toss you both out into the twilight now. We girls have a date with the Pizza Pirate very shortly. No boys allowed."

"Really? You sure?" Overton sounded surprised for an instant, then swung into full campaign mode. "We'll be going right along then. Thank you, ladies, for a most productive and pleasant evening. I think we accomplished a great deal, Ibby. And you, Lee, thank you so very much for any publicity you can give us to promote the idea of memorializing our fallen classmates." He even bowed slightly and took my aunt's hand—holding it a little longer than necessary. *What an act!* "Please bid a good night to Betsy for me. She's a brave woman. I know how fond she was of Bobby—and he of her. I'd like to call you later, Ibby, if I may."

My aunt nodded slightly. "All right," she murmured.

I let the two men out. O'Ryan didn't bother to come with me. I waited by the long window until I heard Coach's BMW start up. _Engine needs a tune-up. A nice Beemer like that shouldn't sound so rough._ By then it was eight thirty. "I'll stay and help you clean up here," I told my aunt. "Pizza should be along shortly."

We cleared the table, carried the empty cups and mugs to the sink, rinsed out the coffeepot, and reloaded it for morning. We did the dishes together, my aunt washing, me wiping and putting away, just as we'd done a million times before. I told her then about the picture of Penelope typing on what sure looked like an avocado-colored Olympia typewriter. "I took a snap of it and sent it to Pete," I said. "What if that typewriter is still in the cottage? What if somebody used it to write that note telling the police where to find Ted?"

She was silent for a while, then said, "Do you think maybe the tipster is one of us?"

There was a different, terrible question on my mind. _Maybe the killer is one of you._

We sat at the round oak kitchen table awaiting the Pizza Pirate. "I think I'll run upstairs and see if Betsy is ready for dinner," she said. "Will you wait for the pizza delivery? I have a nice bottle of cabernet sauvignon chilling in the fridge. Would you get the wineglasses?"

I agreed to both requests. O'Ryan took my aunt's place at the table, and we waited together for the arrival of the Pizza Pirate's delivery person. O'Ryan knew the pizza had arrived even before the bell chimed, and he made a mad dash for the front door—undoubtedly anticipating a slice or two of pepperoni. I accepted the extra-large pizza as well as the antipasto she'd ordered and prepaid. I took care of the tip and carried our dinner to the kitchen without looking at the hall tree mirror even once. I'd already put out place settings and wineglasses when Aunt Ibby and Betsy appeared—each makeup free and attired in robes and slippers. Little Pixie trotted along behind them. O'Ryan greeted her with a gentle nose rub.

We were a relaxed trio that night at my aunt's kitchen table. Betsy's frame of mind seemed much improved, and the two chatted about reunion plans and the amazing job Penelope had done on the scrapbook. "Does Steve always boss her around like that?" I asked.

"She is an employee," Aunt Ibby said—kind of defensively, I thought—"and he's been very kind and generous to her over the years. Her husband left her penniless when he passed, you know."

Betsy helped herself to a second slice of pizza. "That's true enough," she said, and refilled her wineglass. "But does he have to be such a jerk about it? And how about him grabbing all the pictures that he didn't like? He sure hasn't mellowed with age—as I like to think the rest of us have." She raised her glass, drained it, and put it down. "Okay, girls," she said. "Enough small talk. Who do you think killed my Bobby?"

I didn't know what to say. I looked toward my aunt for a clue as to how to handle this. She refilled her own wineglass, then filled mine before she spoke. "What I think, Betsy, is that whoever killed Bobby shot Ted forty-five years ago, and then sent his mother and me all those cards. All those cruel, lying cards."

"At first I thought Mr. Thorne killed Ted." Betsy's voice was angry. "But even if he did, he couldn't have come back and killed Bobby."

"You know those pictures?" my aunt asked. "The ones Steve didn't like? That he said he's going to burn?"

"What about them?" Betsy asked.

"I looked at every one of those pictures." She had a faraway expression. "It looked as though the boys were at one of those parties everybody said Ted had at the cottage."

"All of the boys?" I asked.

"Right," my aunt said. "They weren't very good pictures like Penelope always took. I think they passed the camera around. There'd be a picture of Ted and Bobby and Warren, then one of Steve and Warren and Ted, and so on. Never all four of them in one picture, but beer cans in every picture."

Beer cans in the Mustang too.

"Everybody knew Ted had those parties," Betsy said. "I mean, nobody ever got really drunk. They used to steal Mr. Thorne's beer. They didn't dare take too many cans or the old man would have noticed and Ted would've been punished."

"I didn't know about the parties," my aunt said.

"I know you didn't, Ibby," Betsy took my aunt's hand. "You were so innocent. But Bobby told me about them back when we were seniors."

"Oh dear. Anyway, I snitched one of Steve's pictures," my aunt said. "If I'd thought of it, I would have taken a picture of it and sent it along to Pete like you did, Maralee."

Betsy looked at me. "You sent a picture to Pete? He's the detective boyfriend, right?"

"Yes." I said.

"What picture? Why?" She leaned forward, eyes wide. "Did it have something to do with the murders?"

"I think it might have something to do with who-ever tipped off the police about Ted's car." I explained then about the picture of Penelope typing on an old Olympia typewriter, the kind the police thought the tipster had used.

"We thought, since Laura Thorne keeps so many of the old things in the cottage, the typewriter might be there," Aunt Ibby said, "so Maralee sent the pic-ture to Pete."

"He's going to check on it in the morning," I added.

"Huh. Should have asked me. It's there. An ugly avocado green one?" Betsy laughed. "It's there. I've seen it. It's on the top shelf of the closet in the small bedroom in the back."

"So you've been in the cottage—um—recently?" my aunt asked.

"Fairly recently," she said, looking down at her hands, almost demurely.

"Did you use the key under the stone lion to get in?" Aunt Ibby's voice rose a little.

"Under the lion? Hell, no. We just used Bobby's key."

I interrupted again. "Bobby had a key to the Thornes' cottage? Where did he get it?"

Betsy laughed again. "They all have them. At least they did. Bobby still had his. I don't know about Steve and Warren. Back during our senior year, one of them took the key that was under the lion and had duplicates made. I don't know who took it. Bobby said Ted didn't even know they had them."

Aunt Ibby sat ramrod straight and pointed an accusing finger. "How come you never told me?"

"Because you would have told Ted, silly."

"Did Penelope know, too?" Aunt Ibby demanded.

"I guess so." Betsy fed Pixie a bit of cheese with her finger. "I remember her being there with Warren once when Bobby and I were there. It was in the late fall. Cold. We wanted to build a fire, but we were afraid somebody would see the smoke."

"What were you all *doing* there anyway?" Aunt Ibby slipped the last piece of pepperoni to the waiting O'Ryan.

Betsy rolled her eyes. "Oh, Ibby. You are *so* innocent." Then she frowned. "But why were you going to send a picture to the detective? It's just a picture of kids fooling around a long time ago."

"There was something about them. Something the police need to see. I took them into my office and made a copy of the clearest one before I gave them all back to Steve. I'll give it to you, Maralee, and you can show it to Pete."

"What's in it?" I asked.

"It's a picture of Ted and Warren and Bobby. I suppose Steve must have taken it." She paused. looked away from us, took another sip of wine. "Ted was wearing a Red Sox T-shirt." She reached inside the neck of her bathrobe and lifted out the gold chain. "He was also wearing his half of this."

"Then—oh my God Aunt Ibby! That must have been the night he disappeared." I stood up. "He—

his body—he was wearing them both when they found him."

"I know. Wait a minute. I'll get the copy for you." Walking a little unsteadily toward her first-floor office, she left Betsy and me and the two cats in the kitchen.

"Now I don't know what to think," Betsy said. "If all of them were together that night, they all must have known what happened to Ted." She put her hands up to her face, covering her eyes. "Bobby thought it was us. The girls."

"WHAT? What are you talking about? Bobby thought you and Penelope and my aunt killed Ted?"

She dropped her hands to her sides. "There was a note. Another note. Not the one they thought was a suicide letter."

Aunt Ibby reappeared in the doorway holding a single sheet of copy paper. "What are you saying, Betsy? What other note?"

"It's upstairs in my room. I guess I'd better show it to you. He was awfully drunk when he wrote it, I'm sure. He'd been out on the patio with a bottle of bourbon all afternoon. When he passed out, I took the bottle away from him. That's when I found the note." She stood, backing toward the living room, still facing us. "I'll get it." She turned and ran toward the front stairs. Both cats followed her.

My aunt, still holding the paper, sat opposite me, silently shaking her head. "I don't know, Maralee. I just don't know."

Betsy came into the kitchen, a small, yellow oblong paper held in her two fingers. "It's one of those big sticky notes. He wrote it in marker, same as the other note. Of course, he must have sobered up a lot by the time he wrote the dumb suicide note." She reached over the table and dropped the paper in front of me. Faceup.

In shaky block print it read, "WOMEN DID IT."

CHAPTER 45

"*Women* did it?" I was incredulous. You think—I mean Bobby thought—the *girls* shot Ted? That's crazy talk."

"It certainly is." Aunt Ibby used her most stern librarian voice. "Total nonsense."

Betsy gave an embarrassed shrug of her shoulders, pulling her bathrobe close around her. "Hey. I'm just showing you what the note says. And Bobby wrote it. What else would I think? What *other* women could he mean?

"You should have known better," my aunt said. "It can't mean he thought *we* were killers, for heaven's sake. He meant *some* women did something else."

"If it means anything," I said, "after all, you said he'd been drinking all day."

"True," Betsy said "I'm sorry. I know I didn't do it, and if you and Penelope didn't do it, Ibby, who did?"

"According to those pictures," I reasoned, "the boys were all together at the cottage at some point that night. Would they have gone to the granite pits with a car full of beer cans for some reason?"

"They might. Why not? They were kids," Betsy said. "But what about the gun?"

"Registered to Mr. Thorne, remember?" I said. "What if he kept it at the cottage?"

"That's right, Maralee," my aunt said. "If they were in the habit of stealing his beer, why wouldn't they take his gun?"

"They must have put it back where they found it then." Betsy looked thoughtful. "Mr. Thorne would have raised hell if it was missing."

"We were always careful to leave everything in apple-pie order," Aunt Ibby said. "We didn't want Ted to ever get in trouble with his parents."

"I know," Betsy said. "They were strict. If Ted had screwed up, they'd have taken his car away and we'd all be out of a ride. We loved being seen in that car."

"Anybody mind if I send pictures of these to Pete now?" I reached for the note Betsy had dropped, and the copy of the photo in front of Aunt Ibby.

There was no objection. Both women watched silently as I positioned first the note, then the photo on the tabletop, took the pictures, and hit send. I didn't offer any explanation. He'd get it. He'd be calling me soon. I returned the note and the picture.

Betsy stood, stretched, and yawned. "Guess we've done all we can then. I think I'll take a couple of pills and head for bed. Okay?"

"Of course. I'll be right behind you," my aunt said. She put the wineglasses and plates into the dishwasher and glanced around. "Where are the cats?"

"They were both asleep at the foot of my bed when

I came downstairs," Betsy said. "Is it all right if O'Ryan sleeps over?"

"Sure. He doesn't have cat friends to play with very often," my aunt said. "I'll say good night, too, Maralee. Are you coming upstairs?"

"I am," I said, and followed my aunt. It was still fairly early. I'd put on my jammies, watch the late news, and wait for Pete to call—which I knew he would as soon as he got a look at those pictures.

I didn't have to wait long. He didn't even say hello. "Where did you get these?"

"Betsy had the note. She says Bobby wrote it the afternoon before he died. He was very drunk at the time. Does it make any sense to you?"

"Not really. The picture is more important. I guess you know what it means. Where did it come from?"

I explained about Overton saying he was going to burn them, and how Aunt Ibby had swiped one and made a copy. "It means the three boys were together when Ted Thorne went missing. The T-shirt and the Mizpah necklace prove it."

"Looks that way," he agreed. "Now about Bobby's note. Women did it. I take it the girls weren't at the cottage when the pictures were taken?"

"Betsy and my aunt firmly deny being there. Penelope doesn't know about the note, but I can't help thinking if she'd been there the pictures would have been better."

"But the pictures were taken with her camera?"

"She loaned it to Warren sometimes."

"Warren, huh?" Cop voice. "Was he at the meeting tonight?"

"Yes. He brought Penelope and all the scrapbook material."

"They leave together?"

"No. Steve rode with Coach and Penelope drove the Jag. More room for all the scrapbook stuff," I explained. "Penelope has her own keys to it. I guess she drives it often."

"I see. Thanks for these, Lee. Seriously. Good job. I'll keep you up to speed on all this as much as I can."

"I'd appreciate that," I said and I meant it.

I put on striped pajamas and moccasins and turned on the big TV in the living room, automatically looking around for O'Ryan. We watched TV together most nights, and I missed my furry friend. It wasn't time for the *Nightly News* yet—that's at eleven—followed by River's show. There was a program on about ancient Egypt. Nice, but I found my attention wandering. I thought about the bentwood bench. My apartment isn't very big, so if I was lucky enough to be able to buy it from Mrs. Thorne, exactly where would I put it? It would fit neatly under the bay window, but I loved the way that space looked already, with my vintage carousel horse and lots of beautiful plants. I stood next to the horse and peered from the window overlooking the backyard on the Oliver Street side of the house. All was quiet. There was a half-moon in the sky and the white blossoms of a fringe tree glistened in the pale moonlight. A pretty night.

I went to the kitchen, got a can of Pepsi, and looked, as usual, at the Star card on the refrigerator door. Two of those bright stars had been extinguished. I hated to think that one—or more—of the remaining stars were responsible. I thought of the cryptic note Betsy had shown us. *WOMEN DID IT.* My aunt, naturally, could not even remotely be suspected. What about Betsy Leavitt, asleep in a guest room one floor below. Could Betsy have murdered her high school sweetheart? And what was the secret she and my aunt had argued about? Plain little Penelope was a mystery to me. Exactly how had she fit in with the group of high achievers—those adolescent "beautiful people"—the kids who sat at the popular table? She still didn't seem to fit. Had she been jealous enough of the young Ibby Russell to have murdered Ibby's rich, handsome boyfriend? No. She couldn't have pushed the Mustang over the granite cliff without help. *Maybe Bobby had helped her. Maybe he had to die too.*

My thoughts were jumbled, tumbling things, making little sense, but I couldn't stop them. What hold did Steve have on Penelope and Coach that allowed him to treat them so disrespectfully? Did he have something on them? Or did he keep them on his payroll over the years because they had something on him? What about the picture Aunt Ibby had copied? All four of the boys had been together on the day Ted was shot to death. But were they all still with him when the fateful trigger was pulled? Were any of them? Or had a cruel father meted out the final punishment after all?

I wish O'Ryan was here. I wish we hadn't agreed to the kitty sleepover.

I wandered back into the living room, plumped up the couch pillows, and watched the intro to the WICH-TV *Nightly News with Buck Covington.*

CHAPTER 46

"What!" I sat bolt upright, looked around, blurry-eyed, not quite awake. The TV was on. I was in my living room. I focused on the television screen. Two thirty in the morning. An informercial for the latest miracle acne cure was playing. I'd slept through the news. River's show, too, apparently. A little too much wine with the pizza? *Did I miss my story about the Brookhouse ladies and their book club? Damn!*

Something had awakened me. I stood up. Looked around. Everything was quiet. *It's supposed to be quiet, dummy. It's two thirty in the morning.* Okay then, what woke me? A sound. There was a sound. A small sound. A door closing? A cry in the night? What?

I went down the short hall to the kitchen. There it was again. I opened the door to the upstairs hallway and looked over the railing to the floors below. *Scritch-scratch.* A cat. My cat. O'Ryan was in Betsy's room and he wanted out. I clicked on the hall light, hurried down the stairs, and padded along the burgundy carpeted hall. My aunt's bedroom door was ajar. I hoped the noise hadn't disturbed her. I gently turned the knob of the guest room door. Maybe I could let him out without waking Betsy. Locked. O'Ryan yowled. I tapped. I tapped louder. Knocked. Knocked again. A thin, sleepy voice answered. "Coming." The door opened a crack. It was enough for O'Ryan's escape. He bolted down the hall, skidded to a stop at the top of the stairway, and looked back at me. "I'm sorry, Betsy," I said. "O'Ryan needs to go, I guess. Sorry. Go back to bed." I pulled her door shut.

I was sure the yowling and knocking must have awakened Aunt Ibby by then. I crossed the hall and cracked her door open. "Sorry, Aunt Ibby," I whispered. "O'Ryan needed to get out of Betsy's room. He needs to go potty, I guess. It's okay now."

No reply. "Aunt Ibby?" I opened her door all the way. The hall light shone onto her bed. Her empty bed. I checked her bathroom. She wasn't there. *Probably went downstairs for some warm milk.* O'Ryan was at the foot of the staircase looking up at me.

I fairly flew down those polished stairs. The cat was on the hall tree seat again, and again, the fishes swam through the toy Mustang. I raced to my aunt's empty kitchen.

Heart pounding, I approached her back door and put my hand on the doorknob. It turned easily. Unlocked. Had she forgotten to lock it again? I stepped into the back hall intending to check the laundry room. No need. The door to the outside stood wide open, moonlight spilling onto the welcome mat.

The sound of an engine starting interrupted the silent night. An engine with a skip in it. The years

spent with my NASCAR driver husband made me
pretty savvy about all kinds of cars. Headlights off, the
black BMW coasted out of our driveway and onto
Oliver Street.

I sprinted back into the house, grabbed the kitchen
phone, and called 911. I gave my name. "My aunt has
been abducted," I yelled. "She's in a 2007 black
BMW. I believe it's registered to Warren Whipple of
Salem." I gave her name, her age, her address. "I've
got to go. I'm going to try to catch him. Hurry!" I
hung up on the warning not to chase him and ran
upstairs. I pounded on Betsy's door. "Wake up! Coach
has Aunt Ibby!"

On the third floor. I grabbed my handbag and
phone and raced down the stairs again. Betsy stood
in the hallway, confused. "I've called 911," I shouted.
"Stay here. You might be able to help the police."

By the time I'd pulled the Vette out of the garage,
I'd already called Pete. "I'm going to try to catch up
with him," I said.

"Lee, No! Let the police handle it You don't even
know where he's going."

I thought of those pretty fish swimming in and out
of the toy car. "Yes I do. He's taking her to the granite
pits. Hurry."

I caught sight of the BMW on route 128 and dropped
far back in the sparse traffic, hoping he wouldn't spot
me. When we reached the stretch of road approaching the entrance to the North Shore Granite Works,
I pulled over and turned off my lights, waiting until I
saw him turn onto the road Francine and I had trav-
eled not so long before.

"I'm better off on foot," I decided, and climbed

out. I was still wearing pajamas and moccasins. I wasn't cold, but the light-colored pajamas might give me away. I remembered the jackets Wanda had given us. Were they still in the trunk? Yes! I pulled the navy blue baggy garment over my head covering my hair with the attached hood. *That's better.* Francine's scuba gear was still in the trunk too. I remembered the dive shop lecture. Did Francine have one of those knives? The ones that can save you from fishing lines and underwater ropes? Oh yes, she did. It wasn't very big, maybe one of the fashion-statement variety, but it was sharp, and since I didn't know what I was walking into, it was certainly better than nothing. I thought of my aunt and attached it, in its trim leather sheath, to my ankle. The pajama bottoms covered it nicely.

I scurried across the street, then moved along the rutted road, sticking to the edge until I came to the clearing Francine and I had crossed when we first saw the divers' truck. It was a lot different at night. The half-moon was high in the sky, and its light was anemic at best but sufficient to show me the BMW parked where the divers' truck had been, next to the little maple grove. I stuck to the perimeter of the field and crept closer to the short path that I remembered led to the ledge where we'd met Bill Andrews. I heard a voice coming from the darkness ahead. Reflexively I ducked, crouching beneath the trees.

"Here we are, Ibby. Don't make any sudden moves, my dear. I can break that pretty little neck with one hand."

I wasn't hearing Coach Whipple. This was the now familiar voice of Steve Overton, and he was threatening the person dearest to me in the world. I moved

closer and felt a familiar tickle in my nose and throat.
Goldenrod.

Dear God, don't let me sneeze.

I poked my head up. I saw them, silhouetted
against the white of the looming granite cliff. She was
in her nightgown and barefoot. His hand was at her
throat. A piece of black tape covered her mouth. He
made a yanking motion, and I saw the glint of the
gold chain in his hand. "Here you go, darling. See?
It'll be just like the scene in *Titanic*, when Rose throws
the necklace into the water where her lover had per-
ished." The chain, with its half-heart pendant, made
an arc in the air when he tossed it, falling with the
tiniest splash. "The difference is that you throw yourself in, too, dear beautiful Ibby. Oh, we could have
made a lovely couple, you and me, but I saw in your
oh-so-intelligent face that you understood exactly
what those pictures meant.

"Bobby was right, you know. It was an accident.
After Warren left that night, Ted showed Bobby and
me the spot under a loose floorboard where the old
man kept his gun. We were just fooling around. I
pointed it at Ted. It went off. What do you think of
that, sweetheart?" I heard the tearing sound, and her
quick intake of breath as he ripped the tape away
from her face. "Don't bother screaming. There's no
one around to hear you."

My aunt's voice was calm, steady. "Why didn't you
tell anybody? That was an accident, Steve, a terrible
accident."

"Are you kidding? I'd been accepted at Harvard
Business. Bobby had a scholarship that might take
him to a Stanley Cup some day!" His voice slid up an

octave. "We were eighteen, nineteen years old. We had our lives planned. We would have had to face a manslaughter charge. Our futures would be ruined. We loaded the car up with beer cans, drove over here, put Ted behind the wheel, and pushed it off the cliff."

"An accident," she repeated. "It's not too late. Tell them what happened. You were kids."

"I can't let you ruin it for me now, Ibby," he growled, "and I know you would. Bobby'd already typed that moronic letter that told the cops where to find the body. Said Ted's mother deserved to know where her boy was. Stupid bastard never got past what happened that night. Climbed into a bottle of booze and never got out. Not like me!" *Jesus. He actually sounds proud of what they did.* "I moved on. Put it behind me. Bobby was ready to tell everything. To implicate *me*! So he had to die. Now, so do you. But what a romantic death! Try not to struggle too much, dear. I'm just going to hold your head underwater for a little while."

River's reading. The Eight of Swords. It means imprisonment. I thought of the card. *A woman is bound and surrounded by swords. She's in front of a rocky cliff, her feet in the water.*

Where are you, Pete? I couldn't wait any longer. I knew I had to act. I reached for Francine's sharp little knife. I felt the tickle in my throat. Covered my mouth with one hand. Tried to take a deep breath. Then I sneezed. And sneezed again. Steve whirled toward the sound, losing his grip on my aunt. She scrambled off the ledge, clawing her way up onto the bank.

Lights blazed. Pete's voice. "Put your hands up, Overton, or I'll shoot."

Steve only hesitated for a second, then raised his hands above his head. Things moved fast after that. Officers surrounded him on the narrow granite outcropping. I reached for my aunt, grasping both of her hands and pulling her up onto the safety of solid ground. Tugging off my jacket, I wrapped it around her quivering shoulders. Before I could say a word, Pete appeared beside us. "You okay, Lee?"

"Yes," I said.

He scooped my aunt up into his arms as though she was a child. "An ambulance is on the way," he said, turning toward the wide field. "My cruiser is just over there behind the trees, Ms. Russell. Come on, Lee."

I followed, hearing from behind me the singsong words "You have the right to remain silent . . ."

"I don't need an ambulance," my aunt said, through chattering teeth, "Just a blanket and some nice hot tea."

"They'll want to check you over," Pete said, as we approached his cruiser. "Lee's going to sit in here with you until they get here. I'll turn on the heater." Cop voice engaged. "I'll talk to you both later."

I opened the cruiser door and Pete, ever so gently, placed my aunt in the backseat. He took off his jacket and tucked it around her legs and feet, then—as promised—turned on the heat. I slid in beside her, taking her cold hands in mine and rubbing them. "I'll talk to you both later," Pete said again, closing and locking the car doors.

"Tell me," I said. "What happened. How did you get here?"

"I was sound asleep," she said. "I woke up because I heard something. It was the cat. Both cats, I suppose, carrying on. Scratching and meowing to beat the band. I jumped right out of bed and ran across the hall to the guest room. It was locked."

"I know," I said. "I heard them too. I finally woke Betsy, but you were already gone. How did he get you?"

"Well, there I was, in my nightgown, pounding on Betsy's door with the two cats caterwauling in there. My God, how could that woman sleep through that racket? Next thing I knew somebody grabbed me from behind. I started to scream and that tape went over my mouth lickety-split. It was dark in the hall, you know. I didn't see who was doing it."

Sirens wailed in the distance. "How did he get you downstairs and out of the house?"

"Tossed me right over his shoulder." She squeezed my hand. "I think they call it the fireman's carry. It was terrible. My nightie was hitched way up, I had no shoes. I knew it was a man, but he didn't speak. I didn't even know who he was until we were outside."

"How did he get in?"

"I'm afraid I forgot to lock the door, Maralee. I expect he waited until the house was all dark and just walked in." Her eyes widened. "If those cats hadn't woken me, he would have taken me right out of my own bed. Shameful!"

Is being kidnapped from bed worse somehow than being kidnapped from a hallway?

"Did he tie you up? Couldn't you have escaped from the car?"

"I was in the trunk! He just threw me in the trunk!

I couldn't scream for help. I think it was Warren's car, wasn't it? I hope Warren wasn't part of this. Was he?"

"I don't know," I admitted. "The important thing is, you're all right. You're safe. Oh, Aunt Ibby, he could have killed you." My eyes began to water and I sneezed again. Loudly.

She smiled. "I think your pollen allergy may have saved me, Maralee."

The siren sound drew close and we saw flashing lights moving onto the field. Pete pulled the cruiser door open. "They're here," he said. "Wait a minute. They're bringing a stretcher and warm blankets."

"I can walk." She bristled.

"You're barefoot," I pointed out. "I'll ride with you in the ambulance."

She didn't object too much when the EMTs lifted her onto the stretcher, and she visibly relaxed when they wrapped her in warm blankets and carried her into the ambulance. The sirens blared and I held her hand as we rocketed through the dark city streets on the way to Salem Hospital. She talked all the way there. I listened.

"He parked Warren's car and let me out of the trunk. Just yanked me out of there, stood me on my bare feet and pushed me ahead of him all the way down to that rocky ledge next to the water. Swore at me when I tripped and fell once and called me such awful names." She tsk-tsked and shook her head from side to side. "His dear mother would have been appalled at such language. Then he said that if Penelope and Warren ever figured it all out, they'd have to have accidents, 'bad accidents.' Then he laughed, Maralee. A terrible laugh. He said they were both too dumb to get it, and anyway if they knew which side their bread was buttered on, they'd keep quiet. He said he'd been buying their loyalty for years. Can you imagine that, Maralee?"

I nodded. I could most certainly imagine that. I'd wondered why Overton had kept the two on his payroll. *It's obvious now that it wasn't out of the kindness of his heart.* He'd thought he was buying silence.

"I don't know how much of what he said you overheard before you sneezed," she said. "Did you hear the part about how he was going to blame Betsy and me for the murders?" She didn't wait for an answer. "He's totally crazy, isn't he?" She didn't wait for an answer to that, either. "He was going to say that I shot Ted because of the prom thing, and Betsy helped get rid of the body, then she killed Bobby to put him out of his misery. I suppose he may still try it now that he's been arrested." The green eyes grew round. "That second note Betsy found. The one that says women did it. Did he mean us? Me and Betsy? Why would Bobby write that if he wanted to tell the truth?"

The sirens wailed to a stop and the ambulance doors opened. We'd reached the hospital's emergency entrance. "I don't know," I said, as the EMTs helped her into a wheelchair.

"Well, I think we'd better find out." She leaned forward, gazing at her feet. "And look at this, will you? My lovely pedicure is ruined."

Pete met us in the exam cubicle where my aunt, sipping on a paper cup of hot tea, had just declined an overnight stay at the hospital for "observation," promising to make an appointment with her GP in the morning. I called Betsy, instructing her to bring clothes and shoes for Aunt Ibby and for me, telling her only briefly that Steve Overton had been arrested. I'd already called the station's night number to tell whoever was on hand to get a camera over to the police station to try for a shot of the congressional hopeful being booked for kidnapping and murder.

Pete, although pleased that my aunt and I were alive and well, was not happy with the circumstances that had put us in danger in the first place. She was roundly scolded for leaving her door unlocked despite frequent reminders. I was more severely reprimanded for running off to rescue her even though I'd been specifically told not to do it.

"We were right behind you, Lee," Pete said. "Following that car was a bad decision on your part. You were unarmed. The man was extremely dangerous."

"I know," I said. *I also know if I hadn't sneezed Steve might have already had my aunt's head underwater.* I hadn't been exactly unarmed, either. Francine's sharp little weapon in its neat leather sheath was still well disguised under my pajamas. When I changed clothes in the hospital that night, I hid it in my jacket pocket. When Betsy dropped me off to pick up the Vette, I put the WICH-TV jacket back into the trunk, and I put the knife back where I'd found it with Francine's gear.

Would I have used the knife to stab a man that night? I'll never know for sure.

EPILOGUE

Steve Overton lawyered up right away, and it'll probably be a while before his fate is finally decided. There isn't any doubt about the kidnapping charge, but the various degrees of the murders of both Ted Thorne *und* Bobby Ross are still jumbled up in a veritable tsunami of legalese. He's locked up for now though, and he'll never be a congressman, so that's one worry out of the way.

As soon as she got home, Aunt Ibby began to work on the cards she'd received over the years from *T*. Since she knew by then that Ted hadn't written them, they no longer were special to her, and she willingly turned them over to the police.

Did the *T* scrawl on Bobby's phone book mean that Bobby had sent those cards to Ibby and Laura Throne? Nope. Steve was responsible for all of them.

My clever aunt fed the names of the cities the cards had come from, the dates they'd been mailed, and events of interest in the area into the library supercomputer. What turned up was a picture of a dog—

or rather a man in a beagle suit. The fact that the cards had stopped coming right after Gerard Thone's death was one of those red herrings the world seems to toss in the way of mystery solving. The real connection was grand openings of Omigoodness Bakeries across the country, where Bernie the Bagel Beagle— aka Steve Overton—had been on hand (or on paw) to cut the opening-day ribbons. The cards had stopped when Steve had taken control of the bakeries and the hated dog suit was retired forever.

Penelope and Coach had actually believed that Steve was just trying to help out a couple of out-of-work old classmates financially by hiring them for small duties over the years. They were as surprised as anyone at how it had all played out.

I have my amazing bentwood bench at last. When Aunt Ibby let it be known that I wanted to buy it, Mrs. Thorne said "What? That old thing? Certainly, Maralee can have it." Penelope's photo finisher did a fine job of enlarging and framing the picture of my mother and aunt, and I managed to fit both pieces into my living room, where I enjoy seeing them every day.

Bobby's funeral was a low-key event. Many of his classmates and old teammates not only donated money but showed up for the service too. There was a memorial celebration of life for Ted Thorne, and a good many future Salem High School graduates will benefit from scholarships awarded in Ted's name. Our new friend at Flower Fantasy sent beautiful tributes for each of them.

Betsy has moved back into her home and has torn down the patio where Bobby died, and put in a wonderful memorial garden. She still brings Pixie over to our house for playdates with O'Ryan.

I was the one who figured out where the mysterious letter *T* fit into the puzzle. It belonged at the beginning of the words on that yellow sticky note. I told Pete about it. "Steve had told Bobby about his idea of blaming my aunt and Betsy for Ted's death. Bobby didn't want that to happen. He'd been drinking, though, and part of a word he wrote wound up on the cover of the phone book instead of at the beginning of the note Betsy found."

"The note that said, 'women did it?'" He'd frowned "You mean it said something like 'twimin did it'? That doesn't make sense."

"It does if you spell it out. 'Two men did it.'"

He hugged me and told me again that I'd make a good cop. I hugged him back and told him again that I didn't want the job.

The forty-fifth reunion of the class of 1974 is going to take place as planned and is expected to be a good party. Life, after all, goes on.

I still don't know what the argument I overheard between my aunt and Betsy was about and I'm not going to ask. Also, I still don't know what perfume Laura Thorne's cleaning lady uses, and I'm not going to ask about that, either.

AUNT IBBY'S GINGER PANCAKES
WITH LEMON SAUCE

For the pancakes:
2 cups of biscuit mix
1 egg
1⅓ cups milk
1½ teaspoons ground ginger
1 teaspoon ground cinnamon
½ teaspoon ground cloves

Beat biscuit mix, egg, milk, ginger, cinnamon, and cloves with a hand beater until smooth. Pour scant ¼ cup batter onto hot griddle. (If yours is the kind that needs grease, grease it.) Cook until pancakes are dry around the edges. Turn. Cook until golden brown. Serve with lemon sauce.

For the lemon sauce:
½ cup butter
1 cup sugar
¼ cup water
1 egg, well beaten
Grated peel of 1 lemon
3 tablespoons of lemon juice

Heat all the ingredients to boiling over medium heat, stirring constantly.

TABITHA TRUMBULL'S GRAPE-NUTS PUDDING

Every diner in Massachusetts used to feature Grape-Nuts pudding. Some of them still do. There are some fancy versions around, but this is Tabitha's, and Aunt Ibby says it's the *real* recipe.

⅔ cups Grape-Nuts cereal
½ cup sugar
½ teaspoon salt
4 eggs
1 quart milk
1 teaspoon vanilla

Combine dry ingredients and set aside. Pour milk into well-beaten eggs and stir into the mixed dry ingredients. Add vanilla and stir well. Pour into a greased casserole dish. Put the casserole dish into a shallow pan with one inch of water. Bake at 325°F until the custard is set—one hour. Serve with whipped cream.

LEE'S BREAD DIPPING SAUCE

½ teaspoon crushed red pepper
1 teaspoon ground black pepper
1 teaspoon dried oregano
1 teaspoon dried rosemary
1 teaspoon dried basil
1 teaspoon dried parsley
1 teaspoon garlic powder
½ teaspoon salt
¼ cup really good quality extra-virgin olive oil

Mix all the ingredients except the olive oil. Put in a shallow pan or bowl. Pour olive oil over the spices. Serve with Italian or French bread. (You can add more oil if needed.)

Stay tuned for

more great books in

THE WITCH CITY MYSTERY series

Coming soon from

CAROL J. PERRY

and

Kensington Books

Connect with U s

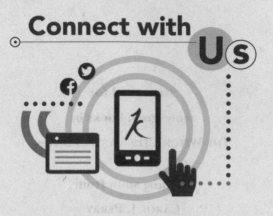

Visit us online at
KensingtonBooks.com
to read more from your favorite authors, see books
by series, view reading group guides, and more.

Join us on social media

for sneak peeks, chances to win books and prize packs,
and to share your thoughts with other readers.

facebook.com/kensingtonpublishing
twitter.com/kensingtonbooks

Tell us what you think!

To share your thoughts, submit a review,
or sign up for our eNewsletters, please visit:
KensingtonBooks.com/TellUs.